A GIRLHOOD DREAM

Sophia Vanderwahl had always dreamed a knight in shining armor would sweep her off her feet, but she knew this only happened in fairy tales. And when she discovers the truth about her philandering fiancé, she decides to track the scoundrel down and confront him in person. So she hires adventurer Jack Mac-Auley to help her find her neglectful husband-to-be. But with every glimpse into Jack's seductive eyes, every tremor she feels at the sound of his voice, she finds her memory of her fiancé fading away . . .

A WOMAN'S LOVE

When the headstrong heiress offers him a king's ransom to find her long-absent intended, rugged Jack MacAuley figures it will be easy money. But nothing is easy when it comes to this willful beauty with the golden eyes and kissable lips, and soon he can't help but think of delicious ways to make her forget her promises to anyone else . . . and to believe that happily-ever-afters really can come true.

TANYA ANNE CROSBY

Happily Ever After

An Avon Romantic Treasure

AVON BOOKS ◆ NEW YORK

This is a work of fiction. Names, characters, places, and incidents either are the product of the author's imagination or are used fictitiously. Any resemblance to actual events, locales, organizations, or persons, living or dead, is entirely coincidental and beyond the intent of either the author or the publisher.

AVON BOOKS, INC.
1350 Avenue of the Americas
New York, New York 10019

Copyright © 1999 by Tanya Anne Crosby
Inside cover author photo by Clay Heatley
Published by arrangement with the author
Library of Congress Catalog Card Number: 99-94450
ISBN: 0-380-78574-9
www.avonbooks.com/romance

First Avon Books Printing: November 1999

AVON TRADEMARK REG. U.S. PAT. OFF. AND IN OTHER COUNTRIES, MARCA REGISTRADA, HECHO EN U.S.A.

Printed in the U.S.A.

WCD   10   9   8   7   6   5   4   3   2   1

This one is for Alaina,
my daughter,
because her happy heart
is like a ray of sunshine
that shines even through the darkest storms.

Prologue

Boston, 1884

It was dark under the covers, but not so much so if Sophie cracked open her little sanctuary to the moonlight shining in through her bedroom window. She'd formed a tent of sorts, with pillows and blankets, and hoped no one could see her if he should happen to peek in her door.

Her mother had forbidden her to get out of her bed, but she hadn't said a word about her drawing. She'd been sent to bed early, just after supper, in punishment for her behavior that afternoon. Sophie had gone to play with the boys, had dirtied her dress, and had ruined her mother's picnic.

But Sophie didn't understand why it should ruin everyone's day just because she was dirty. Jonny and Harlan had been dirty too, but no one seemed to have cared. She didn't like to have to sit on a blanket at every picnic just so her dress would stay clean. It made her feel like she was one of those tarts in a baker's window, getting stale and yucky while they waited for someone to come eat them! Her mother's friends had no little girls, and Sophie always sat alone. She didn't like it. She wanted to run and play like the boys did.

She could even find shark's teeth better than any boy!

She wanted to draw it now. It sat before her on the bed, her afternoon's prize, as beautiful to Sophie in all its mud-encrusted glory as any sparkling diamond. She wanted to draw it shiny and pretty and golden.

As she drew, she thought about Harlan Penn.

Harlan's father studied bones. His house was like a mausoleum—bones everywhere, skulls with no eyes in the sockets, legs and even hands with fingers that dangled. Harlan even claimed he had a cigar box full of glassy eyes he'd plucked from his father's skulls, but Sophie didn't believe him. It didn't matter, she liked to go to his house and wander the corridors, because there was always something new to see. When she grew up, she wanted a house just like Harlan's.

Maybe she would marry Harlan and Harlan would bring her strange and lovely things from far away so that she could display them for everyone to see.

The door to her room opened, and she froze, afraid suddenly that her mother had come to check on her. She rarely did, because she expected no less from Sophie than for Sophie to obey. And usually Sophie did, but she had wanted so badly to draw her shark's tooth before the image in her mind faded away. Everyone said she drew quite well for a little girl who was only eight. It made her beam with pride whenever someone looked at her drawings and smiled in approval.

"Sophia?"

It was her father's voice, and she let out the breath she'd been holding. Relief washed through her. Still, she was supposed to be asleep and she didn't want to upset her father. For the slightest instant, she considered lying back and pretending she was fast asleep, but her daddy would never believe it, she knew.

"Sophia," he said again, and there was only a bit of a reprimand in his voice.

Sophie battled her way from under the covers, leaving her pencil and paper and shark's tooth beneath.

He stood before her bed, looking down on her.

"I'm not sleepy," Sophie complained, lying back on the pillows.

"I wonder why," he said, and pulled the covers up, discovering her drawing. Sophie thought he'd take it away, but he merely let the covers fall again. "If your mother found that, she wouldn't like it, Sophia," was all he said. He pulled the covers up, tucking them in about her, then knelt at the side of her bed.

"Well, she never likes anything I do," Sophie said with a pout. It certainly seemed to be true. No matter what she did, her mother was displeased with her. She could always have done it better.

"That's not true," her daddy scolded her. "Your mother loves you, Sophia. She simply expects the best from her only daughter." He was silent an instant, and then added, "You are all her hopes and dreams rolled into one pretty little package." He reached out and tweaked her nose. "Understand?"

Somehow, the statement disturbed her, but she didn't know why. Her brows drew together as she contemplated.

"She wants your life to be perfect," he told her. "She wants you to be perfect."

Sophie frowned. It was too hard to be perfect. She didn't want to be perfect. But she did want to make her mother happy.

"When I grow up I will be perfect," she promised, thinking of the perfect wedding her mother had described so many times for Sophie. When she spoke of Sophie's future, those were the only times her mother ever smiled at her. "But can I please marry Harlan, Daddy?"

Her father laughed softly, the rich tone of it filling her heart with warmth. "Sophia, my dear, when you grow up, you will marry whomever your heart desires."

Sophie smiled at that, reassured.

"But why Harlan?" he asked her.

Sophie shrugged. "I think he has a very curious house."

Her father laughed again. "That he does, angel face."

"I could walk around it for all my life and

never get bored!" Their own house was far too perfect, nothing out of place, everything sublime. It forbade one to run and play, or even to touch. Only her room seemed a haven from perfection.

Her father touched her cheek with the back of his finger, caressing it softly. "Go to sleep now," he commanded her, "after you show me the drawing you were working on."

Sophie smiled up at him. At once she sat up and lifted her covers, burrowing down until she found her drawings and shark's tooth. She brought them both back up to reveal them in the moonlight to her father. She handed him the drawing first.

He turned it in the dim light of the room, trying to make out the source of her inspiration. "It's . . . lovely, dear."

Sophie knew he didn't know what it was, but he probably had never seen a shark's tooth before. She held out the tooth in her hand. "I found it, Daddy! I went on a expedition—"

"Expedition?"

"Yes! With Jonny Preston and Harlan! At the picnic! And I found it! I did, Daddy!"

Her father's brows went up, and he smiled at her.

"Harlan said there used to be great big oceans over our house! And he said there were a lotta sharks everywhere! His daddy said so!"

Her father nodded and winked. "Well, his daddy would know!" he assured her.

Sophie beamed.

"Put that away somewhere safe," he told

her, letting her keep it. He put his fingers to his lips as if to tell her to hush.

"Mother wouldn't like it," she told him, her voice dire.

"Your mother doesn't have to know everything, my dear."

His declaration seemed to shock him as much as it did Sophie. She peered up at him, waiting for an explanation.

"Hmmm . . . well, there are things in your life as you grow older that you will have to make decisions about on your own," he said. "Mothers and fathers aren't perfect, though we do want the best for our precious little ones. Remember that, and use this." He reached out and tapped her gently on the head.

"Your mother loves you very much," he told her, "but . . . well . . ." He faltered, and then frowned, as though unsure of how to proceed. "Let me tell you a little story . . ."

Sophie nodded eagerly and fell back on her soft down pillow. It wasn't often her daddy told her a bedtime story. He worked so very much. But when he did, she enjoyed it immensely.

"Once upon a time," he began, "there was a little girl who had a mother who wanted only the best for her . . ."

Sophie's brow knit. The story sounded kind of familiar.

"This mother loved her daughter soooooo very much," he told her, "that she put her only in the best dresses, gave her only the shiniest black shoes. She didn't want her playing with the wrong people, and never, ever with the little boys. She was never allowed to get her dress dirty . . . or mud under her nails."

Was he telling a story about her, she wondered.

"But this little girl wanted only to play in the stables, to feed the horses and ride them whenever she could. You see . . . her father sold thoroughbreds and some of the finest most beautiful horses would come through their stables."

Sophie listened intently. "Grandfather sells throwbreds," she commented after a moment.

Her father smiled down at her, obviously pleased with her observation. "Yes, well . . . this little girl was never allowed to ride them, nor even to be in their presence. You see . . . her mother didn't think it was a proper thing for her little girl to do, and only the little boys were allowed to play there. Her brothers and their friends often tended the horses while the little girl watched."

Sophie didn't understand the story at all, and it wasn't as entertaining as the ones he normally told. Still, she listened, because she knew what it felt like to have a mother who never let her do anything at all.

"There was this one little boy," her father continued, "who thought the little girl had the most lovely smile." Her father sighed wistfully and shook his head. "He used to feel very sorry for her when she sat all alone, wishing she could play. He wanted so much to go talk to her, but he knew he would get her in trouble and so he never did, though he promised himself that one day he would take her away from that place and give her a home of her own where she could do whatever she wanted, where she could raise horses if she wished, where she would smile."

"He was a nice boy," Sophie told him.

Her father laughed softly. "Well, he wasn't always a nice little boy," he assured her, "but he really, really liked this little girl."

"Oh," Sophie said, getting sleepy now. She rubbed her eyes.

Her father went silent, staring down at her, though somehow Sophie wasn't certain he was actually seeing her at all. He looked sad suddenly, and far away.

"What happened to the little girl and the little boy, Daddy?"

"Well, they were supposed to live happily ever after . . . but happily ever after isn't something someone can give, Sophia . . . not even a mother who loves a daughter very much. It's a place inside here." He reached out and tapped her on the chest.

Sophie nodded, trying desperately to keep her eyes open, not wishing to hurt her father's feelings. She wanted to hear the end of the story, she truly did, but she was getting so sleepy.

"The boy and girl grew up, and got married. And he took her away, as he promised, but it was too late for the little girl, I think. She was a very good little girl, you see, always did what her parents wanted her to do. She never disobeyed them, ever. They molded her into the perfect little girl . . . who grew up to be the perfect woman . . . just like her mother . . . who never smiled."

Sophie was suddenly too sleepy even to try to understand her father's tale.

"Sometimes it takes a lot more courage," he told her, "to follow your own dreams instead of those of the ones you love."

"What about the little boy?" she asked him.

Her father stood up, drawing the covers up to her neck and tucking her in snugly. He smiled down at her, a little more sadly still. "Well, he grew up to be a terrible daddy, who never was at home and gave his sweet little daughter terrible, terrible advice. Pretend you didn't hear a word of that story, Sophie . . . Go to sleep and dream of angels as sweet as you."

It would be silly to pretend she hadn't heard him, but it was easy enough to put his story out of her mind. She didn't understand a word he was saying to her. "I love you, Daddy," she murmured as he caressed her cheek. "You're the best daddy in the whole world!"

She turned then, cuddling her pillow, her shark's tooth still in hand beneath it. She heard him walk away and close the door . . . and then she dreamed of riding on the backs of great golden sharks over sweeping blue oceans.

She was invincible; she could do anything. And her daddy stood by and watched and waved.

Chapter 1

Boston, 1899

The evidence seemed undeniable.

It was her fiancé's penmanship, but just to be certain Sophie withdrew her most recent letter from Harlan from her private desk, meticulously comparing the handwriting. She studied them both side by side, trying to find some difference in the styles.

Behind her, Jonathon Preston opened the drapes a bit wider, letting in every last ray of afternoon sun, giving her ample light to see by. "I would never have brought it, my dear," he said, somewhat eagerly now that she had begun to take the matter seriously. He came to stand at her side, peering over her shoulder, and his razor-sharp scrutiny of her while she read the letter made her cheeks burn with both anger and humiliation.

She swallowed uncomfortably.

No matter how much she wished to find the letter a forgery, the penmanship was the same;

identical long-tailed y's looping purposely about to cross simple t's . . . precisely dotted i's and j's. Harlan rarely capitalized the names of his acquaintances . . . nor did he ever capitalize hers, though his invariably was—something that plagued her acutely.

"Though Harlan has always been a friend to me, it seemed somehow unconscionable," Jonathon continued, "that you should be treated with so little regard."

Sophie doubted Jonathon's intentions were at all benevolent. He might have sold his soul for her father's favor. Still, she was not the sort who preferred not to know. If her fiancé was making her out to be a fool, then she certainly did wish to know about it—no matter Jonathon's motives for telling her.

And it seemed Harlan *was* making her out to be a fool!

Her entire future seemed suddenly to crumple before her like an old castle in some forgotten fairy tale, all of her carefully laid plans reduced to rubble and her dreams blown away like so much dust.

What a fool she had been.

She peered up at Jonathon to find him staring at her, as though he expected her to burst into heart-wrenching sobs at any instant. Sophie frowned. No doubt he would enjoy that. Well, she wasn't about to! She shuddered to think of Jonathon comforting her.

Strange how before this day she had not thought him quite so nefarious. The boy she remembered from her youth was gone, and in his place stood a gleaming-eyed, calculating man. No, she had no doubt of Jonathon's intentions, and less of his motivations. Her father was a powerful and beneficent man—witnessed by the generosity and support he had bestowed on Harlan. From the day Harlan had departed Boston, his best friend had set out to woo not her, but her father.

Drat men and their love of money!

Her eyes stung as she scanned the letter Jonathon had brought her, this time allowing herself full comprehension of the words scribbled so neatly before her.

God help her, she refused to weep—and certainly not before Jonathon Preston and his feigned concern.

She examined the envelope. It was postmarked April 20, 1899. Two months ago . . . how ironic that he should have written this letter on the third anniversary of their engagement. She wondered if he even realized.

My good friend, the letter began.

Sophie glanced up at Jonathon, wondering implausibly how he could betray his best friend so easily. Her emotions were in tumult. She didn't know whether to be grateful or angry at the man standing at her side. How could she, even now, look to championing Harlan?

Why should she care that Jonathon had played his Judas?

She read the letter.

You really must join me here directly! Give no more objections, jon . . .

It is a wondrous world, indeed, that not merely allows us the opportunity to experience life's most bountiful pleasures, but in fact grants us to do so! Every man should have such an understanding fiancée, eh? And a father-in-law willing to plunk down good money in support of his cause. I count myself fortunate, indeed— yes, indeed—to have won the heart of sophia vanderwahl, but do not think me unappreciative if I do not rush home to the encumbrances of matrimony.

His choice of words stung.
Encumbrance.
So that's what he thought of her?
She took a deep breath and continued.

At any rate, my dear friend, I hardly think you can say sophia is wasting away. She is young enough still that she might bear my children were I to delay our nuptials five, even six more years. And neither are her spirits low; her letters are buoyant and full with interest in my studies. She's a peach to affect such an interest in matters that would only bore her to the grave. Women have not the patience or capacity for such ruminations, jon. But do not concern yourself with sophia, my good friend. She is most loyal, to be sure, and will await me with the grace she was raised to show. Indeed, I could not have chosen better.

Sophie grit her teeth.
Her grip tightened on the letter.

Loyal, was she?

A peach, was she?

Anger surged through her.

Her interest had hardly been feigned! Her questions had been legitimately interested—and how dare he assume she would wait *five, even six more years* until he deigned to return to her! And yet it was hardly that particular narrative that incensed her most. Her eyes skimmed the pages until she came to the paragraph in which he began to *tempt* Jon . . .

> *. . . and the women here are the most lovely any man has ever beheld . . . skin so velvet brown and eyes so deep a black a man may sigh to see his own reflection in her eyes. And hair . . . Christ, I have never had the joy of touching hair so rich it flows through your hands like the mane of a fine riding horse. (And they love to be ridden, jon . . . I know this firsthand.)*

Sophie was not such an oblivious child that she did not understand his meaning. She felt ill at the thought. Her cheeks burned with both anger and mortification.

"Forgive me, Sophia, I did not wish to mask even the worst of it," Jonathon interjected, interpreting correctly the flush on her cheeks. "You had a right to know."

Sophie nodded, too shaken for words, even after reading the letter for the third time.

She forced herself to continue.

. . . never have I known women so earthy in nature. If you experience the carnal joy of one woman's bosom, you must not think her the exception because the next will make you yearn to feel forever her native soil between your toes and run like a savage through the jungles of her birth. You will nearly forget you are a civilized man and never again wish to languish in the misery that is Boston. Not for all the vanderwahl money would I be dragged so soon from this paradise!

Sophie winced at the not so subtle reminder that it was her father's money, not her, that would most likely bring him back—and not even her father's money was enough! He was enjoying himself far too well at Vanderwahl expense!

And he couldn't even be bothered to capitalize her surname, she noticed, growing all the more outraged.

Sorrow was at once replaced with cold fury, and armed with anger, she reread the last passages.

Even here in the wilds I have received word of jack macauley's reckless venture . . . his purchase of that deuced old ship . . . the miss deed, is it? In any case, he must be ready to set sail soon. Entreat upon him, if you will, to give you passage. He would make room for you, I'm certain. His pockets have grown quite shallow, I hear. In the meantime, I shall hand choose the most lus-

cious native girl, and let no man sample her but you.

Join me, jon, and you will hardly wonder why I must convince sophia's father to purchase me more time. Between the two of us we would surely convince him of our potential here. He is eager for grandchildren and alone I will not prevail.

Come, my good friend. Your presence is the one thing I find I sorely miss.

Your loyal friend and associate,
Harlan Horatio Penn III

Jon's company was the *one* thing he sorely missed, was it? Not hers? How telling a remark was that?

How could she not have realized sooner how little interest he held in her? Only the other night she had viciously defended him to her friend Maggie when Maggie had dared imply his interest had waned. Why had it taken a letter from him to Jonathon for her to realize?

She tried so hard to be everything everyone wanted her to be. The best daughter, the best girlfriend, and everything in between. She shouldn't wear her decolletage too high, or too low. She wasn't supposed to weep, nor was she supposed to laugh too loudly.

Numbly she set down her own letter from Harlan, with all its sweet lies, on the desktop, and kept the other in hand, unwilling to relinquish the damning evidence, forgetting just for

an instant to keep her shoulders even—a lady
never slumped, not even in the most dire of
situations.

"Is everything all right, Miss Sophia?"

Sophie straightened and looked reassuringly at their longtime butler, Harold, who
was standing at the door. In her parents' eter-
nal absence, Sophie was the lady of the house.
She had been groomed well by her mother,
and she managed the household meticulously,
but it was only in that very instant, as Harold
looked in on her, that she suddenly wondered
who was doing the supervising. But Sophie
had never felt like a child in her own home.
She had never dared be anything but exem-
plary.

"Everything is fine, Harold," she assured
him. "I'm fine."

He cocked his head at her. "Are you certain,
Miss Sophia?"

Sophie waved him away. "Quite certain. It's
nothing I can't manage."

The older man smiled affectionately at her.
"As always, Miss Sophia." He then cast a suspicious glance at Jonathon and left, assuring
her, "I shall be in the hall should you need
me."

Sophie smiled to herself. Harold was, as
ever, her guardian angel. If she knew him
well—and she did—he would remain just outside the door, dusting the same picture frame
over and over until Jonathon Preston left the
premises at last. In fact, were it up to Harold,
he would have never have allowed Jonathon

entrance at all. He was far more protective of her than even her own father. But then her father and mother always expected her to do the right thing. And she always did. They never doubted that Sophie would always adhere to her good breeding.

"Sophia," Jonathon said.

Sophie looked up at him. He seemed suddenly to take up far too much of her breathing space.

And all at once everything seemed far too confining—her father's house, her predictable manners, even her dress.

She had every right to be angry!

Why couldn't she ever allow herself a single instant of real emotion? Why must she always be perfect? Always be strong? Always do the right thing? She wanted to shout and cry and break things!

She sucked in a breath and stood calmly, clutching Jonathon's letter to her breast. Her fingers unconsciously curled about the parchment, crinkling the fine paper. Fury constricted her throat—not sorrow, not fear, but unrelieved fury.

How dare Harlan take advantage of her father!

How dare he use and discard them both so easily!

"I see how much this has upset you, Sophie. Perhaps I should not have come," Jonathon proposed, setting a hand gingerly on her shoulder.

Sophie shrugged out from under his touch

and brushed past him, swallowing her temper, trying to regain her composure.

Three years ago, with her mother's and her father's avid blessings, she had promised herself to Harlan. Three years and two months she had waited for him to come home and marry her, so that she could go and make them another perfect home. She had gladly rebuffed the advances of all her would-be suitors until every last one of her friends was wed, and only Sophie remained. And still she had waited, content in the knowledge that her *darling* would someday return from some faraway exotic land to claim her for his bride— like some knight in shining armor.

Bah, humbug!

They were supposed to have lived happily ever after . . . together with three children and a miniature pony for their daughter.

A young girl's foolishness.

Yes, indeed, she had been young when Harlan had left Boston, but she was twenty-three now, and no longer some giddy school-miss with girlish dreams that were meant to be broken.

And no longer was she content to make do with straggled letters intended to keep her on a shelf!

Harlan thought he was so smart, did he?

Jonathon's company was the only company he sorely missed, was it?

Well, Sophie had more pride than to allow him to discard her at will, only to reclaim her when it pleased him! She wasn't about to give him the satisfaction!

"I never intended to join him, Sophia," Jonathon assured her, his tone reproachful of Harlan. "I could never join in his sophistry against your father!"

Sophie narrowed her eyes. She was just about tired of hearing about her father. Why was everything always about her father, his money, his connections, his name? Why was it never simply about her? She decided in that instant that she would never again allow herself to be party to such an arrangement—even if it meant she would spend every day of the rest of her life *alone*! If a man could not love her for herself, then she just didn't want him!

By God, she even liked the idea of being alone! And why shouldn't she? She didn't need a man in her life!

She only wished Harlan were here so she could rip up his letter and toss it right in his face—along with his wretched engagement ring and a few well-chosen words.

She felt almost giddy at the thought, suddenly empowered with the decision to leave the wretch.

"Sophia," Jonathon pleaded. "Please don't weep, my dear."

Startled at his request, Sophie straightened her shoulders. Weep?

Oh, but she wasn't weeping!

Though she could certainly understand why he thought so, with her back to him and her head bowed. Her brows drew together suddenly as a thought occurred to her.

Why wasn't she weeping?

Maybe she was simply in shock?

Yes, that was it; she would break down later when Jonathon left. And then she would sit down and write a scathing letter to Harlan, breaking off their engagement once and for all—she only wished she could be there to see his face when he read it—the rat!

She wasn't about to wait about like some ninny for her fiancé to deign to return, simply to tell him to go to the devil. She absolutely would *not* put her life on hold one instant longer than she must for a man who had so little commitment or regard for her!

It was Sophie's father's money and connections that had won Harlan his prestigious grants, and Sophie had supported Harlan with all her heart, wishing him to be happy in all his endeavors, and now it just wasn't good enough to simply see his grants declined.

Resentment crept through her.

Perhaps he wouldn't regret losing her, but he *would* regret losing her father's support. She didn't know what her father would say about this, precisely. She had no idea if he would support her or if he would endeavor to convince her that Harlan meant no harm . . . that all men strayed once . . . that it bore no reflection on his feelings for her . . . but for the first time in her life, Sophie intended to take a stand. She was quite weary of being the good daughter!

A devilish thought suddenly occurred to her.

Why, indeed, should she wait for him to return? Why should she twiddle her thumbs until her father and mother returned from Paris to convince her all was well? And why shouldn't she *see* his face when she tore up his damning letter?

In fact, why should she *send* the letter at all . . . when she could *take* it to him?

She turned slowly to face Jonathon, her thoughts stewing, her eyes narrowed. "I wasn't crying," she assured him.

"Y-you're angry," he sputtered.

Sophie lifted a brow. "Quite."

"Sophia, dear . . . I-I've never seen you like this," he managed to say.

She'd never *felt* quite like this.

With Harlan's betrayal, something seemed to have snapped inside her, something slightly terrifying and exciting at once. The simple fact that she wasn't huddled in a weepy pile at her desk and sobbing should have alarmed her as much as it seemed to shock Jonathon. The poor man was staring at her, mouth agape.

Sophie tried for an even tone as she dismissed him. The sooner he left, the sooner she could make her plans. "Thank you, dear Jonathon, for bringing this matter to my attention." She straightened the parchment against her breast, ironing it neatly, resolved in what she must do.

She wanted to see Harlan beg for her father's money! She wanted him to fall at her feet and endeavor to convince her to stay with him. And most of all, she wanted to toss his letter in a thousand little pieces, and then walk away.

"Sophia," Jonathon began, taking a step backward as she neared. Sophie couldn't help but note his confused reaction. He'd obviously expected a far different response from her. Her brow lifted as she contemplated its meaning. "I think perhaps you are in shock," he told her, recovering himself, and planting his feet firmly.

No doubt he thought so.

Certainly it was unheard of that a woman should respond to such a case with anything other than pure hysteria, Sophie thought irately.

"I'm perfectly fine," she assured her fiancé's best friend, and flashed him a smile meant to placate, even if her eyes felt as though they burned with wrath. "You may go now, and please, please, do not trouble yourself any further, Jonathon."

"Oh, but I must!" he protested at once. "How can I come to you bearing such horrid news and simply go and leave you disconsolate? You need comfort, my dear—comfort and friendship! And I am here to give it to you!"

Sophie began to fold the letter with cool deliberation. "You will find a way," she assured him, her tone as dulcet as she could manage. "As you can see . . . I am hardly disconsolate."

"Sophia, my dear . . . this is quite unlike you!"

Sophie smiled. "Why, yes, it is!" she agreed, and batted her lashes at him a bit mockingly, feeling quite the shrew, though with ample justification.

Men! Her father included, all of them were despotic oafs! Well, she was quite through being a door mat!

She came toward him, laying a hand on his arm. She gripped him firmly and pulled him toward the door. "So thank you, dear Jonathon, for considering me in this."

He had no choice but to follow . . . or make a scene, and Jonathan, like Harlan, had no stomach for embarrassing spectacles.

Her mind at once began to make plans. First she would need to inquire about this Jack MacAuley Harlan had mentioned in his letter. Someone at the university would know how she might contact him. Then she would need to pack. And money . . . she would need money.

And then after all was done, she would write a letter to her mother and father so they wouldn't worry when they returned and found her gone.

Come to think of it, they probably wouldn't even notice, but she should write them anyway. It was the proper thing to do, and she always did the proper thing.

She wondered about Jack MacAuley. She'd heard his name mentioned before . . . a controversial fellow her father had called him, and had heartily disavowed his theories—though Sophie didn't much care if he thought himself descended from blue monkeys; he'd do very well for her purposes. It shouldn't be difficult to find out his story. If he could be bribed to take her aboard his vessel, she certainly had the means to do so.

She hurried Jonathon along. "My father will much appreciate your . . . integrity," she told him, seeing him to the door, "and I will be certain to tell him how sweet you were to consider my . . . interests."

"Of course," Jonathon replied, nodding, confusion furrowing his brow. And then he looked down his nose at her with that mocking arrogance that always managed to clench her jaw. "My dear . . . would you like me to stay and bear witness while you tell your father?" he asked hopefully, and she knew his offer had nothing to do with his concern for her. He wanted her father to know what he had done—that he'd betrayed Harlan for his daughter's honor.

"Oh, no, no," Sophie replied, patting his arm. "Anyway, he isn't in at the moment, but it will go much better if you are nowhere near when he does read the letter, Jonathon. Trust me in this. He will be quite apoplectic, I assure you! I would sorely regret it if you were to endure the brunt of his wrath in Harlan's . stead. After all, you were only looking out for me . . . isn't that true?" She gave him a canny look.

Sophie hoped the question filled him with

guilt, but she knew a moment's discomfort was the most she could hope for. She was coming to understand that women meant little to men like Jonathon and Harlan. Women were mere pawns—expendable for the *greater good*.

She smiled to see that he nodded jerkily. "Yes . . . yes, indeed . . . that wouldn't be good at all." And he withdrew a kerchief from his pocket, dabbing his brow.

Sophie nodded portentously. "He's quite protective, you know." He *was* fiercely protective of their name.

"Of course," Jonathon replied as Sophie opened the door. "As it should be." His brows drew together, and he hesitated, clearly unsure over the fruit of his labors. She knew it had not gone as he'd hoped. Out of spite, she ought to let him be there when her father read Harlan's letter. It would serve him well to witness Maxwell Vanderwahl's wrath . . . except that Sophie wasn't about to show her father the letter . . . not yet.

She lifted his hat from the rack by the door and set it atop his head, smiling up at him. "Goodbye!" she declared.

Her mother would have been proud of her this moment, for keeping her calm when she felt like flying into a rage.

She opened the door wider, barely restraining herself from shoving him out the door and rushing up the stairs.

She was eager to begin preparations.

Her parents would be in Paris until the end

of the month. By the time they returned, it would be too late to stop her. She was no longer a child and she certainly had every right to deal with her fiancé any way she felt necessary.

Jonathon took a step out, then stepped back over the threshold, barring her from closing the door. "But if your father isn't here, Sophia, then perhaps I should stay!"

Sophie pushed him gently backward. "Thank you, but *no!*"

Harold, God bless him, made himself known in that instant, standing like a sentinel at the end of the hall. He said nothing but cleared his throat discreetly, and Jonathon remembered himself at once.

"Goodbye!" she said firmly when he opened his mouth to protest.

"Yes . . . goodbye," he stammered, and left at last.

Sophie slammed the door behind him. She turned to collapse against it, facing a dour-faced Harold. He stood with his hands behind his back, looking at her empathetically.

"If I may be so bold to say so, Miss Sophia, I have never liked that young man!"

She smiled softly at him. "I know." Harold would worry, she knew. "That will be all, Harold," she said, dismissing him. When he was gone, she made her way up the mahogany stairwell that led to the private rooms.

In an instant of weakness, tears pricked at her eyes, and she clutched the banister. This moment she felt ill-used and trampled, but she refused to feel this way for long. The one thing she had determined from observation was that one could lose anything at all—anything, except one's pride—and come back relatively unscathed. It was only when one lost one's sense of worth that one might not come back at all.

Well, she didn't care to carry this scar throughout her lifetime, only to end up bitter and alone at fifty and stealing brandy from her father's cabinets.

No, that just wouldn't do.

She went to her room, closing the door behind her. It was meticulous, but for the drawings posted everywhere, on the dresser mirror, on the walls. They were *her* drawings, and much to her mother's dismay, she hung them everywhere. It was her one small rebellion, but she was proud of every single sketch, and couldn't bring herself to bury them in her closet, like something of which to be ashamed.

Sophie couldn't seem to simply draw things as they appeared. She never truly saw anything the way others did. Every person, every object had a *soul*, and she felt it her duty and her mission to capture its essence in her drawings.

She walked toward her dresser, touching a finger to the face of the sketch of her mother she had posted there. Unfortunately, sometimes her portraits weren't particularly flattering. She smiled to herself at the memory of her mother's expression when she'd first gazed on her own portrait. She'd practically fainted at the sight of it.

Sophie had sketched her eyes abnormally large, because she was ever vigilant, and often affronted. And her mouth was big as well, and her ears . . . and her nose. Sophie just hadn't been able to help herself. Her mother seemed to hear everything, smell everything, know everything—or at least made it a point to.

The few drawings in which Sophie had managed to restrain herself, her mother had proudly hung out in the halls for everyone to gaze on. But these in Sophie's room were all the rejected ones . . . because they dared not to be sublime.

Sophie loved them all . . . from her own interpretation of the Mona Lisa, with her teeth bared in laughter, to the tiny sketch of her cherished shark's tooth she had hung over her bed like a halo-crowned portrait of the Virgin Mary, with its every precious flaw drawn from the store of her memory.

It was all she had left of it. Her mother had found the tooth one morning, and had discarded it long before she'd awakened. It wasn't seemly to play with teeth from dead animals, she'd been reprimanded.

Sophie still missed her little talisman. In some strange way, the little tooth had embodied her hopes and dreams—not the ones she had been schooled to, but those she'd tucked away in the farthest reaches of her soul, deep inside where not a single ray of light could expose them . . . or her.

She wasn't perfect.

Sighing, she looked about her room, littered with drawings of so many precious imperfections . . . flaws in people, as well as objects, tiny flaws that gave every single person and device a spirit of its own.

Sometimes, Sophie feared she no longer had one. She felt she was a shell of a person, a perfect façade.

Just once, she wanted someone to look beneath it and see all the imperfections . . . and cherish her anyway.

She lifted up the portrait she had sketched of Harlan . . . touching the chin with a finger. She had made him perfect . . . perfect as she was expected to be . . . perfect as her mother expected of her life.

This portrait, and a depiction her mother had hung in the hall, were the two paintings Sophie had rendered to absolute perfection. Simply titled *The Wedding Day*, the one in the hall was a storybook picture, her wedding day as Sophie had often envisioned it. From her childhood, her mother had woven every glorious color and every precise detail for her, until the vision had reached an almost sanctified perfection. The pristine white gazebo, decorated with pure snow-white ribbons . . . the golden rays of sunshine penetrating a vibrant, rich green canopy of trees, and shining down like the touch of God himself on the faceless couple within the gazebo. The rays had been so brilliant as they'd shone on the wedded pair that it had washed away every detail in their faces, rendering them completely without identity.

Perhaps she'd always known that destiny was not her own.

As long as she could remember, Harlan had been her mother's choice.

Glancing first at the letter in her hand, she frowned at the picture she held and then set it down on the dresser. Turning it over, she removed the wooden back, and set it, too, down on the dresser. She folded Harlan's letter neatly and lay it against his portrait, then replaced the back once more. Like everything else in her life, his imperfection was hidden behind the unblemished façade.

She would take the picture with her . . . to bolster her when she wavered.

It would behoove her to pack only the most necessary items because she was certain space aboard the *Miss Deed* would be limited as it was. For money she would sell the necklace Harlan had given her as an engagement present. She might have felt a trifle guilty were it some precious heirloom, but it was merely an expensive token he had purchased, gaudy and ugly. Sophie had never liked it.

It wasn't as though she didn't have funds at her disposal, but she refused to allow her father to bear the burden of this, when it was Harlan who deserved the responsibility! He had taken quite enough from her father—and from her. Sophie couldn't do anything about the grants or the surplus money, but she certainly could recover something of her own!

Her pride.

But first things first . . . she had to find this Jack MacAuley . . . What if he had set sail already?

Panic beset her.

No, she refused to think the worst.

Jack MacAuley held the key to her plan, and she wasn't about to let him leave harbor without her—even if it meant she had to stow away on his ship!

But he wouldn't turn her down, of that she was certain. Sophie fully intended to give him an offer he couldn't refuse.

She removed from her drawer a few sheets of paper and a pencil, then sat on the bed, needing to express her emotions. But this time, instead of drawing, she wrote a letter to Harold, explaining to the faithful old man what she was compelled to do. She'd place it somewhere later where he was sure to find it, though not too soon. Next she wrote a letter to her parents, hoping her sarcasm wouldn't cause them too much concern, and she felt considerably better when she was through.

It read simply:

Dearest Father and Mother . . . Please don't worry, I'm off to the Yucatan to murder Harlan. Will tell you everything when I return! My love to you both!

And she signed it.

Love and kisses, your daughter Sophia.

Chapter 2

"Did you ever find out who was sniffing around about you at the university?"

Jack MacAuley tossed a neatly bound bundle of newly repaired sailcloth from the pier onto the ship's deck, eyeing his longtime friend irritably. Kell Davenport was his best friend and a damned good sailor, but he was worse than an old woman with his gossip.

"No, and I couldn't care less who was nosing around or why!" He lifted up another bundle and hurled it after the first. "I quit caring a long time ago about anything that had the remotest connection with that damnable institution—or any other, for that matter—and it would seem to me you would've, too!"

Jack had, by stubborn will, earned his degree, but Kell had been forced to withdraw in his second year. He hadn't been *university material*, so they'd claimed, but Jack hadn't met many more qualified than Kell. A few barroom brawls weren't enough reason to deprive the man of an education. He'd earned his way into the university through scholarships and hard work, but his background was as ordinary as could be, and when pressure came to throw grant money elsewhere, elsewhere it went.

That simple.

Despite that, Kell's mathematical genius was incomparable, and that, more than his sailing ability, made him indispensable in this particular venture. It worked in Jack's favor that Kell had been forced to resign his studies so early, and that he'd taken up odd fishing jobs on old schooners to make his living, but it was a damned shame that he'd been reduced to using good brainpower on idle gossip. Jack fully intended to put his noggin to good use once again.

"Think maybe it was one of Penn's team nosing around again?"

"Does it matter?" Jack tossed another bundle aboard the ship's deck. Sweat ran in rivulets down his temple and face, and he swiped them away with the back of his arm. "You'll need to check those right away," he instructed Kell. "I have no idea what to look for myself and we're behind schedule as it is."

"All right," Kell agreed, reluctantly giving up his topic of conversation. He pulled one of the folded bundles of sailcloths aside and began to work tediously at the knot that bound it. In the meantime, Jack hauled the remaining bundles aboard, hoping the cloth and rigging were all in order. He'd have to trust Kell's judgment, in any case, because he didn't know the first thing about sailing. That he was captain of this mass of tar and lumber didn't mean a damned thing. He'd merely bought the old ship; the title fell to him by default.

The *Miss Deed* had once been christened *The Adventurer*. It had been decommissioned at least fifty years before, and had sat rotting in the shallows off the New England coast until he had happened on it. It had taken some coaxing on his part for the owner to agree to part with it, because it had apparently held some sort of quasi-historic value. But the rotten ship was barely worth what he'd paid for it. It had even escaped the Civil War draft, and Jack could, on closer inspection, see why. He'd had to reach deep into his pockets to complete the repairs necessary just to get the bugger seaworthy, and it was on the verge of becoming a very expensive dinosaur.

Kell cast him a sober glance. Giving up on the knot at last, he pulled out his pocket knife and severed the rope with a single slice.

Jack winced and had to restrain himself from cautioning Kell to take care with the knife. There wasn't money enough to replace the sails. They were just skidding by as it was.

Kell returned the knife to his pocket and met Jack's gaze. "You realize . . . it doesn't matter what you find down there, *they* won't go for it no matter how you present it."

They were the powers-that-be, those who decided which anthropological discoveries were worthy of academic mention and which were simply hogwash. Jack had had one go-round with them already, and had been raked over the coals, rejected, and dismissed, all in the blink of an eye. His findings just hadn't fit in with the blueprint they were busy creating.

"I'm not going down there with an agenda, Kell. I could give a damn if what I come across proves or disproves my original findings. I wouldn't be any better than the rest of 'em if I did, would I?"

"Maybe," Kell agreed.

"I'm going down there to do my job, because it means something to me. *Period*."

"Yeah?" Kell began recounting bundles. "Well, you're a better man than I am, Jack, because I *am* going down there with an agenda!" He stopped to face Jack, arms at his hips. "Personally I'd like nothing better than to find something to rub into their damned elitist noses. Even if they don't come about to our way of thinking, I'd like to see them squirm just a bit. Wouldn't you? Admit it." He stood there grinning, egging Jack on.

If the matter weren't so close to his heart, Jack would have relented and laughed.

"You would, wouldn't you?"

Jack declined to answer. He couldn't afford to make this a personal vendetta, not for his own sake, not for the sake of his studies.

"They should have at least given you an ear," Kell persisted.

"It doesn't matter."

But the truth was that Jack didn't like it any better than Kell did that they had dismissed

him so easily. He'd worked hard, and it grated
on his nerves that they would disperse grants
so easily to a man like Harlan H. Penn III, who
liked his image far better than he did his
work—only because of who he chose to
marry!

In fact, Jack would be surprised as hell to
find dirt under Penn's nails—the pantywaist!
He had no idea what the man was doing
down in South America all this time—drink-
ing mint juleps probably, and sitting on his
duff!

"They should have given you that grant,"
Kell said harshly, and then returned to count-
ing the bundles, and Jack wondered just how
transparent his thoughts were.

He let the comment go because it didn't do
any good to mull it over and over. It wasn't
going to get him anywhere but in a sore mood.

"I think we're missing a sail," Kell told him,
scratching his head in frustration. "But who
knows until we get them up."

Jack sighed. "Figures."

"It'll be a miracle if we get these up by tomorrow. That rigging is a deuced nightmare—
clear from the Middle Ages, if you ask me."

He wasn't kidding.

Looking up at the miles of rigging, Jack
wondered just how seaworthy the thing really
was. With his luck, she'd break up just out of
harbor and they'd end up swimming back to
shore. But beggars couldn't be choosers. He
walked over to where he'd tossed his shirt

over the ship's railing and lifted it up, shrugging into it.

"I'll go after it."

"Send Shorty," Kell suggested. "He knows where to go."

"No, he's saying g'bye to his gal, and everyone else has his own job to take care of. I'll go'n get it."

"You shouldn't have to," Kell told him.

Jack tried not to sound impatient, considering Kell's loyal defense of him. "Shouldn't . . . oughtn't . . . they'll drive you nuts if you'll let them, Kell." He didn't bother buttoning his shirt. Half the men on the docks worked shirtless on a day like today. The sun beating down on them was so hot a man could fry an egg on his head. All that was missing was Satan and his damned pitchfork. Hell couldn't be hotter.

"There are a deuced lot of things that shouldn't be that just are," he told Kell. "You just do what you have to, and to hell with the shouldn't be's!"

Kell shrugged. "Maybe. All right, I'll get these inspected while you're gone," he said, "but I'll need help to set the rigging and hoist them."

"I'll be back soon," Jack promised him. "Don't go off saving the world while I'm gone."

Kell was that sort of man. He bore the weight of the world on his shoulders—always pulling for the underdog. There wasn't a finer man Jack could have at his side.

Kell shook his head. "No chance of that. It's gone to hell already." He peered up at the sun, shielding his eyes. "Blasted heat is gonna kill us!"

Jack took one last look at the rigging, and his blood began to simmer with excitement.

Almost there.

As soon as the sails were hoisted and they made one final inspection of the ship and supplies, they would raise the anchor and be on their way. He couldn't wait to see the sails billowing and rippling in the wind—his proud lady of the sea with her breasts puffed in pride. He could almost feel the wind in his hair and the undulation of her sweet lithe body beneath him.

Old as she was, rickety as she was, she was all his, and the pride he felt in that moment choked him.

To hell with Penn and his sugar daddy-in-law.

This tremendous feeling of accomplishment was worth the struggle. He felt damned near invincible this moment, and it showed in his stride as he left the ship to retrieve the last of the sails.

Nothing was going to stop them now; they had God's wind in their sails.

They'd had little to say about Jack Mac-Auley at the university, but from what Sophie had gleaned from sources close to her father, he was a pretender of sorts.

An Irish immigrant, his father had belonged

to Boston's growing fraternity of new money. He'd apparently received his inheritance this past year, on his father's death, and had already squandered most of it on this venture, deemed politely, by his peers, as reckless.

Sophie didn't give a fig whether his comrades respected him or not. Nor did she care if his theories were poppycock, or if he would be taken seriously by respectable academia. None of that was any of her concern.

She only wanted passage aboard his ship.

Jack MacAuley himself was of no consequence to her—nor was any other man for that matter.

She'd had quite enough of them all, and they could just go to the devil!

The *Miss Deed*, they'd informed her, was scheduled to set sail sometime today or tomorrow, and Sophie fretted that she would miss it.

Just to be certain she didn't give Jack MacAuley any reason at all to waver in his consideration, she came with her bags packed. She wasn't going home without having accomplished what she'd set out to do. Somehow it was crucial to her sense of self-worth that she salvage her pride. She had tucked away in her purse a considerable sum she intended to use as *persuasion*, and was prepared to offer quite a bit more if necessary. In fact, she felt so confident that she had gone so far as to open a small account in Jack MacAuley's name and had already placed the sum of five thousand dollars in it. And there was more where that came from if she should need it, but she hadn't turned a blind eye in all these years of watching her father's ruthless negotiations.

She intended to offer enough and no more.

It was good business sense all around, she decided. Jack MacAuley needed the money, and she had it to give. She needed him.

It would be a mutually beneficial arrangement for both of them.

She'd left her trunks safe in her carriage, under the driver's watchful eye, while she'd set about on foot to find the elusive *Miss Deed*, and she was heartily glad she had done so because she scarce could move amid the swarming crowd of workmen, passengers, fishermen, and pickpockets.

A particularly dirty little boy of about thirteen latched on to her purse and tugged with all his might. With such a precious lot of money in her possession she was far too vigilant to fall victim to his thievery. She jerked her purse back and the boy went stumbling onto his backside. He peered up at her with a mixture of fear and annoyance. Before she could speak, he scampered to his feet and scurried away.

"You ought to be ashamed of yourself!" she shouted at his back, though guilt pricked her. She had so much and the boy so little. Perhaps, though, he'd think twice before attempting to steal again.

He disappeared into the masses, leaving behind only a greasy stain on her pale silk ivory purse where his grimy hand had been.

"Brat," she muttered to herself, brushing off her purse. Were she not so angry at men in general and so resolved against marriage and children, she might have been a little more sympathetic. But she couldn't afford to soften her heart. She didn't want children! She didn't want a husband or kids, or a blasted pony either, for that matter!

Wretched men!

She was quite content all by herself, thank you very much!

At least she would be, after she plucked her darling fiancé's head bald as a baby's bottom!

In the struggle, she had dropped her address card on the ground, and she bent to retrieve it. They had given her a port address that seemed to be wrong. Lifting the card, she inspected the ships at anchor ... *The Lady Ann* ... *The Alaskan* ... *The Prodigious* ... no *Miss Deed* ... but the address was near, she was certain.

"Pardon me, sir," she said to a passing gentleman.

Apparently he was in too much of a hurry to be bothered, because he kept walking past her, though not without casting her a harried glance.

Sophie glared indignantly at his back, loathing men all the more in that instant.

The caw of seabirds filled the air as she turned once more to inspect the throng. Spying someone who appeared as though he belonged on the docks, Sophie lifted her skirts

and hurried after a shortish fellow with sun-
bleached hair who stood leaning against a
lamppost smoking a cigarette.

"Sir!" she called out, waving at him. As she
neared, he tossed down his smoke and tamped
it out, then turned and walked away, blatantly
ignoring her.

Sophie gasped in outrage. She was unaccus-
tomed to such outright rudeness! Surely he
hadn't just walked away from someone in
need? Perhaps he just hadn't heard her.

"Sir!" she shouted quite a notch louder than
before, and started after him, deciding it must
be so. No one had ever just ignored her! Still
he didn't turn, merely continued along his
merry way, walking at a brisk pace, and Sophie couldn't keep up. She spun abruptly,
dithered, and smacked into something solid
that hadn't been there previously.

She banged her cheekbone against a chin.
"Ouch!" she cried. A strong arm caught her,
holding her steady, before she had the chance
to bounce back onto her rear.

It was a man . . . by the strength of his
grip . . .

"Oh my!"

Yes, it was very definitely a man.

His shirt was undone, and wide open. That
was the first thing Sophie noticed. She blinked,
and for an instant was transfixed by the sight
of a very well-defined, very muscular chest. It
was smooth and bronzed by the sun, as
though he'd labored shirtless for long hours.

The summer heat dizzied her.

"Oh my!" she said again.

She stood there an instant, dumbfounded, rubbing her cheek with one hand while clutching the address to her breast with the other.

Or rather, she was clutching her breast, only she didn't realize . . . until . . .

"Pardon," he said, with some surprise.

"Pardon . . . me," Sophie stammered, and had yet to look into his face. His bare chest held her transfixed.

Good God, didn't they arrest people for running about like that?

She glanced up at last, her cheeks warming, into the most vivid green eyes she had ever seen . . . green eyes crinkled with amusement.

At her expense, no doubt.

Sophie wasn't in the mood.

And still, it *was* her fault. *She* had run into him.

She knew she must appear addled, but she couldn't help it. Not even her father had bared himself so shamelessly. As an only child she had no brothers to offend her so easily.

Flustered, she stared up at the man who held her, despising him if only for his gender.

His gaze flicked downward, and she realized almost at once the indelicate position of her hand.

He had the audacity to grin at her then.

"Oh!" she exclaimed, wriggling free of his scandalous embrace. *"Do you mind, sir!"*

His hands dropped at his sides and she cast him a disapproving glance.

"Not at all," he answered much too glibly,

and had the audacity even to wink. "It was my pleasure," he added, and his lips curved into the most infuriating smirk she had ever witnessed.

Sophie gasped softly, her cheeks burning. Outrage tied her tongue. She hated being reduced to an impotent rage.

All men were the same!

"Sir, you are no gentleman!" she exclaimed, narrowing her eyes at him.

"Madam," he replied, mocking her, "I never claimed to be."

Sophie took a step backward, gathering her composure. Somehow it didn't give her the distance she needed.

"I do believe they've a word for your state of undress, sir," she enlightened him as coolly as she was able. "It's called indecent exposure! And I believe you could be arrested for it!"

His grin widened. "Oh, really?" And his tawny brows arched in obvious amusement, irritating her all the more intensely.

Cad!

If there had ever been anyone in her life she had taken an instant dislike to, it was this man without a doubt!

Sophie cocked her head in reproach. "You think that's quite amusing, do you?"

"Actually," he replied, affecting a mock-serious expression and tone, "yes, I do." But his eyes fairly twinkled with good humor and she wanted nothing more in that instant than to box him in the nose!

"You are an arrogant churl!" she accused him.

"And you are blushing, Miss . . ."

"My name is none of your business! And I most certainly am not blushing!" Sophie denied hotly, but she was, because she could feel it. Her face flared with heat and her hand went to her cheek. She rose on her tiptoes to face him squarely. "And even if I were, sir, you are quite rude for pointing it out!"

He swiped at his chin, and lifted a brow. "Did you know that you spit when you yell?"

He was absolutely insufferable!

"Ohhh!" Sophie exclaimed, infuriated. "I do not!" She shuddered with outrage. "Why am I even talking to you?" she asked herself, frustrated, and dismissed him at once. "If you will excuse me, sir, I have business to attend!"

She didn't even bother to ask him about the address she was looking for, because his very presence unnerved her.

She attempted to go around him to the left, but he apparently had the same instinct. When she moved to the right, so did he.

Exasperated, Sophie glared at him and, without thinking, lifted her hand to his bare chest, standing him off.

"Please!" she begged him, and realized at once where she had touched him. She jerked her hand away as though his flesh had burned her.

He chuckled in reply, and Sophie felt hot with indignation. She glowered at him, and if she could have barreled through him in that instant, she would have. She pushed her way past him, then and didn't look back, even when his robust laughter followed her.

She'd be glad never to set eyes on the man again!

Rude, infuriating creature!

Even if he did have the most incredible green eyes she had ever had the misfortune to see, he was the most common wretch she had ever met!

Her face burned hotter at the memory of his glance. What absolute crudeness to have pointed out the indelicacy of her hand's position on her breast!

How utterly embarrassing!

"Miss!" he called after her. Sophie's heart fluttered at the sound of his voice, but she refused to turn. She kept walking, clutching her . . . purse—her purse! Oh, God, where was her purse!

She spun about, her heart leaping into her throat, to find him standing there smiling incorrigibly at her, dangling her purse, with its precious burden, from a single finger.

"I think you dropped something," he told her, his tone filled with repressed laughter.

Without a word, Sophie marched toward him and snatched her purse from his hand, then turned and left him staring after her, his green eyes glinting.

It was men like that, she thought, that made her eternally grateful to be a woman.

She didn't know why Harlan was so obsessed with discovering primitive man. All he had to do was look about him: *Man*kind certainly hadn't progressed very far!

Chapter 3

The *Miss Deed* could scarce have passed for a ship, more like an oversized boat.

Sophie discovered it hidden between two bright shining vessels, a fossil of days gone by, with its sails stripped bare, the rigging dangling like some long thirsted vine.

Several men worked aboard the vessel, but one stood out, kneeling over yards and yards of material, inspecting it . . . or so it appeared.

"Excuse me," she interrupted, "I'm looking for Jack MacAuley."

A reply seemed to die on his lips as he turned to look at her. For an instant he merely sat staring, as though he were somehow dumbstruck by her presence. Sophie hardly thought of herself as the sort to render a man speechless, so she concluded that it was her manner of dress. Judging by his own attire, she doubted he was accustomed to seeing a *lady* call on a man so boldly—certainly not here on the docks.

Stepping carefully down onto the deck, Sophie approached him, though warily. She had heard horror stories of women abducted and abused, their bodies tossed into the river, never to be heard from again. But she had to trust the man if she intended to take passage aboard his ship.

Really, she told herself, there was nothing to be afraid of . . . except this rotting deck.

She grimaced as she stood there looking down at it, half-afraid it would give way and she would plunge down into the bowels of the vessel.

Her stomach rioted a bit and she experienced an instant of panic, but she took a deep breath and stared the man in the eye.

He had yet to speak.

"Hello?"

Maybe he couldn't speak English, she decided. Many of those who found work here on the docks, she remembered, were immigrants who hadn't the linguistic skills to work elsewhere. Dark-haired and dark-eyed, he could have easily been of Latin descent, and it certainly would make sense that Mr. MacAuley would employ a Spanish-speaking crew, considering the destination.

"I am looking for Jack MacAuley," she repeated more slowly, enunciating her words more clearly.

"He's not here," he answered without any accent at all.

"Oh, good!" Sophie said. "You speak English very well!"

He gave her a bemused sort of look.

Smiling reassuringly, Sophie approached him once more. "Do you know where I might find him?"

"Jack?"

Sophie clutched her purse before her, taking comfort in the persuasive nature of its contents. "Mr. MacAuley, yes. Have you any idea where he might be?"

He had yet to rise to greet her, but Sophie excused his manners . . . considering.

She extended her hand toward him, introducing herself. "I am Sophie Vanderwahl, and I wish to speak to Mr. MacAuley concerning a business matter of sorts."

The man blinked, and his big brown eyes looked suddenly wary, she thought. "Did you say Vanderwahl?"

Sophie kept her smile and nodded, though he appeared distinctly guarded suddenly.

"Damn. Sorry," he said, rising, seeming to remember himself at last. After wiping it first on his trouser, he extended his own hand. "Not sure where my manners ran off to. Kell Davenport, Miss Vanderwahl. Nice to meet ya."

Sophie nodded. "And you," she countered politely.

"Jack's not here, but he'll be back soon if you'd care to wait." He motioned for her to sit perhaps, but there wasn't any place Sophie cared to seat herself. Her gaze swept the deck, and she suppressed a grimace of disgust. Somehow she felt transported to a distant past, where comfort and the barest necessities were luxury.

"Yes, thank you," she replied, but stood, clutching her purse to her breast.

He interpreted her reluctance correctly. "It's an old ship," he remarked in explanation, though it didn't seem to be an apology. Instead there was a note of pride in his voice.

Sophie nodded pleasantly and tried not to sound disdainful. "Oh, really?"

"Yep." He swept a reverent glance over it. "An old warship, we think, reconstructed to serve as an exploratory vessel. We found it nearly unseaworthy, and refurbished it. It turned out pretty well," he told her, and clearly believed it.

Sophie had doubts it would even remain afloat.

She tried not to look as skeptical as she felt.

"Why yes, it did," she agreed, swallowing at the lie. She looked about, trying to see what he saw. "Very quaint," she relented, and decided the man was utterly blind.

Still, if he had faith in the vessel, who was she to question it?

Good lord, what was she getting herself into?

"It's just that . . . I didn't expect it to be soooo . . ." She tried to find the right word to express her uncertainty without hurting his feelings.

"Ancient?" He laughed, and the sound somehow put her at ease.

Sophie let out a breath. "Yes, that's it!"

"She is *very*, but she'll do all right." He smiled at her, and Sophie decided she liked him well enough. He might not have the finest manners in the world, but his presence was affable. "She's really a beaut if you consider her age. It'll feel almost nostalgic out there. Can't wait to get the sails up."

He stared up the masthead, and Sophie took the opportunity to walk over and inspect a baby cannon, one of two that adorned either side of the aft of the ship. Her fingers brushed over the blackened hull, and she couldn't help but wonder . . .

"Is it real?"

"As real as they come, but just for show these days. I doubt we'll find ourselves in a position to use it."

Sophie smiled. "I don't suppose one makes a good impression by firing on the natives."

"I doubt these babies will do more than knock out a tooth, but no, I don't suppose they'd appreciate the gap in their smiles."

Sophie giggled, and looked up when she heard a new male voice.

"You were right. We were missing a sail," the man said, tossing down a bundle before Mr. Davenport.

"That was quick," Kell answered.

Sophie gasped softly at the sight of him.

"He had it already set aside for us and was ready to bring down himself."

"Good man!" Mr. Davenport said in praise.

"You!" she exclaimed in recognition, and his gaze sought and found her at once.

"You," he echoed.

Looking amused, Mr. Davenport peered from one to the other and back, and then said, grinning, "Apparently you've met?"

Sophie straightened her spine and lifted her chin.

"What are you doing here?" She moved toward Mr. Davenport, unconsciously seeking his protection, though she truly had no reason to expect harm to come to her. The man's presence merely disturbed her.

He didn't bother to respond to her question, but answered Mr. Davenport's instead. "Yes, I've had the pleasure."

Sophia bristled at his wink. "I'm not quite sure I would call it a pleasure, precisely!" she demurred hotly. "I see you haven't yet bothered to dress yourself!"

"And I see you've managed to hold on to your purse, if not your tongue," he countered.

She was clutching it so hard that her fingers had turned white.

"No thanks to you!" Sophie replied smartly, and then turned to Mr. Davenport. "I rather doubt you'd appreciate a pickpocket in your employ!" Dressed as he was, he couldn't have been more than a dock hand, arrogant though he certainly was.

Mr. Davenport laughed as he asked the question, not of Sophie, but of the exhibitionist. "You stole her purse?"

"What do you think?" the man answered.

"I'd watch those hands were I you!" Sophie warned him.

Davenport cast her an amused glance and shook his head, as though he found the prospect quite humorous. "You're definitely not the first to complain of that, miss." And then he began to chuckle, and Sophie didn't see what was so wretched funny.

Sophie felt her cheeks begin to burn.

She couldn't stay here! Good lord, she couldn't even look at the man! He'd managed to button a few of his lower buttons, but had neglected to finish the consideration, and her eyes seemed unable to dismiss it. His smug expression set her teeth to grinding and his smile was far too unnerving in its perfection. His eyes bored into her with too much familiarity.

"I do believe I will wait for Mr. MacAuley elsewhere!" she informed them both, lifting her skirts, intending to disembark, when Kell Davenport burst into renewed peals of laughter.

Sophie was certain these were the two rudest men on the face of the earth!

"Blast!" she exclaimed in sheer frustration, and turned to face Kell Davenport, who somehow suddenly seemed unable to control himself. "I don't see what is so amusing, and you can be certain I will report this to Mr. MacAuley at once when I see him!"

"Oh, hell!" Davenport's laughter brought him suddenly to his knees, and Sophie felt the flush of anger cloud her brain. "Sorry . . . sorry—Christ!" he sputtered, and clutched at his side, pointing. She peered down at him,

trying to understand the words he was gar-
bling through laughter that had suddenly rendered him an idiot.

"I don't understand!" She glared down at
him.

"You just did!" he burst out at her.

Sophie's brows drew together in confusion.
"What do you mean I just did? I just did
what?"

He continued to laugh.

"Mr. Davenport?"

"What he's trying to tell you is that you
should consider the matter reported," said the
voice at her back. "Jack MacAuley, miss. What
can I do for you?"

Chapter 4

She froze at his introduction, and then turned slowly. *"You're* Jack MacAuley?"

Her expression was clearly disbelieving and Jack knew it was more than their scuffle on the docks that made her dismiss him so completely. It grated on his nerves. She was a spoiled little rich girl, no doubt, judging by her manner and dress, who was used to getting her way, no matter the consequences.

Apparently he had something she wanted.

She wasn't going to get it.

Even if she did have the deuced most kissable lips he'd ever had the pleasure of trading insults with.

"I am," he assured her, and watched the emotions that flitted across her face; uncertainty, then horror, then wariness, and then as she lifted her purse to her breast, a little smugness, he thought. Curiosity filled him, but he waited for her to divulge herself in her own time.

She took a deep breath and nodded. "I see."

Kell grew quiet, though his grin remained to taunt Jack. They'd been friends too damned long.

"I suppose since we have not gotten off to the best start," she reasoned, "I should be direct."

A refreshing notion.

"My name is Sophie Vanderwahl," she stated, coming forward, extending her hand as any gentleman would. Jack met Kell's gaze over her shoulder. His friend's brow lifted, partly in amusement, partly in curiosity.

The name for an instant stunned him.

"Vanderwahl?" he said after a moment.

She held her hand outstretched, waiting. "Yes, my father is Maxwell Vanderwahl." Amber eyes sparkled with challenge.

She said it with such self-importance that Jack wanted nothing more than to toss her off his ship on her delightful little fanny. When he'd watched her saunter away on the docks, those delicious hips had swung with unmistakable feminine allure—not to mention a cockiness that surpassed the egotism of most men. He had nearly laughed when she'd realized she'd abandoned her purse. The expression on her face when she'd spun to face him had been worth the wait.

Lovely little vixen.

Reluctantly Jack accepted her handshake, though he couldn't quite keep the sarcasm from his voice. "To what do I owe this dubious pleasure, Miss Vanderwahl?"

His body stirred, an unwelcome reaction to

the warmth of her hand in his own.

The same hand she'd held to her breast.

A vision of the scene, slightly revised, his own hand in place of hers, accosted him, and he released her hand, unnerved. It was the same response he'd had when faced with her on the docks, even though she'd looked at him with such deep revulsion. He didn't particularly enjoy his lack of control.

He preferred to choose the women to whom he was attracted.

Arrogant little brat.

"I would like to buy passage aboard your ..." She glanced about, wrinkling her nose. "... ship."

Her obvious lack of appreciation for the historical vessel Jack had procured and then spent long hours laboring to repair, provoked him. "Would you now?"

He didn't need the distraction of a woman aboard his ship.

Particularly when she was the first to attract him in far, far too long.

She nodded, resolute. "Yes, indeed, I would! And I am prepared to offer you a substantial sum for it." She cradled the conspicuous purse, rocking it in her arms.

"Are you?" Jack asked her, and then without ceremony went on, "What the hell for? We're not on a pleasure cruise, Miss Vanderwahl, and neither are we some poor little rich girl's private yacht to be paraded into the harbor of her choosing!"

"Mr. MacAuley!" she protested. "There is

absolutely no need for such rudeness! And I would *hardly* have mistaken this ship for either!''

"The answer is no," Jack told her, dismissing the proposal without discussion. He turned and walked away, leaving her for Kell to deal with.

He didn't want her around.

Period.

He could tell right off she was trouble. She'd turn his ship upside down faster than a monsoon. He turned to climb down the ladder to the lower deck to find her standing there, hands on her hips, and her purse swinging violently in her grip.

"You can't say no!" she informed him rather indignantly. "I haven't even given you my offer!"

"I can, and have," he said resolutely, and dropped down to the lower deck so he couldn't see her.

He heard Kell's chuckle and stifled an expletive when he glanced up to find she was peering down at him. "Three thousand dollars!" she exclaimed. "I'll give you three thousand dollars, Mr. MacAuley!"

"*No.*"

He wasn't going to waver.

She had a lot of nerve asking him for help when her fiancé was the bane of his existence and her father was Penn's deuced ally.

Jack didn't want any part of any of them.

"Five thousand!"

Jack stooped to enter the mess hall, ignoring her.

The ship had been refurbished so that its two previous levels had been made into three. The lower deck housed the kitchen, the cook's office and chamber, the mess hall, two officers' quarters, the captain's dining area and cabin. The bottommost level was used predominantly for storage, and also housed four smaller cabins, in which Jack wondered how any grown man could sleep much less stand or piss. Everyone else slept in the mess hall, in hammocks hung from the ceiling and put away each morn. It was a primitive arrangement but it would do just fine.

Still, it was cramped quarters below, and Jack foresaw a permanent backache maneuvering the lower decks. Only the kitchen and captain's dining area and cabin had any real comfort to them—comfort meaning a man could actually stand upright.

He heard her feet drop on the polished wood, and then her dainty footsteps followed behind him. He rolled his eyes.

"I'll give you five thousand dollars!"

"I don't need your money, Miss Vanderwahl."

He heard a thump, and presumed it was her head as she entered the mess hall. It was a low ceiling.

"Ouch!"

"Watch your head," he warned her too late, and kept walking. He couldn't suppress a grin as she cursed softly in his wake.

"It looks to me as though you do need my money!" she countered, sounding quite determined.

Jack clutched the rung of the ladder that led to the captain's dining room, ready to hoist himself up.

"Wait, please!"

She sounded almost frantic now.

"Please listen to me, Mr. MacAuley!"

Why the hell should he?

He climbed halfway up, then stopped. Neither her father nor his committee had truly listened to a word he'd spoken in their presence. He didn't have to listen to a damned thing his daughter had to say.

Still, curiosity made him linger.

"I'm desperate, Mr. MacAuley! Please!"

He peered down at her, tilting her a curious glance. "Desperate?"

"Yes, please!" she begged him, and Jack found he liked the sight of her down there, her cheeks rosy and her eyes smoldering up at him like molten gold. She had a hand to her forehead, rubbing it gently, as though soothing a wound.

She *had* whacked her head, and he might have been concerned, except that she was as full of fire as she had been on the docks.

Contemptuous, spirited—no, passionate—and desperate, her own word.

Why?

"You have a knot on your head, Miss Vanderwahl."

Why did she want passage aboard his ship?

Her hand flew to her forehead once more, and she covered it daintily with her hand. Her brows knit. "How kind of you to point that out."

Why had she chosen him?

"I do believe it's going to bruise," he taunted her, thinking she must be vain to be so bloody beautiful. Those lips made him crave the taste of her. "A nice fat one, deep purple maybe."

"Really, Mr. MacAuley!"

She scowled up at him but held her tongue, and Jack had to smile because he knew she was struggling to keep her temper. She couldn't hide the fire in her eyes, however. He could swear they were glowing up at him.

Saucy chit.

She really *was* desperate.

"Why?" he persisted. "Why *my* ship, Miss Vanderwahl?"

She cocked her head backward a bit, looking as though she were suddenly at a loss for words.

"Why?" she echoed, looking stupefied.

"Yes, that's what I want to know . . . *why*?"

"W-well," she stammered, "why else?"

He started back up the ladder.

"Because you are bound for the Yucatan, are you not?" She sounded desperate again, and Jack had the fleeting suspicion that Penn might have sent her to spy on them. He wouldn't put it past the idiot. *Someone* had been checking up on them, and Penn had made his name by stealing the theories and grants of others—Jack's in particular.

He stopped, looking down once more. "My destination isn't a secret, Miss Vanderwahl."

"Yes, I know . . . I know . . . but you just don't understand." She pressed her hand to her head, and her expression turned pitiful. "I simply must go with you!"

"Must you?"

"Yes! You see, I can't stand being away from Harlan so long, and I just think I will die if I don't see him soon!"

Irritation welled up inside him.

The last thing Jack needed just now was a spoiled little rich girl who was *missing* her fiancé—particularly when that fiancé had all but stolen grants right from under his nose, grants Jack had worked hard to win.

Harlan Penn had worked with him a year, had been privy to all Jack's research. Jack had just about had a grant pinned down, had worked hard to woo the powers-that-be, and then Harlan had run to them, twisting Jack's research, both against Jack and for himself, snatching the grant money Jack had been waiting for right out from under his nose. Before Penn's interference, Jack's theories had been deemed "bold and innovative, free thinking." Afterward, Jack had been named a blasphemous charlatan, and accused of wanting nothing more than press. Penn had known just what to say to them to turn their heads. He had plucked out bits of radical summations from Jack's theories and used them against him, his only counterevidence being conventional theology, and then had walked away with the rest, using it as his own.

"I'll give you seven thousand dollars!" she exclaimed. "Seven thousand dollars and the first thousand is right here!" She thrust her purse at him.

So that's why she'd been looking so smug; the damned thing was filled with bribe money. Everyone had his price, and she thought his would be mere money.

"I've taken the liberty of opening an account for you at my bank," she continued presumptiously, "and I can deposit the remainder at once!"

Damn her.

He wouldn't carry the little fool to her own funeral, much less to exchange spit with the man he most held in contempt.

Everybody knew, it seemed, except his china doll fiancée and puppet father-in-law-to-be, that Harlan Penn used his academia as a convenience. The man no more took his studies seriously than he did his fiancée. He had accompanied Jack on his first trip to the Yucatan, and Penn had spent most of the time entertaining women in his tent rather than working. Penn was lazy and oversexed, in tune only with his own pleasures. Jack had felt sorry for the fiancée Penn never spoke of. It had been obvious to Jack, even then, that it was Maxwell Vanderwahl's fortune to which Penn was so intent to be married.

Still, it irked him that Sophie could toss around money so easily when he had paid out of his own pockets nearly every cent he had for this meager little ship. He'd had to scrounge so deep into his personal finances that he hadn't even had money enough for all the extensive repairs the ship needed. Most of his crew were volunteers as committed to their expedition as he was, scholars, not seamen, who cared enough about their journey to put little things like comfort and pay aside.

"Let me get this straight . . . you want me to take you to the Yucatan because you miss your boyfriend so much that you can't live without him?"

Something like fury flashed in her eyes, but the expression was so fleeting that Jack had to wonder if he'd seen it at all.

"Yes," she replied firmly.

"No!" Jack exploded. "Ask your *daddy* for a ride!" He dismissed her once and for all, hoisting himself up the ladder, muttering about the overconfidence of men—and women—with money. He'd like to build a bonfire and burn every last bill.

"You don't understand!" she cried, and he could hear the ladder creak under her slight weight. He made a note to fix the thing before someone took a nasty spill. "My father wouldn't let me go!"

Jack spun on her, giving her his fiercest glare, hoping it would scare her away. She was nearing his cabin, and in his present mood, he'd just as soon tell her yes, drag her into his bed, and seduce the haughtiness out of her.

In fact, he'd almost enjoy doing that *only* to get back at her weasel of a fiancé.

But he liked to think he was a better man than that.

He liked to think so, but damned if those pouting lips weren't begging to be kissed. And he wasn't a gentleman. He hadn't been born to seasoned manners and cultured words. He and Kell had come from a different world.

"Maybe your daddy isn't so brainless after all," he suggested.

"I beg your pardon!"

"Poor little rich girl . . . you should listen to your papa!"

She hesitated just a moment and then lifted herself onto the lower deck. "That really isn't a very nice thing to say!" she reproached him.

Jack stood there staring at her in disbelief, and had to restrain himself from taking her into his arms, kissing her brutally, teaching her a bloody lesson for following strange men practically into their bedrooms.

She stood facing him without backing down, without fear, and he thought she was either stupid or truly desperate . . . the sort of desperate that made you truly stupid.

She reached out and touched his arm tentatively, but Jack could feel the plea in the barest touch. "Mr. MacAuley. Please, you don't understand how important this is to me. Please . . . please . . ."

Jack wavered, seeing the sincerity in her eyes.

Penn didn't deserve such loyalty. He didn't

deserve the passion so apparent in her resolve.

"I'll give you ten thousand dollars," she offered him, and he knew that she had reached her limit. There was, for a moment, fear in her eyes while she waited for his answer. "This is possibly the most important thing I have ever done in my life!" she appealed to him. "Please . . . I will make myself useful . . . I will do anything you say . . . please . . ."

Dammitall.

If Sophia Vanderwahl wanted to squander good money to spend two weeks spewing her guts out over a ship's rail, who was he to stop her?

Jack might be principled, but he sure wasn't stupid. He could use the money, and his crew could use some pay . . .

"All right, dammit!" he said, and grumbled after.

Her eyes lit up.

With the light shining down on them from above through the nets, her eyes looked almost like nuggets of gold . . . with specks of green.

Beautiful.

"Oh my, did you really say yes?" She clapped her hands together joyfully.

He was going to regret this, he could tell already, and he'd be damned if he'd let her dripping enthusiasm dampen his irritation, so he said sternly, "Be here before four P.M. tomorrow, packed and ready to go, or we leave without you."

She shrieked so loudly, Jack winced at the

sound, and then she hurled herself at him with the force of a cannonball.

The feel of her body pressed to his sent a jolt through him. He let her hold him as she laughed with glee, not daring to touch her. He kept his hands in check before him, his senses reeling.

"I'm already packed!" She jumped up and down, hugging him happily, her arms going about his neck, choking him. "Oh, thank you! Thank you! You won't regret this! You won't! I promise!"

He already did.

With every little leap of joy, he could feel her nipples, aroused with excitement, clear through her dress. The sensation tortured him mercilessly.

He stared up through the nets, trying to get hold of himself, holding his breath, trying not to notice anything at all . . . not her sweet feminine scent or the mint of her breath . . . especially not the sudden burst of heat in his groin . . . and saw Kell peering down at them.

The bastard was grinning.

Chapter 5

It was going to be a long voyage.

Sophie dragged what Jack would allow of her baggage down one ladder and up another. She peered up through the netting at clear blue skies and white billowing sails and wondered irately why she couldn't have just removed the netting and tossed down her luggage rather than tow it after her up and down ladders.

He hadn't even bothered to help her, merely carried on with his work, and even if she was feeling just a wee bit grateful that he'd refused to allow her to bring aboard three more pieces, she wasn't about to relinquish her annoyance.

He'd placed her in a tiny cabin near his own that was barely big enough to sleep in. One couldn't even stand upright in it. Nor could one wash within it, or do the necessary. Absolutely primitive!

Sophie thought perhaps he'd been hobnobbing with savages far too long.

The water closet, for example, was disgraceful. It was no more than two donut-shaped seats on the fo'castle that hung out over the side of the vessel. Really, what did they expect her to do? Hoist up her skirts in full view of his crew and let it rain down on the little fishies in the sea? The very notion made her shudder. Men were absolutely shameless.

However, she was determined to make the best of the situation. She began to whistle a merry tune, telling herself that she would make do, that she would not complain, because she had promised to do nothing that would make him regret his decision—but mostly because they weren't so very far out from shore, and she wouldn't put it past Jack MacAuley to toss her overboard and make her swim back. He was *that* rude.

So she tried to whistle as she made her quarters more comfortable, giving it as much of a homey feel as she possibly could. She couldn't quite manage a tune, because she didn't really know how to whistle. It wasn't seemly for a lady to whistle, and of course Vanderwahls never did anything unseemly.

Removing her portrait of Harlan from her suitcase, she set it on a small shelf at her bedside—not because she adored him so much that she couldn't live without his image, but because it served as a reminder of her mission . . . and because she'd hidden his letter in the back of it. She didn't want it out of her sight.

She was going to get satisfaction from him if it was the last thing she did. Harlan was a rotten louse, and she wasn't going to rest until she gave him a piece of her mind—not until she had the pleasure of seeing him wretched at the thought of losing her father's money.

She had misjudged him. She had thought him an honorable man.

Suddenly feeling the urge to draw, Sophie retrieved her pencil and pad from her baggage. She couldn't go anywhere without it. Somehow, it was as essential to her as breathing.

She sat back on the cot and began to draw.

She'd hoped Harlan would love her—as her grandfather had loved her grandmother. Her own parents were merely tolerant of each other, partners of a certain, but confidants . . . or lovers . . . she didn't think so. They traveled together often, but rarely told the same tales on their return, and Sophie had long ago surmised that the only time they spent together on those extended trips was the time spent en route.

She sighed at the thought, but hardly blamed her father. Her mother had always been a trifle overbearing. As their only child, Sophie had been expected to behave as an adult from the instant she had been able to walk and talk. Her mother had allowed nothing less.

Her father was a dear soul, but he hadn't been happy as long as Sophie could remember. He seemed to spend his entire life trying to live up to her mother's expectations. Sophie wanted to believe he would applaud her this moment, wanted to believe he would revel in her courage. She wanted to believe he would understand, he above all others, but she knew he couldn't allow it. Never once had he taken a stand against her mother, and Sophie thought it rather sad that, for love, he had lost his own spirit. And yet some little part of her could feel him just now ... some slightly rebellious piece of his soul. In her mind's eye, she could see his secret smile and single nod of approval.

Taking a rest from her sketching, she glanced at Harlan's picture, allowing herself a moment's sorrow. She wouldn't mind so much being alone. There would be no one to tell her what to do, but to tell the truth, she was lonely already. She might deny it, but she couldn't lie to herself. With a sad smile she recalled the days so long ago when, as a child, she'd snuck away to play with the boys. Her mother had been furious but those had been the only times that Sophia had felt a sense of communion with other human beings. She often wished she'd had siblings ... if for nothing else than simply to share confidences with.

She missed that desperately.

Yet how could someone miss something so fiercely when she'd never had it to begin with?

Deep inside, she was lonely, empty, and more so now with Harlan's betrayal. He had offered her so much hope, and she had clung to it. She had built all her dreams around him. And now they were all gone.

But she was stronger and wiser.

She went back to her drawing, working absently.

It had been all she could do not to be physically ill when she'd claimed to miss Harlan so fiercely. The louse. She hadn't planned to explain anything at all to Jack MacAuley, because she really didn't feel it necessary. It was none of anyone's concern *why* she wished to see her fiancé—ex-fiancé.

She stopped to cast a malevolent glance at the portrait by her bedside. It wasn't as though she were begging passage anyway. She had paid handsomely for the privilege of traveling aboard this wretched vessel, and doubted any man in her shoes would feel obligated to disclose his personal affairs. She simply hadn't known what else to say to convince Jack MacAuley to let her aboard, and didn't particularly like that she had been browbeaten into revealing what she had. She knew Jack was not Harlan's closest friend, but men tended to band together, and she doubted Mr. MacAuley would be party to some woman's attempt at reprisal.

Maybe she had even said it a little out of embarrassment. It wounded her pride not a little that Harlan could use her so meanly, and it made her feel a bitter shrew to admit to wanting revenge.

And maybe she *was* a bitter shrew, but as soon as she recovered some measure of her pride, she could let it go, and live unencumbered by this terrible feeling . . . this sense that she had been trampled on—and more, that she had allowed it.

This was unlike her, this ever-simmering sense of rancor. The sooner she rid herself of it, the better.

"If you'd've left at least one more of those monster pieces of baggage behind, you *might* have some room to sleep in."

Sophie started at the unexpected intrusion.

She turned to find Jack MacAuley peering in on her, his head in the door. Her heart fluttered a little at the sight of him, but she ignored the sensation, refusing to explore the reason for its manifestation.

She blinked down at the sketch she'd been working on. Jack's face peered up at her, his eyes staring at her intensely, and she started, clasping it to her breast in shock. Her heartbeat quickened. She hadn't even realized!

"Would you mind terribly knocking next time?" she snapped at him.

He smiled mockingly. "I did knock." He knocked again on the doorframe so as to prove it. *Cad!* Glancing at the picture of Harlan, he said, "You were so lovelorned staring at that picture you just didn't hear it."

Lovelorned?

Sophie cringed that he would think so, though she didn't deny it. She clutched Jack's caricature possessively, lest he see it. The blood seemed to rush into her brain, and her head suddenly hurt. "A fiancée is *supposed* to be lovelorned in the absence of her loved one," she told him, trying to sound aloof, though she felt anything but.

"Is that so?"

Sophie thought so, but it occurred to her only after saying so that she had never really languished over Harlan. She considered that fact. "Yes," she replied, but continued to puzzle over the realization. She had been engaged to Harlan for three years and had never felt as though she'd missed him terribly—anxious, perhaps to begin a new life with him, but miss him? Never.

Perhaps because she'd spent so little time with him before he'd left?

She resisted the urge to turn his picture over. The sight of him only seemed to elicit her anger.

"I wouldn't know," Jack said a little acerbically.

Neither would she, if the truth be known, but she wasn't about to admit it.

"Anyway, if you can bring yourself to stop pining long enough . . . I have a favor to ask of you."

The man had no respect at all, and it was probably her imagination but the portrait of his face pressed against her breast seemed to burn her even through her dress.

She wondered irately if he had ever been taught his manners. It certainly didn't appear so.

"I am *not* pining!"

"I beg to differ."

He cast another glance at Harlan's picture

and lifted a brow when his gaze returned to Sophie. "What else would you call sitting, gazing at a picture of your lover with that wistful look on your face?"

Sophie sat straighter, irritation crawling the length of her spine.

Certainly not pining!

"Not that it's any of your concern," Sophie corrected him, "but he's my fiancé, *not* my lover!" She cast him a malevolent glance.

And if her look had been wistful at all then it surely had little to do with any desire to see Harlan Horatio Penn III. There was only one thing Sophie wanted from her fiancé, and that was satisfaction.

Jack merely grinned at her.

Why did that simple statement please him?

"Why are you doing that?"

"What?"

"Smiling!"

Jack lifted a brow. "Am I smiling?" He took another look at the little portrait, and concluded that the man had a weak chin.

"Yes, and please stop! It makes me uncomfortable!"

She did seem a bit fidgety so he frowned at her. "This better?" He made an exaggerated face, wanting a smile, just a tiny one out of her. Uncertain why it mattered, he nevertheless wanted to know what she looked like when she dared to.

She rolled her eyes but couldn't quite hide a faint smile that came to her lips. Her face didn't crack.

"You are absolutely despicable, Mr. Mac-Auley!"

He ducked his head back out the door and said to anyone and no one at all, "Hey, I think she likes me!"

He heard her laugh, though her expression was sober when he ducked his head back in the door.

"If it makes you feel better to think so," she conceded, and he watched her mood sink as she glanced at the portrait of Penn.

Funny, it had the same effect on him . . . but it was a strange reaction to have to the man you intended to marry.

He watched her more closely, trying to decipher her mood. Was she truly missing Penn? Or was there another reason for that forlorn expression?

He shouldn't give a damn, but he'd found his mood soured by the sight of her brooding over her bumbling boyfriend, and quickly restored by her admission that they were not yet lovers.

"Women are not all so base," she reproached him, seeming to read his thoughts.

He couldn't keep himself from wondering if her lips were as soft as they appeared.

"They are if their man is worth a damn," he told her, and dared to wink.

She leapt to her feet, smashing her head against the low ceiling. "Ouch!" A rosy hue crept up her cheeks as she rubbed her head, and she clutched the sketching pad almost jealously to her breast. He noticed it for the first time. "Mr. MacAuley!" she protested. "I hardly think this conversation is appropriate!"

"Watch the ceiling," he warned belatedly.

She glared at him and tried to stand defiantly, but couldn't quite manage the effect in this miniature room. He wasn't certain precisely why he seemed to need to bait her, but he liked that she didn't stand down.

He gestured at her pad. "What is that?"

She crossed both arms over the item in question. "What is what?"

"That, in your hand."

She shook her head. "Nothing."

"I see . . . and what is it you were doing with that nothing?"

He didn't know why, but she seemed suddenly guilty, and his curiosity needled him harder. "Nothing," she answered again, her tone slightly raised.

"I see," he said, and refused to beg. "Speaking of what's appropriate," he told her, changing the topic, "I hardly think your beau is going to appreciate the fact that you are alone on this ship . . ." *With me*, he almost added. ". . . in the company of so many men. Have you thought of that?"

Her chin jutted toward him, though her glance was suddenly wary. "Are you telling me your men cannot be trusted?"

"We aren't barbarians if that is what you're asking, *Mizz Vanderwahl* . . . though your kind often likes to think so."

"My kind?" She drew back at that, taking offense, and probably rightly so. Jack knew he was being unfair, but years of fighting the system had left him slightly rankled and ill-tempered—something he usually managed to overcome, but not when faced with Sophia Vanderwahl, the fiancé of his nemesis.

"About that favor?" he prompted, changing the subject.

She narrowed her eyes at him. "You have a lot of nerve, insulting me and then asking for favors. The answer is *no*, whatever it is! Now if you don't mind leaving me to the *comforts* of my *state room*," she said haughtily, and turned, dismissing him to rummage through an open bag.

Jack allowed himself a moment's appreciation of her pert little backside, then, knowing they had reached a standoff, he conceded. "Suit yourself, *princess*."

She whirled to face him, standing abruptly once again, smashing her head. "Don't call me that!" This time she didn't yelp, only rubbed her head, but her eyes flared with anger.

The devil on his shoulder jabbed him. "If the shoe fits . . ."

She rubbed her head harder, looking beautifully indignant. "You know, I really don't think I like you, Mr. MacAuley! Not at all!"

"Don't worry," he told her, "I don't like you, either."

But he wanted her.

He didn't have to like the woman to feel desire for her. The proof was in his trousers, firmer now after their encounter.

He left her, closing her door behind him,

and couldn't help but smile at her fit of temper that followed. He heard her through the door though she tried to muffle her scream. More than he should, he enjoyed pricking her anger. She was far too easy a target, and he concluded that there was more to Mizz Vanderwahl's trip to the Yucatan than she was willing to let on.

The question was what.

Whatever it was, Jack was certain of one thing . . . Penn was at the heart of it, and it wasn't that Sophia Vanderwahl missed him. He didn't take her for the type to chase a man about even with a ring on her finger, and she'd already admitted they were not lovers.

No, there was more to the story, and Jack intended to find out what it was.

He determined to keep a close eye on Sophia Vanderwahl, and if Penn had put her up to spying for his own gain, Jack was going to make him regret ever having tangled with him.

As would his golden-eyed fiancée as well.

In the meantime, since Sophie had refused his favor even before hearing it, he was going to have to find someone else to cook for them since they seemed to have accidentally left Shorty behind.

How long did it take a man to say goodbye to his gal, anyway?

It was just as well that she hadn't heard him out . . . He tried to, but couldn't quite picture Sophia Vanderwahl with an apron on and standing behind a lit stove. He could see her better sitting on a throne with a yapping mutt in her lap.

Damnable woman ... she was too distracting by far.

Chapter 6

"You have the most wonderful hands,
dear girl!"

Harlan Horatio Penn III writhed under gently caressing fingers. He had taught her well, he thought with some pride, and felt only remotely guilty for not remembering her name.

He couldn't be expected to remember anyway; their names weren't made for the American tongue. Positively foreign.

He turned to admire her dark skin and features, and she caught his expression and smiled. How wonderfully intuitive she was! He smiled in return, and she renewed her efforts. How eager to please she was!

How spoiled he was becoming.

The thought of going back to Sophie, with her little-girl expressions and her unpracticed kisses, appealed not at all. He grimaced as he thought of the letter he had received from her father. It seemed Maxwell Vanderwahl was eager for grandchildren. He had decided out of the blue that Harlan was wasting his time in the wilderness, and had summoned him back to Boston posthaste. Harlan had little doubt he would exercise his considerable power to achieve that end, if Harlan did not comply soon. He needed Jonathon to help him persuade Maxwell to give him more time.

He sighed wistfully and turned around to let the girl labor over his back, settling into a comfortable languor and thinking he would like to spend his entire life here and nowhere else.

"It's not that she's unattractive," he told the smiling native girl, knowing she didn't understand a word he was saying. "She just . . . has no passion," he explained, and turned to glance over his shoulder. "Understand?"

The girl's smile widened, and she nodded enthusiastically.

"Of course you do," he said anyway. "Smart girl!" He didn't need a woman who talked incessantly, asked questions interminably. He wanted someone who would shut up and tend loyally to his needs.

She rattled off something in her native tongue, and giggled, making him smile. The simple fact that he could not understand her Spanish made her every utterance seem like music to his ears.

"I wonder if Jon booked passage with that rabble-rousing pretender," he said thoughtfully. "I think he'll like you very much!" He turned to her. "You'll take good care of him, now, won't you?"

She giggled and nodded, seeming to understand that he wished her to.

"Good girl. Good girl."

He lapsed into a thoughtful silence, then
turned, raising a brow and grinning a bit las-
civiously. "You'll have a bit of making up to
do, I think." He wiggled his brow at her. "I
promised Jon you would be exquisite, and the
poor chap will likely have had a rough journey."

He'd also promised the girl would be un-
used . . . but that particular promise was one
he couldn't seem to keep.

She mistook his expression.

Again she smiled, only this time much more
seductively, and began to move her hands
down his back to his buttocks, eager to please
him.

He sighed in pleasure, deciding that Jon
would simply have to make do with leftovers.

Anyway, it would be far better fare than he
would be getting aboard MacAuley's wreck.
Harlan had finagled a little gift for the entire
crew. They'd all be lucky if they didn't die of
food poisoning before the journey was over . . .
thanks to one sordid character who went by
the name of Shorty.

Too bad for Jon, but Harlan hadn't dared
risk telling even his good friend. It just
couldn't be helped. The girl would just have
to soothe his wounds when he arrived.

The last thing he wanted to see was Jack
MacAuley on the same site he was working.

She suddenly lowered her lips to the small

of his back, startling him as she lapped gently at his back.

"Oh my!" he exclaimed, and chuckled softly.

Fast learner, she was!

He only wished his *linguistic* skills were as fine as her own . . . so he could understand what the hell she was whispering to him in that sweet musical tone.

With another sigh he relaxed completely, giving himself over to her ministrations.

"Professor Penn!" a voice intruded.

Startled, the girl stopped her tongue exercises abruptly, and Penn's mood soured instantly.

Didn't anybody ever knock? Christ!

Rolling his eyes, he sighed again but didn't bother to move. His voice was muffled by the towel he was using for a pillow. "Go away, Borland, can't you see I'm busy!" he reproached the boy.

"Yes sir," he answered, and stammered like an idiot, "but . . . well . . . you see . . ."

"*Later!*" he told the young man firmly, and laid his head down again.

Eager beavers these young apprentices were—annoyingly eager, at that!

"But sir . . . it's just that . . . you've a telegram!"

Harlan lifted his head once more. "A telegram?"

The boy nodded and came forth, offering it.

"Well, don't just stand there! Give it to me!" Harlan demanded.

The youth handed it to him and scurried out before Harlan could dismiss him. That simple disrespect irked him.

He opened it.

It said simply: *Missed the boat period your telegrams are on board period they'll be burned first time they use the stove period don't want your blood money period*

It was from Shorty.

Letting out a string of oaths, Harlan bounded up from where he lay, fury engulfing him. "Suffering idiots!" he shouted, and ripped the telegram.

Sophie knew they were working hard on deck: She could hear them laboring without rest and without complaint as she sat on her bed and sketched diligently.

The camaraderie between the men was easy and full of banter, and she found herself feeling quite the outsider among them . . . and not a little bit envious.

She couldn't help it.

She couldn't remember ever having such an easy fellowship with anyone at all, not her parents, not her friends, not even Harlan. Always she had been on her best behavior, afraid to show anyone anything other than what was proper, or what was expected.

And in truth, she'd had reason to be afraid. She was an anomaly, wanting things that were hardly conventional for a woman of her position.

Though she wanted desperately to make her

parents proud, some little part of her had admired Harlan's rebellion against his father. His parents had wanted him to become a lawyer, to replenish their coffers, since his own father's career had nearly broken them. Harlan had defied him, following in his father's shoes, despite the protests, and some little part of Sophia had wanted to follow his example.

Some little part of her still did.

While Sophie had snuck out to search for ferocious shark's teeth with the little boys of her age, her friends had all been busy learning their manners and reciting the beatitudes. As adults they had become so very somber—no giggling with their heads together over anything at all, while Sophie still dreamed of attending the university and studying Plato's *Ethics* or the origins of nature and the limits of human knowledge.

But it was an impossible dream.

Her father would never permit it. Their world was an unforgiving one, and a woman's *duty* was to be a proper showpiece at all times.

How dare Harlan belittle the interest she had shown in his work!

How dare he make light of her mind!

It was as though he didn't believe her capable of meaningful thought.

It was as though he had entirely dismissed her because of her gender.

She had thought he respected her more, but she was a fool for believing it, because all the signs had been there. She had only refused to see them.

She didn't want to be a wretched showpiece; she would die inside.

She would certainly become one if she married Harlan.

All her friends—every one—as mistresses of their own homes seemed to have metamorphosed into their mothers, ready to raise their daughters in the same manner in which they had been brought up. She looked into their eyes and saw but a remaining flicker of that curious fire every child is born with—boy and girl alike. For a time, it had nearly smothered within herself. She could see that now.

Only now, when she should be weeping with grief over Harlan's betrayal, did she feel truly alive for the first time in so long.

She could feel.

And smell.

And see.

And it was quite likely melodramatic to think so, but she could do these things with far more clarity and intensity than she had experienced ever in her life.

She sighed wistfully, feeling restless.

She had completed the first sketch of Jack and set it aside, determined to capture his essence on paper. Somehow, every time she finished one, she was compelled to begin another. Jack might be a demon, but his was no simple façade. No matter how many times she drew him, she seemed somehow to be missing something essential to his persona. And so she kept trying. And kept trying . . .

and kept trying . . . until she was wading in a veritable sea of Jack's face.

She wondered what they were doing above deck, wondered what it would feel like to be one of them—to be allowed one's own opinion, to tell bawdy jokes . . . to wear pants . . . and even more scandalous yet . . . to wear no shirt.

Unbidden, a vision of Jack MacAuley's broad, bare chest materialized before her, and her heart began to beat a little faster. She started to draw shoulders below the neck, and stopped herself, forcing the pencil once more to the exaggerated arched brow.

She blinked the other image away and tried to visualize Harlan, but his face remained a blur. Certainly his body was no more than a shadowy blob.

Odd that she suddenly couldn't even recall him clearly. Reaching out, she lifted up the portrait and studied it, trying to recall what it was about him that had attracted her to begin with.

She had known him forever, it seemed, but she supposed she had first admired Harlan's intelligence. He had been her first real friend and confidant.

But somehow, her heart was not broken at the thought of losing him. Anger she felt in spades over his betrayal, but heartbreak, no.

He had been everything her parents had wished for in a son, and everything Sophia had wished she could be—intelligent, witty, adventurous . . . unafraid to stand up to his own father.

Secretly, Sophie had yearned to live Harlan's life, visit the places he visited, talk to the people he talked to, learn and learn and learn, and experience life to its absolute fullest!

It was her true dream, though she was a practical woman, and if she couldn't live the life she wished, she had determined to do the next best thing—to be the best mother and wife she possibly could be, and live vicariously through her husband. Even if he *would* have been mostly absent, she was certain absence was bound to make their hearts grow fonder.

Bah humbug!

He had forgotten her the instant he had departed Boston!

She set the picture down and began to gather her drawings, afraid someone might see them.

The voices above deck had quieted with the sun's descent. Faint murmurs reached her ears, but otherwise only the sound of the wind through the sails was discernible.

The air was stuffy and stale in the tiny cabin. For propriety's sake, she was forced to keep the door closed, and not a whisper of air penetrated the small room. It was rather like being in a coffin. In fact, the longer she remained, the more morbid became her thoughts—she glanced at the portrait of Harlan—the more delicious was the thought of her revenge.

If she sat here dwelling on her anger, she was going to murder Harlan in truth.

He looked far too serene in the portrait—far too noble with his patrician nose and rounded chin. And his blue eyes shone with far too angelic a light. His smile was far too kindly.

With a growl, she tossed her pencil down and reached out to slam the picture facedown, so she would be spared his magnanimous gaze.

How could she have been so blind?

No sooner was it down then his face blurred before her eyes completely . . . replaced by another, and Sophie tried in vain to erase it, too, from the canvas of her brain.

Green eyes and tawny hair . . . full lips. His lips . . . that was what she had failed to capture . . . the pure sensuality of his lips. Sophia shuddered at the sensations that assaulted her with the vision. Her body flushed with heat. She resisted the urge to retrieve her pencil.

He was far more handsome than he deserved to be.

Nor was he anything at all as she had supposed.

Because he was a student of anthropology she had visualized him more like Harlan—soberly dressed and staid, slightly wayward perhaps, but certainly not someone she might mistake for an arrogant dock hand!

She wondered what he was doing up there, and then berated herself for thinking about him at all.

Why should she care what he was doing?

She didn't think he'd come back to his cabin . . . else she would have known it. He would have had to pass her room, as his was the only other cabin on this level—at least on this end of the ship, and Sophie found herself suddenly curious to know if his quarters were as "plush" as her own.

She'd be willing to wager his own quarters weren't nearly as meager.

Well . . . there was only one way to find out.

She crawled out of bed as quietly as she was able, leaving her papers in a neat pile and rose carefully so as not to whack her head again. Prowling like a thief, she crept out of her room, into the captain's dining hall.

In this room was a medium-sized table, with six chairs around it. Snuggled within a nook, a washbasin sat. Bookshelves lined the length of one wall.

Above her, the sun had set completely and cast the lower deck in shadows. She heard voices near, but not so near that she could make out to whom they belonged—not that she would know at any rate. The voices filtered down from somewhere above deck . . . and somewhere below, but she decided the immediate coast was clear.

Feeling a little like a skulking thief, she made a dash for the captain's cabin, and threw open the door.

Chapter 7

Sophie shrieked in startle at the sight of Jack seated at his worktable. Throwing up her hands in fright, she clutched at her breast, trying to catch her breath and regain composure.

"What are you doing here!" she asked, her heart thumping fiercely.

His brow lifted, and he gave her an assessing glance, but otherwise didn't move from where he sat. He was half-dressed once again, shirtless entirely, but this time she had no right to complain.

She was in his cabin.

Uninvited.

He gave her a pointed look. "I would ask you the same."

Sophie knew she had been caught in the act of snooping, but she couldn't quite bring herself to apologize—especially after seeing the differences in their quarters. The least he could do was feel just a little guilty! Good God, his room comprised half the lower deck, with windows along the back to let in the sunshine and moonlight. He had the shutters open, and a cool breeze shuffled through, teasing her hair and face.

A tallish wardrobe occupied the wall behind her, and a private washroom the niche beside it. Behind the desk where he sat was another massive bookshelf that spilled over with books. His bed was a hammock that occupied practically half the room and there was room for a second hammock above the table where he sat. Lanterns, six of them, two per wall, were lit against the setting sun, throwing warm golden light over the floors and polished maple table.

"I didn't hear you come down," she said, looking around, feeling a bit outraged.

She had paid an exorbitant fare of *ten thousand* dollars for passage aboard this accursed ship! The *least* he could have done was to have offered her better living quarters!

"I'll be sure to warn you next time," he told her, and the sarcasm in his tone was not lost on her.

Sophie's face heated, but she ignored the barb, inviting herself in. "How novel. One can actually *stand* in *your* cabin."

He set down his papers, making a point to turn them over, as to hide them, and Sophie wondered what it was he was reading to guard them so jealously.

"Your powers of observation are astounding," he countered.

Sophie gave him her most winsome smile,

liberally laced with derision. "You give me far too much credit Mr. MacAuley. I hardly think it takes a keen eye to note the difference."

He ignored her subtle complaint. "So tell me," he prompted, "was there any particular reason you came bursting into my cabin... seeing as how you were evidently surprised to find me here?"

Sophie frowned, noting the way he had begun to collect his papers and set them inside a drawer as though to remove them from her reach. It was a ridiculous notion, but he was staring at her a bit accusingly. "To steal all your theories, of course," she answered flippantly.

He didn't laugh at her jest.

In fact, his frown deepened and he stared at her a bit more intensely. Those green eyes of his seemed entirely too perceiving. They bore into her, and Sophie's heart began to beat a little faster under his careful scrutiny.

He was handsome, stunningly so, with his rugged good looks. His jaw was strong, with the slightest cleft that seemed to invite the delicate brush of a lover's thumb. His tanned skin, she realized, came from long hours in the sun, but not laboring on the docks as she'd first supposed. She could well imagine him burrowing shirtless in the dirt, searching for buried treasures.

She envied him fiercely.

All Sophie had ever wanted was the chance to learn—a chance to travel and discover new worlds. Her dream to mother Harlan's children had been second to all her own. Only now that she was suddenly free of Harlan did she see it all so clearly. It was almost as though a burden had been lifted off her shoulders. She didn't want to be married. Shocking as the idea was, it took root and began to grow.

Jack studied her, trying to determine if she were telling him the truth.

He had joked privately to himself that she had come to spy, but hearing it so baldly from her lips gave him reason for pause. Could she truly have come spying for Penn? He wouldn't put it past Harlan, but would Sophia Vanderwahl lower herself to such a level?

"So you miss your fiancé?" he asked her, his voice laden with sarcasm as he watched her changing expressions.

"I do?" she replied, and blinked, drawn out of private thoughts by his question. And then with a great deal more enthusiasm, she declared, "Oh, yes, I do!"

"In fact, you miss him so much that you are willing to piss away ten thousand dollars just to see him?"

"Mr. MacAuley!"

"Is that true, Mizz Vanderwahl?"

Once again that flash of anger appeared, but then it was gone as quickly as it presented itself, and her tone was even when she spoke. "Yes."

"You miss him so much that you are willing to travel with an entourage of strange men in less than stately accommodations?"

The fire in her eyes was back. "*Yes.*"

"You miss him so much, actually, that you are willing to travel against your father's wishes just to see him?"

"I am not traveling against my father's wishes!"

"No?"

"He doesn't know, Mr. MacAuley. I didn't tell him. He would have worried."

"I see . . . so you were so hungry for the sight of him that you left without even bothering to tell your parents where you were going?"

Her chin lifted a bit. "I left a letter, of course."

"Lucky man."

Of course, what she was saying might be true, but he didn't believe her. That wasn't her reason for seeking Jack out. She was on this boat for a reason, and he intended to watch her closely to find out what it was. He'd be damned if he'd just hand over his hard work to Penn so easily.

He stood, his gaze never leaving her.

Her gaze locked with his, and her expression was wary as she watched him . . . as it should be. "What are you doing?"

Certainly not what he'd like to be doing.

Without a word, he came around his desk, physically forming a barrier between her and his research—not that he thought she would dare go after it in his presence, but he hoped it sent her a message. He knew what she was after, and he wanted her to know that he knew. He leaned casually against his desk, though he felt anything but casual in her presence.

Every muscle in his body was tense with anticipation.

"What does it look like I'm doing?" he asked her.

"Staring rudely!"

His brows lifted. "Am I?" he asked coolly, shifting his weight to relieve the growing ache in his trousers.

"*Again!*"

He made no move toward her, resisting the urge. He wanted to go to her ... wanted to teach her a lesson about entering strange men's cabins without permission or protection.

He wanted to show her what her presence did to him. He wanted her to see it, *feel* it. She had no idea what thin ice she was treading on. If he were a different man that bravado of hers wouldn't keep her safe enough.

She stood a little straighter. "Do you always stare at women that way?"

"What way?"

"*That* way."

"Enlighten me, Mizz Vanderwahl."

"As though you will swallow me up like some lion and spit out my bones!"

He *was* hungry—intuitive little vixen.

"No," he answered truthfully. It had been a long time since a woman had distracted him so completely. He'd like to slam that door at her back and pin her against it, kiss those soft-looking lips until her knees buckled and he swept her into his arms . . . put himself out of his misery.

And he *was* in misery at the moment, aroused for no reason at all, except that she had dared walk into his bedroom . . . into the lion's den.

It was going to be a long journey.

He decided it was high time to set some ground rules. With purpose, he moved toward her. It'd be in her best interest to learn before, not after, what dangers lurked for a woman alone in a man's bedroom. He had given her the cabin nearest his for her own protection, but he was beginning to realize that there was no one around to protect her from him. He wasn't Harlan H. Penn III, and he wasn't accustomed to tiptoeing around his desires.

She didn't retreat, merely watched him, and he told her, "You're a brave woman, Mizz Vanderwahl."

She took a step backward then, but otherwise held her ground, and he knew she had no idea how close she was to finding herself thoroughly kissed.

Her chin lifted higher as she watched him approach. "Whatever do you mean?"

He fully intended to show her.

He stopped directly in front of her, entering her space, and waited to see what she would do.

She must have read the desire in his eyes, because she said, "You wouldn't dare!"

But he would.

"Dare what?" he taunted her, knowing she wouldn't say it.

She didn't answer, and he knew she was suddenly uncertain of his intentions. She looked so adorably confused that Jack only craved her more.

He smiled. "Call me Jack, Sophia."

She lifted her chin higher yet, but didn't retreat, and her response pleased him immensely. She wasn't a coward, but she might just be naive. If she only realized what thoughts were going through his head at the moment, she would run, without question.

His mouth went dry with desire.

How would she respond to his kiss?

Would she slap him indignantly and walk away?

Or would she kiss him back, offering that sweet tongue for him to suckle?

She was near enough that he could easily find out . . .

Chapter 8

Sophie lifted her chin. "What if I don't want to?"

She knew she sounded petulant and childish but she couldn't help it. When he looked at her like that she just couldn't think at all. He came nearer, standing so close that she could almost *feel* him, and she held her breath as he spoke.

"Then don't. I am a great advocate of free will, Sophia . . ." Staring at her still, he reached out and lifted a strand of hair from her face, brushing it gently aside. The gesture was such an intimate one that Sophie swallowed any response she might have uttered. "Man must always follow his greatest impulse," he told her.

Sophie lifted a brow. "Man?" She tried to retain her coolness though her heart beat like native drums. "And what about woman, Mr. MacAuley?"

"Of course, I'm an advocate for women, as well," he answered softly, and Sophie quivered at the sultry timbre of his voice. He winked at her, but he hadn't quite answered as yet, and she wasn't so addled she hadn't noticed.

He was standing too close, but she found she didn't want to move. What was wrong with her that she didn't just walk away? This was an entirely inappropriate position she was in, and yet . . .

"That's not precisely what I meant, Mr. MacAuley."

"Tell me what you meant, Mizz Vanderwahl."

He came closer, she thought, though it didn't seem as though he'd moved at all, and his proximity dizzied her. His breath was warm against her face, teasing her. His scent drew her nearer . . . sunshine and sea . . . and something more.

She tried to keep her train of thought. "Do you believe in free will for women as well?"

"Of course."

She tilted him a smart glance. "Even for your own?"

He bent closer, his eyes sparkling with mockery. "Personally I have never owned one," he whispered, "but if I did, then certainly."

"*Owned* one?"

He grinned slowly, and Sophia realized he was toying with her. Her eyes narrowed.

"What a bigoted thing to say!"

She straightened indignantly, but the response merely brought her face nearer to his.

"In defense I would argue that yours was a

confrontational sort of question, Mizz Vander-wahl, including even its phrasing, and that I was merely answering as you wished."

Their lips were entirely too close now, their breath intermingled as intimately as that of lovers, and his voice was seductively low. Sophie felt strangely exhilarated by his nearness. Harlan had never made her heart pound so fiercely. Nor had her skin felt so hungry for his touch. Jack's simple gesture of removing her hair from her face had left her wanting somehow.

Did he intend to kiss her now?

Did he want to?

Sophie held her breath, gazing up at him.

"I wasn't looking for an argument," she assured him, and her voice sounded strange even to her own ears.

"No?"

She lowered her lashes, lest he guess her thoughts.

"No."

"Then what were you looking for?"

Sophie blinked at his question.

What *was* she looking for?

And why was she still here?

He reached out and touched her forehead with his thumb, a soft caress. "Definitely a bruise, but not too bad."

Her knees felt suddenly soft. She lifted her hand, brushing his in search of her bruised forehead. "It doesn't hurt," she said softly.

He smiled, and the smile glistened wickedly

in his eyes. "Need someone to kiss it and make it better?"

The very suggestion took her breath away.

She took a step backward, and he followed. Did she appear as wide-eyed as she felt? The sensations she was experiencing were awakening for the first time in her life. Suddenly she couldn't catch her breath.

"Why did you book passage on this ship, Sophia?"

"I . . . I wanted to see Harlan," she stammered, but it seemed suddenly the most ridiculous notion.

He leaned against the doorframe at her side. "Did he put you up to it?"

Sophie swallowed, uncomfortable with the look in his eyes. She shook her head, and took another step backward. "He doesn't know."

"What doesn't he know?"

"That I'm coming . . . to see him. I didn't tell him."

His expression changed suddenly and something flickered in the depths of his eyes . . . concern perhaps. For her? Her heart squeezed just a little. Had everyone known about Harlan's dalliances but her? Anger welled once more within her.

She didn't need Jack MacAuley's pity.

But he was looking at her suddenly as though she were some wretched little girl whose heart had been broken by her favorite beau. Well, her heart was *not* broken! Harlan was not the one calling the shots here!

She was not a victim!

Sophie didn't know what came over her in that instant—anger perhaps, but not anger alone.

By God, she was not to be pitied!

She flung herself at Jack, wrapping her arms about his neck, and kissed him smartly. He was so startled by the embrace that he scarce had the good sense to hold her. Sophie pushed away just as comprehension seemed to reach him, and spun on her heels, leaving him open-mouthed and staring after her.

It was only as she fled the scene that she even realized what she'd done.

"What the hell was that all about?"

Jack was still fingering his lips and staring at the door when Kell poked his head inside.

"Damned if I know," Jack answered, dazed.

"She ran right into me on the way out. Don't think she even noticed."

Jack was having a tough time refocusing himself.

He'd fully intended to kiss the wench, teach her a lesson, and what did she do? She kissed him first! And not tenderly at all. She'd done it in anger, and he hadn't the first clue what had gotten her prickles up. One minute he'd had her under a spell, and the next she was angry and in a tizzy.

Why the devil had she kissed him?

It didn't make sense.

"Bit of a she-wolf, isn't she?"

Jack shook himself out of his stupor. "Con-

fusing is what she is. I can't quite figure her
out, Kell."

Kell gave him a look and then sauntered in
as though he knew something Jack didn't. It
infuriated Jack when Kell seemed to think he
knew everything.

"She's up to something," Jack disclosed.
"And I want to know what."

Kell smiled and turned to him. It was only
then Jack noticed the papers in his hand.

"Well, if you can tear yourself away from
playing sleuth where Miss Vanderwahl is concerned," he said. "I have something to show
you that might shed some light."

Curiosity outweighed his annoyance.

"Then again, it might not." He winked at
Jack.

Jack nodded at the papers, ignoring Kell's
jab. "What are those?"

He tossed them down on Jack's desk and
said, "Come see for yourself."

Chapter 9

What in God's name had come over her? She'd kissed a complete stranger— and worse, she had thrown herself into his arms!

Sophie had no excuse for it, except that she'd been blinded by her pride. Inevitably, Jack would discover the reason for her journey, and when he did, she couldn't bear it if he were to feel sorry for her. She didn't want him to see her as a victim. She didn't want him to think her a fool.

Even if she was one.

Harlan had used her from the very first. He'd never loved her, that much was evident, but she'd wanted to believe he did.

The night air was cool on the sea, and the sounds of the ocean waves comforted her. She stood at the bow of the ship, staring out over the midnight-blue horizon at the diminishing skyline that was Boston. All that was left of it now was a dim indiscernible glow that was, at best, poor competition for the bright half-moon. The moonlight cast a ghostly hue over the sea.

If she dared forget everything but the place in which she stood, time almost seemed suspended.

In that moment, she understood why Jack MacAuley had chosen this experience. Well, maybe he hadn't chosen it, but she could certainly see why he'd embraced it. It was, indeed, nostalgic in a way nothing else had ever been. It wasn't a luxurious private yacht, nor was it some elegant ocean liner, laden with newfangled gadgets, but it held a charm all its own.

Those crewmen who had remained on deck had drifted from their chores now and lounged about the helm, trading quips and jokes with the helmsman. Sophie heard bits of their ribaldry and found herself smiling despite her mood.

"Damn I'm hungry!" one man declared.

Come to think of it, so was she.

She frowned, wondering why no one had bothered to call her to dinner. Surely Jack didn't intend to starve her?

"Yeah, what the hell happened to Shorty?" she heard someone ask.

"Who knows," she heard another man reply. "Probably smothered himself between her breasts. Did you see those sisters?"

Sophie's brows lifted, and she put a hand to her mouth, stifling a horrified giggle. She wondered if they knew she was there.

"Who could miss them!" she heard the first

man exclaim. "Anyway, he'd better be dead as a doornail, else I'll kill him myself for leaving us high and dry! Squirrely little bastard!"

"Oh my," Sophie whispered, and sat down so as not to be seen. She felt terribly guilty for eavesdropping and suddenly couldn't bear it if they discovered her presence. Her cheeks burned fiercely, and she wondered over the wisdom in traveling alone with a ship full of men—not that it hadn't crossed her thoughts before.

She just hadn't expected it to be quite so intimate a journey. In truth, it was as though they were all under the same roof, very little privacy to be had for anyone at all—except Jack.

"If he went running back to the docks on those short li'l legs of his," someone quipped, "he's prolly running still . . . stubby little bastard."

The others chortled.

"Damn . . . it's gonna be a long two weeks if we have to eat bread and cheese the whole time!"

Shorty must be the cook, Sophie gathered, and from their conversation she surmised he'd been left behind . . . or had abandoned them? Either way, it seemed they'd been left to fend for themselves when it came to supping.

Maybe she could offer her assistance somehow?

Sophie hadn't the least knowledge of how to cook, but it couldn't possibly be so difficult to learn. Could it? All she would need was a little direction. She was sure she could do it. And anyway, if she was to be stuck on this ship for the next few weeks, she was bound to make the best of it.

In the morning, she decided, she would surprise them all with breakfast, but this instant, she thought a trip to the kitchen would be fitting. Sophie had never used a stove, and it would be in her best interest to acquaint herself with the tools of the trade.

Certainly Jack would appreciate her effort, and she hoped it would serve as an olive branch between them. They'd gotten off to a terrible beginning, and Sophie needed allies just now, not enemies.

Besides, Jack didn't know it yet, but *someone* was going to have to bring her home, and she didn't intend to wait about for Harlan to do it. And if Jack couldn't do it straightaway . . . well then . . .

She smiled to herself.

She would simply have to hang around the dig site, now wouldn't she?

It wouldn't be the most terrible fate, Sophie decided. In fact, she rather hoped Jack would let her remain in his company. There was no better time to begin learning than the present. As far as her reputation was concerned, what did it matter? If she didn't wish to marry, then what did she care what people thought? Life was far too short, and she intended to live it to the fullest.

All her life she'd wanted to do this, and the opportunity was there for her to seize.

It was time to make herself indispensable. She didn't want him to have any reason to regret her presence.

Looking for some proof of ownership, Jack reread the crumpled telegrams.

Not one of them contained a name, or even much clarity of direction—merely simple instructions that would be apparent only to the recipient.

What was clear was that there *was* foul play at hand.

"You found these where?"

"In the kitchen," Kell told him.

"All of them?"

Kell nodded. "Stuffed in the stove, ready to be burned ... except that whoever put them there hasn't had a chance to get rid of the evidence yet."

"I can't believe that s.o.b.!" Jack exploded, slamming his fist down on his desk.

"You think it's Penn?" Kell asked him, making himself comfortable on the desktop. He turned one of the telegrams so that he could reread it himself. *"Find out his agenda period Make sure he doesn't get here before the board reconvenes period."*

"Who else would benefit by our absence from the Yucatan?"

"But you aren't really a threat to him, either, Jack. He has backers. You don't. Why should he give a damn whether you show up on your own or not?"

"Because Penn is a lazy, cheating pretender, that's why! I'd be willing to wager that he hasn't the first clue what he's doing down there. Even Penn will need something to throw at the investors. If they think he's sitting there twiddling his fingers and diddling howler monkeys, he won't see another dime."

"Is the expedition up for review?"

Jack rubbed his chin thoughtfully. "That I'm not sure of. To tell you the truth, I thought he pretty much had free rein, with his father-in-law on the board."

"They aren't married yet, Jack," Kell interjected, and Jack had the impression it was meant as more than a mere statement of fact. He eyed his friend curiously, and was certain by the look on Kell's face that it was a suggestion, in fact.

"Might as well be," Jack countered.

"You think Penn put her up to spying?"

Jack eyed the papers, thumping his fingers as he considered them. "Who else? And why wouldn't she? She loves him, right? She's his fiancée."

"That's not what I see," Kell argued, his brow lifting suggestively. "She doesn't look to me like any woman who is missing her lover. And if she's concerned about Penn's affairs, I would think she'd simply ask her father."

Jack's gaze returned to his longtime friend, and he peered up at him through narrowed brows.

"*They aren't lovers,*" he corrected Kell, disturbed at the very prospect—and more at himself for giving a damn whether she'd spoken the truth or not. He ignored the last of Kell's observation, needing to keep up his guard.

What did it matter if they were lovers? They *were* engaged to be married, for Christ's sake. Why should he give a damn whether Penn had bedded her or not?

Kell's brow raised, and that annoying halfsmile of his returned. "Defending her, are we?"

"Hell no!"

Kell's grin actually widened at his vehement response, and Jack nearly turned the table over, dumping him on his ass. His brows collided. "You're a bastard, you know that, Kell?" But he really didn't mean it. Kell knew he didn't as well.

Kell merely laughed at his slander. "Keep telling me that, buddy, and I'll let you sail this prehistoric ship all by yourself."

"You do that," Jack warned him, his own smile returning, "and I'll send you back to Boston on a deuced raft!"

Kell shook his head and laughed again. "No the hell you won't! Who'd you argue with then? You'd die of boredom, MacAuley!"

Jack grinned, knowing it was probably true, but he jabbed back anyway. "I'd get a better debate out of a bag of bones!" He couldn't help himself. Their friendship had spanned most of his lifetime, though they'd never spoken a kind word to each others' faces, but Kell was probably the best friend a man could hope to have. Jack respected him as he did no other.

"I can see you now, ya stubborn bastard . . . wandering aimlessly about the South Seas—'cause no damned body will put up with you, Jack, you know that—babbling to yourself like an idiot."

Jack was forced to laugh at the picture Kell painted.

"Hell, you're not far from that now!"

"You're a bastard," Jack said without meaning.

"Yah yah," Kell agreed. "What can I say?"

It was true. Kell *was* a bastard, but he knew Jack didn't mean it that way, and he really didn't seem to have any problems about it anyway. It was just a fact his friend lived with.

Jack reached out and punched Kell lightly on the thigh. "Not a damned thing to say. Just don't go changing streams on me now. At least I know what to expect from you."

Unlike someone else he knew.

He'd be damned if the notion hadn't crossed his mind when she'd first come to him, but he'd blown it off, thinking it too far-fetched. Well, he should have followed his gut—the papers scattered before him told him that much. He would from now on. He hadn't achieved all that he had by ignoring gut instinct.

"So how do you intend to handle it?"

Sucking in a weary breath, Jack thought about it a moment as he considered the telegrams. No names mentioned . . . no proof . . .

no real evidence—not really, because they didn't even say clearly what they were about.

All of it was purely circumstantial.

"Nothing for now," he said after a moment's deliberation. "Personally, I think we should just sit back and let her hang herself. She's not going anywhere."

Kell nodded in agreement.

"But I'm not letting her out of my sight," Jack added. "I don't trust her."

"Yah, right!" Kell's grin returned. "You mean you don't trust us!"

Jack smiled. "That too."

"She's a sweet one, for sure!"

He knew damned well Kell wasn't referring to her disposition.

"Hell, Jack, she's had your name tattooed on her forehead from the instant you saw her. No one would dare touch her, you know that." He jumped down off the desk before Jack could object, and continued, "Anyway, I'm sure watching her won't be a hardship for you. It's not like you know a damned thing about sailing this dinosaur. Guess you have to keep busy somehow." He winked at Jack. "Have fun, buddy!"

"You never let up, do you?"

Kell shook his head in answer. "Someone has to keep you in line," he countered, and left with a chuckle. "I'm going to count some sheep before my shift. I'll leave Mizz Vanderwahl to your capable hands."

Jack's thoughts had already drifted to their

unexpected guest. "All right," he said absently.

When Kell was gone, he gathered the evidence, then set it neatly within his desk . . . and went in search of his beautiful little spy.

Chapter 10

ᔕophie found the kitchen.

Like the matron's desk in a school-room, the stove sat in the center of the kitchen, facing a multitude of tables, so that the cook would be forced to face the men he would feed. It was probably that very thought that had sent Shorty into hiding!

She couldn't blame him.

She could well imagine the room filled with hungry men, all of them waiting on their supper, banging impatiently on the tables with enormous wooden spoons. The pressure to deliver would be high, and Sophie resolved to come early in the morning to begin cooking.

After looking at the sooty old contraption, she was glad she'd come to inspect it. Though even after close scrutiny, she couldn't quite understand how it was supposed to work.

Opening the oven door, she stared into its bowels, trying to decide whether it was in fact an oven . . . or whether one was supposed to burn wood within it and cook on top. There

wasn't any wood to be seen, or coals, either
... but then there might possibly be another
compartment for that beneath. She poked her
head into the dark chamber, trying to see what
she could see. It was spacious enough to roast
a man! And she found herself inside the oven
up to her forearms, trying to peer down into
the lower compartment.

There, indeed, she spied wood, though how
the devil one was supposed to get new wood
down inside there, she had no idea.

Carefully, so as not to get herself dirtier than
she already was, she began pushing against
the sides of the oven, testing it, looking for a
removable panel. Nothing budged, and it occurred to her that she could probably remove
the grating on which she was leaning.

She had already checked the supplies, and
there was ample bread to be heated and slabs
of meat to go with it. It was probably best to
do something simple with her first attempt,
and leave the more difficult tasks for later.

Still ... she would need the oven to heat the
bread ...

"Well, well," came a familiar voice.

Sophie gave a startled little shriek and instinctively tried to look to see who had come
in.

She banged her head on the roof of the oven
and yelped in pain as she dropped once more
onto the soot covered grating. Much to her dismay, she discovered the way into the lower
chamber and plummeted, hands first, into the

gray ash and what remained of the charred wood.

"Ouch!" she cried, and tried to lift herself out before she could cause more damage. A log rolled beneath her palm and she lost her balance entirely, toppling head first into the ash. A cloud of soot exploded in her face, and she sputtered and coughed.

His voice was sarcastic, as always. "Imagine finding you here."

She heard his footfalls as he came around behind her, and was at once mortified at the sight she must present with her bottom poking indecently out of the oven and her feet waving at him.

"What are you doing, *Mizz Vanderwahl*?"

By Jude! She was beginning to loathe the way he said her name, as though it were a blasphemy! "What does it look as though I'm doing?" she snapped at him, and coughed as she stirred another cloud of ash.

Wretched man!

"Looking for something?"

Yes! Sophie thought at once. Her dignity— something that seemed to be stubbornly eluding her these days!

"Go away!" she begged him, but knew he was too much a cad to adhere to her wishes.

"And miss the show?" he taunted her. "I don't think so."

Wicked man!

By the sound of his tone, Sophie thought he must be enjoying this immensely. She dearly hoped he was! The rotten louse! This was the thanks she got for trying to help? Some days it just didn't serve to get out of bed.

There was only one way she knew to salvage her pride ... with a sense of humor and her grandmother's wit. Her father's mother could curdle milk with mere words, but she'd rarely meant a single unkind word she'd said. It had merely been her way of showing affection.

"Gee, I thought I'd dust just a bit," she told Jack sweetly, her voice echoing within the cavernous oven. "Your hired help has been remiss, I think." She wiggled backward, and managed to get her feet on the floor.

His sarcasm doubled. "Is that so?"

"Yes," she informed him coolly, trying to extricate herself with as much aplomb as she was able, "I wasn't particularly looking forward to grease with my bread in the morning. You should see it," she told him. "I really think you'd be quite appalled!"

With her feet back on the ground, she backed out of the oven all the way, wincing at the sting in her left hand as she put pressure on it to lift herself out. It hurt enough that she daren't use it again. Bracing a hand behind her, on the oven door, she used it as leverage to drag herself up, and yelped in surprise as the oven door fell off, then again in pain as it landed on her heel.

"Ouch!" she exclaimed. Tears pricked at her eyes, but she refused to cry. She pushed the oven door aside, and once removed from the oven, she stood as straight as she was able and faced him squarely, refusing to cow before his acid tongue.

His brows were both arched high, and Sophie could tell he was trying hard not to laugh.

The awful wretch!

He placed a hand to his jaw, appraising her, as though she were a work of art to be studied. Let him be amused at her expense!

"I take it you were personally mopping up the grease?" he asked her sardonically.

She ignored the insult. She knew she was an awful sight, dirty as she was, though it wasn't very gentlemanly of him to say so. "It might have been polite of you to help," she chided him, and kicked the oven door away in outrage, wishing it were his shin instead.

Jack eyed her with amusement. It might have been polite of him to help . . . but he wasn't in the mood to help Penn's appointed saboteur.

He bit his lip, trying not to burst into laughter at the sight of her. His anger half-fled now. He'd be damned if she wasn't standing as straight and tall as a bloody totem. Proud little chit.

He couldn't help himself: She was easy prey.

He lifted a finger and dragged it softly across her cheek, smearing grease, then inspected his finger. "Looks like you missed a spot," he told her, and then did laugh at her answering expression.

She actually fumed. She shook her head indignantly, and ash rose like smoke from her hair.

"You are an insufferable man!" she burst out suddenly, her cheeks blushing pink wherever there wasn't grime.

Never in his life had he seen a more amusing sight.

From her waist up she had grease marks on her dress and skin where she had been pressed against the grill—her face included! Her hands were black with soot, and when she lifted them off her dress they left a print as dark as night. The tip of her nose was as black as a dog's nose, and her hair was covered with a blanket of ash.

To tell the truth, she didn't look the least bit threatening, and more than slightly comical.

"I really don't see what's so blessed funny, Mr. MacAuley!"

Jack's laughter erupted. No longer could he keep quiet. "You would if you had a mirror!"

She stomped her foot, and ash billowed from her hair once more.

His laughter continued, despite her outrage—or perhaps because of it. He couldn't tell. She just didn't bring out the best in him.

"Oh, but you do look lovely, *Mizz Vanderwahl*!" he teased her.

She had the nerve to look wounded then.

He'd caught her practically red-handed looking for the telegrams and she had the gall to look hurt! He wanted to take the beautiful little shrew over his knee and paddle her delicious backside—and oh, it was delicious. He couldn't have gotten a better look at it if he'd asked for it. Pert and round as it was, it had made him yearn to pat it.

"Will you please stop calling me Mizz Vanderwahl!" she railed at him. "You manage to make it sound an obscenity!"

His laughter subsided a bit, and he gave her a pointed glance. "You're the one who refused my request to be on a first-name basis."

"Well, I've changed my mind!"

Infuriated, she swiped her hand across her nose and managed to paint it blacker. Jack barked again with laughter.

Sophie's feelings were hurt.

She would have liked to have said that his hilarity didn't affect her, but it did. Tears pricked at her eyes. She'd tried to do something nice and he had the audacity and bad manners to make fun of her misfortune!

She doubted there was a shred of her pride left to salvage, but still she tried. "If you'll excuse me, Mr. MacAuley," she said evenly. "I think I'll go wash!"

"You do that," he allowed, and fell back into another fit of laughter.

With as much self-dignity as she could muster, Sophie walked past him to the door, casting him an indignant backward glance. And by Jude, she would have kicked him if she'd not been raised better.

She glared at him. "You are . . ." She wanted to call him bad names but not a single one came to mind, much less to her tongue. ". . . a bully!"

He guffawed once more, and Sophie turned her nose up into the air and marched away, leaving him to his merriment. His laughter followed her through the mess hall and clear to her cabin.

She looked down at her hands when she reached the captain's dining hall and saw that they were black as coal. With her left hand she reached down for the knob to let herself into her room and shrieked in pain.

"Ouch!" she cried out, and jerked her hand away without opening the door. It felt as though half a dozen tiny needles had pricked her, but she couldn't see anything but accursed black when she inspected it. Then again, the light was dim and she could scarce see much at all.

She wanted to cry.

Whatever had made her think she could have repaired the damage between them? Why did she care so much what he thought of her? Who on earth was Jack MacAuley to make her feel subhuman?

He'd followed her, and had the effrontery to sound concerned.

"What's wrong, Sophia?"

Sophie swallowed her tears. "Why should you care?" Her nerves were near the point of shattering. It had been a terrible day—a terrible week—ever since she found out about Harlan's letters! She had wasted three whole years of her life and wanted some justice done for his making her out to be a fool! How could he waste her father's money so that he could spend his time in the Yucatan dallying with other women?

"I hope it rots and falls off!" she declared wrathfully, and spun around to face Jack MacAuley. "Nothing is wrong!" she lied, sounding too much as though she were trying not to cry. "Nothing at all!" she said a little hysterically, and then added, just to be sure there was no mistake. "I don't like you, Mr. MacAuley!

He pulled himself up the ladder and came toward her, but Sophie stood her ground.

"I don't like you much, either, *Mizz Vanderwahl*!" His green eyes turned almost gray in his anger. With his laughter gone, his jaw was set, and his words were heavy with meaning. "You're a spoiled, rotten brat used to getting your own damned way—no matter whom you have to step over to get it, but at least I don't seem to need to list your shortcomings every time I see you!"

His accusation set her aback.

Did she really do that?

"Look," he continued, having won her silence, "I know I don't fit into your crowd!"

Sophia blinked at the wounded sound of his voice.

"Your kind never lets a man forget where he came from," he told her. "He can work his ass off to earn his degree and prove himself, but no dice! Well, I've news for you, Mizz Vanderwahl, because you're no damned better than I am!" His green eyes were dark with wrath.

Sophie winced at his animosity, at the anger apparent in his words.

She didn't know how to respond.

"There is no need to use profanity," she protested weakly. "I'm quite capable of understanding your frustrations without it." Her gaze fell to her injured hand, and she studied it, unnerved by the heat in his eyes.

If he'd intended to make her feel responsible for all his ills, he'd succeeded. Sophie felt properly chastened. There was truth in what he said. Everything derogatory she had heard about him at the university had been in reference to his upbringing.

Harlan had been assured even the most basic things . . . such as attendance at the university . . . but this man standing before her had likely had to fight to earn every last honor he had achieved. A new sense of respect welled up inside her for him, but it didn't matter, because he really didn't like her at all, and he hadn't felt the least hesitation over telling her so.

The silence between them was deafening.

Sophie peered up through damp lashes to judge his expression. His fury had cooled a bit from his eyes as he stared at her upturned hand, and when he met her gaze, it expressed mostly concern.

"Let me look at it," he demanded.

Sophie nodded and offered him her hand, palm upturned.

He brushed it softly with his fingers, and Sophie winced in pain. He tried to blow the ash away to no avail, and then peered up at her with a sympathetic expression.

"It's full of splinters from the wood," he told her, and stared at her until she was forced to avert her gaze once more. Somehow, she couldn't hold his glance without feeling heat in her cheeks. "Will you trust me to get them out?"

Someone had to do it, and she hadn't the least idea how to proceed. The last time she had gotten a single splinter in her finger, her mother had stuffed a kerchief in her mouth so she wouldn't scream, and then had squeezed until Sophie thought her heart would stop, all the while railing about how men had lost entire hands from infections that had set in after getting splinters. She'd been admonished to behave properly, and not to slide down banisters like pernicious little boys.

But Jack's expression begged her trust, and she took a deep breath and nodded.

Chapter 11

Taking her by her good hand, he led her inside his cabin, kicking the door shut behind them.

Sophie felt a moment's hesitation as she heard the click of the latch as it closed. Her heart leaped a little at the sound. But he merely dragged her over to his washbasin and released her hand long enough to fill it with clean water. That done, he turned around and seized her good hand, then held his hand out for the other. Sophie stepped forward, and he positioned her in front of him, before the washbasin. He then stood behind her and placed his arms around her, embracing her.

Sophie swallowed convulsively at the feel of him standing behind her, his body hard and very male. He took her hands in his and began to wash them, the gesture such an intimate one that Sophie suddenly found it difficult to catch her breath. He reached up, releasing her only long enough to seize a bar of soap, and then he returned to bathing her hands. The soap slid through their fingers with silken ease, and his big hands moved with amazing finesse. A quiver went through her at the sensation. He washed both her hands but took great care with her injured palm, making certain to clean the area thoroughly but gently . . . patiently, never speaking a word to her as he worked.

Sophie was mesmerized by the sight of their hands intertwined.

His arms were around her. They were alone and the door was closed. The realization shuddered through her.

The moment seemed endless, and the air suddenly thick with anticipation . . .

Nothing happened . . . except that he put the soap away and lifted up a towel, then guided her over to his desk. Still without a word, he lifted her up, as though she were no more than a child, and set her atop the desk.

But Sophie was not a child.

She was a woman.

And she was far too aware of his hands on her ribs, beneath her breasts as he lifted her. Fleeting though the embrace was, it left her breathless and titillated in a way she had never felt before. She watched him light a lantern and turn the flame up so that it was bright enough to see by, and then he dragged his chair before her and sat. Sophie's heart beat erratically. Her breath quickened.

The lantern cast a golden hue on his face, turned his tawny hair a deep, rich bronze. He was really quite stunning a man, and she couldn't help but stare. She knew it was far too bold of her, but he wasn't watching her this instant, and she allowed herself the liberty . . .

"This is going to hurt just a bit," he warned her, looking up into her eyes.

His green eyes seemed to glitter by the flame, hypnotizing her. She tried to find her voice to speak but couldn't. Again she nodded, swallowing, far too aware of the man sitting before her . . . her hand cradled within his.

He tried to be gentle, Sophie could tell, but tears sprang to her eyes as he began to work to remove the splinters. Closing her eyes, she took a deep breath and tried not to cry out.

He knew she was trying hard to be brave.

Jack tried not to smile at her expression.

She looked so much like a little girl, with her eyes scrunched shut and her lips tightly pressed, as though bracing herself for her punishment.

Despite the truth of his accusations—she *was* a spoiled brat—he admired her grit at the moment, the telltale tears welling in her eyes.

Christ, when he'd looked up into those huge wide eyes, he'd wanted to draw her into his arms and hold her, tell her everything was going to be all right.

His emotions warred now as he watched her.

On the one hand he wanted to despise her for what she was doing—spying for Penn. On the other, he wanted to care for her, keep her from harm, soothe her. And at the heart of it all was an intense attraction between them that set him on his ass every time he was in her presence.

He didn't trust her, but even less did he trust himself.

He couldn't seem to think straight when he was around her. His body took over and his brain turned to mush.

Damned Penn!

"Ouch!"

He hadn't met to hurt her. His gaze jerked up. "Sorry. I know it hurts, Sophia."

She nodded, her eyes watering. "It's all right," she absolved him, "I know you have to."

He returned to working on her palm, squeezing out the slivers as gently as he was able, unnerved by the way her pained expression made him feel.

"You really did a number on it," he told her.

She laughed softly, nervously perhaps.

He'd like to say it served her right, but he couldn't find it in himself to wish her harm. Her leg brushed his knee and his body stirred.

Dammit.

What was wrong with him?

He was getting aroused just taking splinters out of her hand. The sweet, feminine scent of her teased him. The softness of her hands preoccupied him, taunting him with images of her gentle caresses. He couldn't stop himself from imagining the pale skin beneath her bodice . . . the rise and fall of her breasts . . . remembering the taste of her mouth.

She had teased him only, giving him the briefest sense of what she would taste like. Her closed-mouth kiss had been far too brief, and he found himself craving the taste of her on his tongue.

He wanted her.

There was no denying it.

He swallowed thickly and reached down to draw his knife from his boot, trying to ignore the heat simmering in his groin.

Seeing the blade flash, she cried out and jerked her hand back. "You are *not* going to use *that* on *me*!"

"Actually, I am," he said, and smiled up at her.

Both her hands flew up at his declaration, and her expression turned suddenly combative. "*No*, you most certainly are *not*!"

Her temper was a good thing, he decided.

He was far more at ease around her when she was being a spitfire. Timidness just didn't suit her. Nor did it suit him at all, either.

It confused him, brought out conflicting emotions that he'd rather not deal with.

He held his dagger in an open hand. It had been a gift from his father, and to him from his father before him. With its heavy metal handle and curved blade, he was well-aware that it seemed far too dangerous a tool to be using on her tender flesh, but it was all he had.

"It's up to you, Sophia. Live with them, or I can take them out." He left it up to her, making no move to return to the task until she gave him leave.

She lowered her hands, but kept them out of his reach.

"I'll just use the tip," he promised her, sensing her hesitation.

Her huge eyes slanted, and he stared into them, trying to decipher their strange color—greenish-gold at the instant, but a green so dark they were almost black . . . and dancing flecks of red maybe from the flame of the lantern.

"You won't let it go in too deep?"

Jack blinked at her question.

The allusion was completely lost to her, but not to him. His body hardened at the images that assaulted him—his body poised over hers, coaxing her to open for him. He glanced down at his knife, then back into her wide eyes.

She couldn't know what he was thinking.

Need clawed at him, and he resisted the urge to *readjust* because she was staring at him too intently. His body strained against his trousers, and he shifted uncomfortably.

"I'll only push it in a little," he swore, and his voice sounded raw even to his own ears.

If she happened to look down . . . would she understand what she saw?

Was she as innocent as she made herself out to be?

He wanted to know. He willed her to look, wanting to see her reaction.

"If it hurts," he added, clearing his throat, "I'll . . . uh . . . pull out at once." He studied her expression. She wanted to trust him, he could see that.

Too bad he couldn't return that trust.

"Promise?"

"Promise," he swore, and winked at her. "I'll be gentle."

Her brows knit. She took a deep breath. "Well ... all right then," she relented and offered her palm once more. "But don't push too hard!"

His body hardened fully.

"You ... uh ... have my word."

Damn, he had to stop thinking about this or he was liable to slice off her hand. He swallowed hard, trying to clear the cobwebs from his brain.

"Forgive me," she said, concern tinging her voice. "I know I'm being a ninny, but it just seems so ... big!"

Jack choked suddenly.

She couldn't possibly know what she was doing to him with no more than a simple conversation.

Or maybe she did?

His eyes were drawn to her bodice, searching for some sign that she shared his bawdy thoughts, but the thickness of her dress completely hid what he most wanted to see.

If he reached out and embraced them, would her nipples be hard through the layers of her gown?

Like the Princess and the Pea ... a man's fingers knew instinctively what lay beneath.

His thumb itched to brush her nipple with a lover's touch.

The handle of his knife was a poor substitute.

He cleared his throat, and tried to change the direction of his thoughts, reminding himself what he had caught her doing.

He peered up at her and found her staring at him, deep in thought.

What was she thinking?

Was she wondering where the telegrams were?

She blinked down at him, her expression vulnerable. "Sophia?"

"Yes?"

He went back to working at her splinters. "What were you doing in the kitchen?" he asked her outright.

He must have pricked her a bit too hard. "Ow!" she exclaimed, but didn't jerk her hand away.

"Sorry," he murmured, glancing up at her, and almost meant it.

"Well . . ." She frowned at him. "I was . . . ummm . . . well, you see . . . I was . . ."

She was searching for an excuse.

He tried to sound casual, though he was anything but. "Looking for something?"

"I suppose you might say that," she replied, sounding a bit uneasy. He glanced up to gauge her expression and found her eyes narrowed on him.

He watched her intently.

"What exactly were you looking for?"

Her cheeks turned pink again. "Actually," she told him, averting her gaze, "I was trying to figure out how to use the oven." She peered back at him with lifted brows as though she expected a reaction from him.

"You were trying to figure out how to use the oven?"

She nodded once. "Yes."

"Why?"

"Well . . . you see . . . when I was on deck . . . I couldn't help but overhear what they were saying about the cook . . ."

Jack's brow lifted. "What about him?"

Clever little liar.

She smiled shyly, looking every bit the virtuous little miss, and Jack clenched his jaw. "When I heard that he'd been left behind . . . I thought I'd surprise everyone and cook breakfast in the morning."

He didn't even try to keep the sarcasm from his tone. "Oh, really?"

"Yes." Her smile brightened, and she seemed oblivious to his skepticism. "You see . . . I truly meant it when I said I wanted to make myself useful." She batted her lashes, looking quite pleased with herself.

She was waiting for him to pat her on the back, he realized, and Jack just wasn't going to do it.

He didn't believe her.

"How good of you," he replied, and dropped her hand. "I think that's all of 'em," he told her, and stared up at her in disbelief.

She was either a very good little actress, or she was telling the deuced truth.

He just couldn't tell which.

The evidence, however, seemed undeniable.

For an instant, he considered pulling out the telegrams and confronting her with them, but he wasn't quite ready to give up his poker hand. There was time enough to figure out how best to handle this. She wasn't going anywhere.

In the meantime, he decided, Mizz Sophia Vanderwahl was fair game.

As far as Jack was concerned, with her kiss, she had declared herself available to him.

If she had misrepresented herself, well then . . . he sure as hell wasn't about to feel the least bit guilty over taking what she willingly offered.

And if she was telling the truth . . . he still felt not one iota of loyalty to Penn. He had no respect for the man, so why should he honor the man's engagement?

Either way, he knew only one thing for certain . . . Sophia Vanderwahl had the damnable most beautiful mouth he had ever sampled.

Chapter 12

J ack awoke to the smell of bread baking.

The tantalizing scents drifted into his cabin, teasing him out of bed. Like a zombie, he made his way into the mess hall, and true to her word, he found Sophie fast at work in the kitchen, and his crew salivating mindlessly at her skirts.

He smiled at the sight she presented, adorably unkempt, skirts mussed and hair escaping pins as she labored diligently despite the distraction of thirty-five men hounding her heels. He would have stepped in, but she handled them easily enough, putting them to work—Randall gathering silverware and Kell delivering plates, Pete in charge of forming a line for those who had already received their dishes. For their efforts she gave them a smile that endeared her to one and all.

But despite Sophia Vanderwahl's killer smile, they should have all stayed in bed.

The bread he'd drooled over turned out as

black as the oven itself and the smoked meat as ashy as carbonized paper.

Peeling away the charred layers of his breakfast, Jack took a glance around the room. It was like looking into a mirror with thirty-some faces—every expression the same. No one wanted to hurt Sophie's feelings, but the question was the same in every gaze.

How could anyone screw up something so simple?

Sophie stood over them, looking as uncertain as a newlywed bride with honeymoon jitters. When no one spoke up, she finally took her own plate and sat in the only empty seat remaining in the mess hall . . . right in front of Jack, next to Kell.

"I think it's a little burned," she told Kell as she sat.

Kell smiled and nodded, pushing a rock-hard piece of loaf into his mouth. "It's all right," he told her, his words muffled.

As they watched, he crunched down on his food, and Jack thought maybe it hurt him to chew, because he winced with every bite.

Sophia looked at him then, apologizing with those honey-colored eyes that left him dazed every time he stopped to look into them.

"The fire burned a little too high," she explained, and shrugged nervously. "I didn't realize . . . until they were already . . . done."

Jack coughed.

Overdone, he wanted to say.

He lifted up a piece of incinerated ham and put it into his mouth. It tasted just like ash, and he resisted the urge to spit it back out. She was watching him too intently, and the look in her eyes told him that she really had tried, that it seemed to matter how he responded.

Unsure why it was important to him that her feelings weren't hurt, he swallowed, wincing as a jagged piece of ham tried to make its way down his parched throat. He attempted a smile for her then, and closed his mouth when he looked at Kell's ash-blackened teeth.

"It's really . . . good," Kell offered politely, nodding just a little too enthusiastically.

Jack stifled his laughter.

Kell was a poor liar, he decided, but a better man than Jack was, because Jack couldn't seem to muster the words to give her the assurances she seemed to need.

Sophie's brows lifted when she saw Kell's teeth . . . and the black inside his lips . . . and thank God she broke the ice with a horrified little squeal.

"Oh my!" she exclaimed, dropping her own bread and slapping a hand over her mouth. "Tell me you aren't missing teeth because of me!"

It sure as hell looked like it, and it sounded that way as well.

Kell looked panicked for an instant, his eyes going wide as he shoved a finger in his mouth to feel for missing or broken teeth. There were none, and his relief at finding them intact was evident in his sigh.

"Damn!" he said, casting an uneasy glance at Jack. "Scared me for a sec."

Sophie turned to Jack then, pursing her lips and trying not to laugh.

Jack grinned at her, knowing his smile would be as flattering as Kell's, and was rewarded with her sparkling laughter.

The sound of it sent a shudder of desire through him.

Christ, she wasn't merely lovely when she laughed, she was dazzling. Her laughter glistened even in her eyes.

He wasn't prepared for the way it affected him.

He found himself completely disarmed.

Even Kell seemed to hold his breath until her laughter subsided, and then he turned to meet Jack's gaze, and Jack groaned inwardly, recognizing the instant infatuation in his friend's eyes.

Damn, but she was going to turn out to be trouble . . . in more ways than one.

And Jack was in trouble as well, if she could win over his motley crew with a lousy breakfast like that!

And judging by the expressions on all of their faces, she'd somehow done exactly that.

As far as Sophie was concerned, the morning's efforts had not gone in vain.

She didn't try to fool herself. She knew her first attempt at cooking had been a disaster, but it obviously had not gone unappreciated. The crew either felt terribly sorry for her, or they had taken her gesture for what it was . . . a hand in friendship.

In either case, they seemed to have adopted her as one of their own—Kell in particular.

Sophie liked him.

The tall, dark-haired giant was a Bohemian of sorts. His shoulder-length hair was bound at the nape like some old-time pirate's, and his dress, as well, was reminiscent of another age. His mirth never faded from his bright blue eyes, and his patience was remarkable. For that Sophie was indebted to him.

Without having been asked, he had taken the time to show her how the stove worked so that she might do better with her next effort. And then he'd given her a tour of the ship. She had only to ask about the cannons, and he had determined to show her how they worked.

"Are you certain it's no trouble?" she asked him, afraid to become an inconvenience. He had spent practically all afternoon amusing her, and she was beginning to feel guilty about monopolizing his attention. She knew he had work to attend to.

"No trouble at all," he assured her, and winked, then drew her aside to watch from a safe distance as he properly packed the cannon.

Sophie clutched her hands togther as she watched him work. The prospect of actually seeing the gun go off left her with a strange sense of anticipation—like a child waiting for a display of fireworks.

"You say this was a vessel used for exploration?"

"Yep," he told her. "Primarily by topographers."

Sophie's brows knit. "Why would a topographer need cannons, I wonder."

He stopped what he was doing to answer her question. "It's an old ship, Miss Vanderwahl. It was their sole means of protection on highly ungovernable seas."

"Oh, please!" Sophie exclaimed. "Call me Sophie!"

He nodded. "All right, Sophie," he replied warmly.

The crew on deck began to gather round them, watching as well, curiosity snatching their attention.

"They are so small, though!" she declared, speaking of the cannons. "Why so small?"

"Well, she was never a warship," Kell disclosed. "No reason for heavy guns."

Her brows knit as she watched Kell struggle with the preparations. "What a tedious process!"

"Yeah, sometimes it was," he agreed. And then he finished at last and lit the fuse. "Ready?"

Sophie nodded.

He backed away from the cannon and took her by the shoulders, pulling her out of harm's way.

The cannon went off with an explosion that nearly left her deaf.

"Oh, my!" Sophie exclaimed.

The cannonball landed in the ocean with a

lame splash, not more than fifty yards from where they were.

Sophie laughed. "How pitiful!"

Kell nodded. "Yah, and at this point, the ships are crashing," he told her, donning his storyteller's cap. "The crew is off and running to grab their guns . . ."

Sophie grinned at his boyish gestures. He brandished his finger at her as though it were a pistol.

"No swords?" she asked him.

"Nope, no swords," he said. "Guns . . ." He stopped and winked at her. "Or maybe a few poison arrows . . . we're going into savage country," he reminded her. "Wanna try the cannon?" he asked abruptly.

Sophie blinked in surprise. "Me?"

"Yes, you. C'mere, I'll teach you how."

Sophie followed him. It was, after all, just a baby cannon, hardly much bigger than a rifle.

What harm could possibly come of it?

Kell walked her through the entire process, and she felt almost like a pirate standing beside him, packing the powder to his boyish utterances. "All right, here they come!" he encouraged her. And, "Hurry . . . they're almost on top of us!"

Never mind that this wasn't a pirate ship at all, it felt dangerously exciting to play along.

The crew joined Kell in his banter, and Sophie never felt so much a comrade in arms. She giggled as she rushed her preparations, trying to arm the ship before they could be overtaken by their imaginary foes.

Someone lit a match and came running to light the fuse for her, and Sophie stepped back, plugging her ears as she waited for it to go off.

"What the hell is going on here?"

His voice thundered over the decks and Sophie heard it despite her muffled ears.

She spun to face him, her heart leaping at the prospect of seeing him again. He'd been locked in his cabin working all afternoon with strict orders that he not be disturbed. As she turned, her feet tangled in a coil of rope and it sent her tumbling backward against the cannon. She merely skimmed it and tumbled past it onto the deck, onto her rear, but the impact of her weight tipped the cannon upward, small as it was.

Sophie only had time to realize what had happened when the cannon exploded.

"Hell's bells!" someone exclaimed.

It might have been Kell.

Sophie lay there helplessly as the ball went flying upward.

Every gaze followed it.

Complete silence fell as it rose above the sails . . . and then it seemed to pause in midair for an interminable moment. Chaos broke loose as it made its descent, plunging toward the stern. It ripped through the sails, and Sophie gasped in alarm.

She met Jack MacAuley's murderous gaze for the briefest instant before he sprinted after his crew toward the hole she had just put in his ship.

Chapter 13

She was afraid to move.

Sophie watched the crew gather around the damage she had done, and she was taken with the most overwhelming urge to jump overboard.

Had she sunk the boat?

His silence was terrifying.

In fact, everyone seemed suddenly mute. They all gathered like mourners about a casket, curious and grim. Jack had disappeared into the mob of his crew, and had yet to resurface, but Sophie could tell by their stoic silence that she had done something really, really terrible.

Her heart beat frantically, and though it wasn't her way to fly from trouble, she might have done so . . . if she'd had somewhere to go.

But there was nowhere to go, nothing to do but face him.

Deciding she couldn't avoid it, she picked

herself up and brushed herself off, then went to view the damage.

Instinctively she hid behind Kell, peeking between him and Randall.

"Someone get down there," Jack barked at them. He gestured with his hand, and several men obeyed at once. He got down on hands and knees and peered into the cannonball-sized hole. It was a moment before he spoke.

"I'll be damned," he swore, and Sophie held her breath, waiting to hear the report.

"Do you see it?" she heard Jack ask after a moment. Apparently the men had reached the damage site.

Sophie couldn't hear their muffled responses, but she heard the chatter of voices below deck. Kell suddenly seemed to notice her standing beside him and put a hand on her shoulder, as though to comfort her, but he said not a word. The gravity of the situation did not escape her. If the ball had managed to go through the hold and bottom of the ship, would there be anything they could do to stop it from sinking?

Her heart raced wildly.

"Are you sure?" Jack shouted through the gaping hole.

More chatter below.

"What stopped it?" he asked.

A thousand sighs exploded around her, and Sophie thought that might be a good thing.

She nibbled her lip anxiously.

"You've got to see this!" she heard someone below deck shout up at them.

"I'm coming!" Jack told them at once, and bounded up from his knees. As though he had sensed her presence, his gaze seemed to find her at once, and the look in his eyes sent her pulse skittering.

He came toward her, pointing rudely, and Sophie froze. "You!" he said. "Come with me!" And he seized her by the arm.

"Hey, Jack, it wasn't her fault," Kell said in defense of her.

No one else dared to speak up.

Silence followed them.

Sophie's heart pounded with fear as he dragged her behind him. He came to the ladder and released her, practically jumping down, not bothering with the rungs, and then he motioned for her to come down after him. Sophie didn't dare resist.

He pulled her through the mess hall and then down another ladder, and up into the captain's dining hall.

Sophie had yet to see any sign of the cannon damage.

And then she did.

Several crewmen were gathered around her cabin, staring inside. They parted for Jack, and he released her long enough to go inside and inspect the damage firsthand.

"Lucky thing she packs like a woman, eh?" she heard one man whisper.

"There went her summer wardrobe," snickered another.

Sophie groaned inwardly and stepped forward to see for herself.

There, indeed, went her summer wardrobe.

The cannonball had come through the roof of her cabin and had landed, of all places, on her suitcases . . . which were of course stacked on her bed. She had dragged them out to find a suitable dress and then had stacked them on top of one another, smallest on top, because there just hadn't been room to do anything else. She had left them there, intending to set them aside later when she went to bed.

The first and smallest bag had been tossed aside. It had been crushed, actually. Sophie winced at the sight of it . . . her mirrors and toiletry. The scent of perfume permeated the cabin. The second, too, had been destroyed along with its contents and now sported more than abundant ventilation, but the third remained in place, the cannonball snuggled deep within the folds of her very expensive gowns.

Sophie cringed at the sound of her mother's voice in her ear, shrieking with indignation.

As she watched, they dragged that suitcase aside as well, and then her bedclothes, and found the cannonball had stopped short of destroying the wooden cot that was her bed. It was cracked and dented from the impact, but otherwise intact.

She blinked at the sight of it.

It was, indeed, fortunate for them all that she had packed heavily. After it had ripped through the sails and crashed through the deck, and then three suitcases, her gowns had provided adequate stoppage for the ball.

Her gaze was drawn to the picture of Harlan she had placed face up on the bed this morning. Less than a foot or so to the right and his face would have been plastered to the cannonball...but it had been spared... more's the pity.

"Isn't that...*lucky*," Sophie managed to say, her stomach roiling.

Now what was she going to wear?

Jack glared at her, his green eyes smoldering with ire. "For the first time I can honestly say I'm damned grateful a woman *never* travels light!"

Sophie didn't know whether to be relieved or offended by his remark. Since she couldn't very well defend herself, she might have been inclined to defend all womankind in that instant except that she was afraid to even open her mouth.

"If there is a God out there," he told her, "we've seen proof of it today!"

She thought he meant because they had been spared. The ship was intact and they weren't going to plummet to the bottom of the sea to be eaten by little fishies.

"Out of everywhere on this ship that ball could have landed," he continued angrily, "this is the *one* place where justice is served!"

Sophie opened her mouth to speak in self-defense and indignation, but nothing came out.

She closed it again.

It was true—even though he didn't have to be so blessed gleeful over her loss!

She peered up at the hole in her ceiling to find half a dozen pair of eyes staring down at them, and turned to face Jack again, wincing at his wrathful stare.

She straightened her shoulders. "You really don't have to shout," she told him with as much dignity as she could muster.

She had tried so very hard to make up for their first meeting. She sighed. So much for the morning's efforts.

It seemed she and Jack were destined to remain at odds.

Jack MacAuley was an insensitive brute!

Sophie came to that decision as she lay in her bed, staring at the stars through the hole in her roof.

She wondered how a man could grow to be so hard, but she didn't really wish to explore the answer to that question because she didn't want to feel sorry for him. If he'd had a hard life because of his upbringing, well, it wasn't Sophie's fault. Nor was it her fault that her life had been made easier by her own birth circumstances.

And neither was the afternoon's mishap entirely her fault!

He didn't have to come storming into their midst, shouting in anger. He'd frightened her, and she'd tripped, and she had just as much right as he did to be angry. She could have been hurt, but he hadn't even stopped to think about that!

The look in his eyes had been terrifying—

almost as terrifying as her mother's had been to her as a child.

Her father had been soft-spoken to the extreme, bowing to her mother's every wish, and no one in her household had ever dared go against Olivia Vanderwahl's edicts. Only Sophie's grandmother had ever dared scold her mother, and then only with subtle undertones that Sophie hadn't understood for many years.

In truth, she hadn't even realized her father had any backbone at all until she had seen him at work in his own environment, and then it had left no doubt in her mind who was truly in charge of their household. Despite the emotional berth her parents seemed to give each other, her father had humored her mother in most things. Sophie supposed a man didn't always have to exert his dominance . . . not if he had nothing to prove, and her father hadn't had a thing to prove.

Jack MacAuley was somewhat of a different animal, she decided.

He didn't actually exert his dominance over anyone . . . but those in his presence seemed to bow to him anyway—even Kell to some degree. It was obvious the two of them were friends, but Kell hadn't even stood up to him to defend her, beyond his simple statement that it wasn't all her fault.

Aside from that, they'd all thrown her to the proverbial wolf!

A pall had been cast over all their moods for the remainder of the day, while the damage had been assessed and repaired. Their chores had been attended to in a sort of contemplative silence—and Sophie doubted they were all having life-altering revelations triggered by the simple fact that she'd very nearly killed them all today. No, everyone's mood was a reflection of Jack's—including her own.

He hadn't bothered to fix her roof, though, and Sophie thought he wanted to see her suffer just a little.

What had she done to deserve his animosity?

She frowned as she considered that...

Besides yelling at him on the dock for his lack of dress... accusing him of thievery... breaking his stove... burning his breakfast... and nearly sinking his ship.

She sighed.

Her demerits were adding up.

She heard voices above and tried to ignore them, wholly grateful they had chosen to do the same. Out of consideration, they seemed to be avoiding the gaping hole in their deck.

Which was more than she could say for Jack.

Her attention caught by their conversation, she strained to hear him. His voice was unmistakable. He was talking to Kell, she surmised—mostly because Kell seemed the only one willing to question His Holiness, for he clearly believed he had never done anything wrong in his entire life! No, Jack MacAuley was untouchable, never culpable, perfect!

She gritted her teeth as she listened to them.

"Maybe we should throw a tarp over it," Kell suggested, and Sophie knew they were discussing the gaping masterpiece in her ceiling.

"Hell no!" he answered. "Let her sleep with it tonight."

Silence a moment.

She heard the shuffling of feet, and Sophie wondered if he'd intended for her to hear this particular conversation. Probably so. He didn't strike her as the sort of man to leave anything to chance.

"Jack," Kell protested. "It feels like rain tonight."

"Good," Jack retorted, without the least pause.

Sophie bristled.

She had paid good money—ten thousand dollars to be precise—for the dubious privilege of boarding this blasted ship! Why should she be forced to sleep under the stars? It wasn't as though she hadn't suffered already. She had no clothes to wear!

"If she wants a tarp over it, she can damned well put one over it herself," Jack continued, his tone adamant. "She has two legs and two hands, Kell, and this isn't a cruise expressly for her pleasure. I told her that to begin with, and we aren't here to do her damned bidding!"

"I really don't mind," Kell countered.

"*I do.*" Jack's tone brooked no argument.

Silence again.

Then Jack exclaimed, "My God, man, have you forgotten what we're dealing with here?"

Kell's answer was softly spoken, almost reluctant. "No."

"Good, because they're both in cahoots, and the last thing I intend to do is to make her job easier!"

Sophie's brow knit.

Their conversation was no longer making sense.

What were they dealing with? Who was in cahoots? Whose job? Was he talking about her?

Her mind raced, searching for possibilities, but none seemed to manifest itself.

In that moment, thunder rumbled overhead, distant but the sound of it fraught with menace.

"Jack," Kell said, and it sounded much like a plea in her behalf. Sophie wanted to hug him for his concern.

Jack, on the other hand, was unmoved. The cur. "If she wants out of the deuced rain badly enough, she'll figure out how to do it for herself."

She heard his footfall ebb, leaving Sophie to gnash her teeth in helpless frustration over his uncharitableness.

Only she wasn't helpless at all!

He was toying with the wrong woman!

She wasn't going to take insult from Jack MacAuley any more than she intended to suffer it from Harlan Penn! They could both go to the devil!

Another rumble of thunder rolled overhead, and Sophie sat up in her cot and looked about the tiny cabin with disgust. She was cramped and uncomfortable in a room she could scarcely share with her luggage! Not that she had to worry about that particular inconvenience any longer!

So he wanted her to figure it out, did he? Well, she intended to do just that! Only if he meant to make her suffer, then two could certainly play at this game.

If he wanted a battle waged between them, then a battle he would get! And her volley this morning would be nothing compared to what she had in store. She had learned something from her mother.

This was all-out war.

Chapter 14

Jack tried to make sense of his anger.

He knew that afternoon's accident wasn't entirely her fault. It was his own—and Kell's, as well, for showing off. They had purchased the powder out of sheer curiosity—a toy of sorts for them to explore together. It damned well annoyed him that *his* friend had spent the entire day showing off to *his* woman—not that any of it made *any* sense at all.

She wasn't his woman.

Kell's defense of her had only provoked him all the more. The man had never defended anyone against him—even when his anger had been unreasonable! Jack had once damned the entire faculty of the university, taking a stand against capitalistic exclusionary academics, putting his career on the line for something that had been of minuscule importance in the grand scheme of things. His fury had been tangible. Kell had backed him the entire way, only injecting the voice of reason when it was appropriate . . . to keep him from cutting off his nose to spite his face.

The fact was that Kell had every right to spend the day with Sophie. She wasn't his!

He still didn't like it.

Her door was open, he noticed, when he passed her cabin on the way to his own, but she wasn't inside. Where the hell could she be? She wasn't above deck, he was certain. It wasn't a big enough ship that he would have missed her. Anyway, she would have had to pick her way through the mess hall where at least half his crew was fast asleep in their hammocks, and he doubted she would have braved the course. If their snores weren't enough to keep her at bay, their half-naked torsos would have sent her scurrying back to her room.

It didn't take him long to figure out where she had gone.

He heard a ruckus in his own cabin, and his hackles rose. What the hell was she doing? Snooping again? This time he was going to catch her red-handed.

He threw the door open, expecting to find her going through his papers, and froze in shock at what she was doing instead.

She was dividing the room with sheets, setting up house in half. She'd already found and strung a hammock on the second set of hooks and stood there looking like a beautiful vixen in her white nightgown. The hem of the otherwise pristine gown was shorn and stained, but the gauzy material lifted and fluttered behind her when she spun to face him. Bathed in the lantern light, she looked a little like a banshee in the moonlight—ethereal in her beauty and fierce . . . seductive . . . like the breeze on a hot sultry night.

"What the devil do you think you're doing?"

Jack had never seen such fiery determination in a woman's eyes. Beautiful eyes, despite their furor.

"What does it appear I'm doing?"

He stood in the doorway with his hands on the knob, his jaw slack. "Besides making a mess of my cabin?"

"I am not making a mess!" she said, splitting hairs as far as Jack was concerned. "I'm making myself comfortable!"

"I see that," Jack countered, raising a brow. "What I want to know is *why*? Who the hell gave you permission to set up house here?"

She let her sheet fall from her grasp and advanced on him suddenly, thrusting her finger into his chest. "*I* did!" she declared.

Jack blinked down at her.

Her eyes sparked, it seemed, flashing with ire. "I paid good money for passage aboard this ship and I *will not* be crammed into a wretched little cabin to suffer a perpetual shower!"

Her finger rested between his ribs, jabbing him lightly, and her determination was more than evident in her stance. He almost admired what she was doing . . . except that it was bound to make his life miserable.

"How about I just give you your money back and send you home on a raft," he offered, without any real intent.

For just an instant, she was taken aback by his suggestion, seeming to take him seriously. Jack nearly smiled at the look of shock on her face. But she only stood straighter at his threat, and faced him squarely.

"Put me out on a raft, Mr. MacAuley, and I will . . . I will . . ." She frowned, unable to come up with a suitable retribution.

He arched a brow. "Tell your daddy?"

"No!" she exploded, and jabbed her finger a little harder. Jack winced. "I would see that you suffered the greatest indignity for it!"

Christ, she was beautiful.

"The greatest indignity, huh?"

Her cheeks were flushed with color and her eyes fairly glowed with indignation. They reminded him just now of fine whiskey . . . the rich amber clarity of the liquid against crystal. Her hair was a rich, silky auburn that turned to flame under the soft, warm light of the lanterns, and he resisted the urge to pull it back out of her face . . . to touch her.

He wanted to taste her just now, silence her with a brutal lover's kiss. His body tightened with the realization that she would be alone in his cabin.

Fair game.

But she had come to him.

He came in the door, forcing her backward as he advanced on her. She retreated as he kicked the door closed behind him. And yet still she stood her ground, crossing her arms, glaring at him as fiercely as a wild mustang who refused to be broken.

He wanted to ride her: The very thought aroused him.

Would she wrap her legs around his waist and cling to him, urging him deeper with soft little cries?

Or would she make love to him with as much passion as she fought, digging her hands into his buttocks and drawing him deeper.

"Can't have me suffering great indignities." he told her. "Stay, then," he conceded, his voice taut, though not with fury, but with barely restrained desire.

She didn't seem to know the difference.

She smiled in victory, and Jack very nearly smiled back at her, but he didn't.

Let her think she'd won.

He took her by the shoulders to move her gently aside, and his body experienced an instant shock at the touch. It startled him. She felt it as well; he saw it in her eyes, heard it in her gasp of surprise.

Sophie's breath left her in a rush.

For the briefest instant, she stood stupefied, staring into eyes that seemed to see far too deep into her soul. Her heartbeat quickened painfully, and she swallowed convulsively.

The shock of his touch left her dazed.

He felt it, too; she could see it in his eyes.

She'd never felt so affected by a simple touch.

Without another word, he set her aside and walked around her. Like a booby, she merely stood there, staring at the door a bit stupidly. His touch had startled her far more even than his capitulation.

She'd expected a battle from him, and had been more than prepared to wage it. Now that she had her way—and worse, the door was closed—and she was alone with him, there seemed a far different battle raging inside her.

He sat down at his desk and she went back to hanging the sheets. Determined to give herself some privacy at least, she tried to ignore him as best she could.

She'd strung the blankets over ropes she had tied to each wall, forming a curtain of sorts. In the mornings, they could push them aside, so the room would be accessible to both. At night, they would simply close them. Sophie claimed the side of the room with the washbasin and no door. She gave him the door, just in case someone needed him in the middle of the night for some emergency, such as if the boat decided suddenly to fall apart and they were all going to die and they needed Jack to stand around and yell at everyone.

"I really hope you don't snore," she told him, feeling querulous still, although he hadn't said a word since his initial protest.

He didn't bother looking up from his work to answer her. "I hope you don't, either."

Sophie had started this particular altercation; still she took offense. "Of course I don't!"

He didn't look up, and his continued dismissal grated on her nerves—almost as much as the derisive brow that shot up at her declaration. "That's what they all say."

"Hmmph!" she declared and closed the curtain so she wouldn't have to see him.

That's what who all said?

All his women?

His answer needled her.

Why should she care if he had a thousand women? She didn't, she told herself. She scarcely knew him, and more, she didn't want to! The man was insufferable.

She ripped open the curtain to find him shuffling papers. Maybe he hadn't felt the same thing she had? How could he continue to work when she was feeling so . . . irritable?

"I really have never snored a day in my life!" she persisted.

He began to read, ignoring her, and Sophie pouted inwardly. "I'm sure you don't," he said much too agreeably.

He was mocking her, she thought, but she couldn't tell.

He peered up from his papers suddenly and smiled roguishly. "But time will tell, won't it?"

She didn't snore, she told herself—she didn't!—and if she did, she didn't care, blast it all!

In fact, she *hoped* she did, because she hoped it would keep him awake all night long!

She might even snore just to spite him.

"What are you doing?" she asked him petulantly, curiosity getting the best of her.

When he didn't answer, she abandoned the sheets for his workbench, making a pretense of dusting off the portrait of Harlan she had placed on his desk. It was her reminder, and she was very proud of herself for being so strong.

In fact, she didn't remember a time in her life when she'd felt more alive, more stalwart, more content . . . more pleased with herself.

Almost lovingly, she dusted the picture with her sleeve, then blew at it, and set it down.

He seemed to notice it for the first time then, and he glared at it, then turned to glare at her.

"What is *that*?"

Sophia didn't understand the question. "You've seen it before," she told him matter-of-factly. "You know what it is!"

"Yes," he argued, "I do know what it is, but what I want to know is . . . what is it doing on my desk?"

"Perhaps you should have asked *that* instead," Sophia reprimanded him with a nod and smile, and then answered his question, "I had to put it somewhere."

She thought perhaps he resented sharing his desk with her.

His eyes glittered with animosity. "*Try the garbage.*"

She tilted him a curious glance.

He was staring at the picture with utter revulsion, as though it were some atrocity she had heaped on his desk. Judging by his expression, she thought he didn't like Harlan—

and considered that maybe it wasn't entirely her to whom he objected.

Harlan had never done anything to Jack that she knew of, had never even mentioned him, in fact.

Then again . . . if Harlan had done something to spur Jack's animosity, it wasn't likely that Harlan would come right out and say so.

In any case, why would Harlan have suggested Jonathon secure passage on Jack's ship if the two had no love for each other?

Interesting, she thought, and studied him more closely.

He dismissed her again and returned to his reading. She set the portrait down and walked boldly around the desk to look over his shoulder.

Harlan had rarely discussed his affairs with her, much less worked in her presence, though Sophie had practically begged him to. Her mind thirsted for knowledge. She had so many questions, and not nearly enough answers. It just wasn't fair that women weren't encouraged to pursue an education.

She envied both Jack and Harlan with all her heart.

"Mizz Vanderwahl," he protested, sensing her at his back. His tone lacked any patience at all, and Sophie crossed her eyes at him. Whatever had happened to his simply calling her Sophie?

Mizz Vanderwahl, she mouthed, mimicking him, and felt strangely pleased with her brattiness. Never as a child had she dared speak out of turn. Even if she was far too old to indulge in such impishness, it felt wickedly good to do it privately.

He very nearly caught her.

He turned his papers over and looked up at her, and she donned a pleasant expression and smiled.

"Can I do something for you?"

Sophie shook her head, smiling sweetly, and he turned away once more to read. She frowned at his back, pouting really, though she had no notion why. Why should it matter to her if their acquaintance had gone beyond any form of reparation?

It didn't matter, she told herself.

And yet a feeling, something like a lead weight, sank in her belly.

"I was just curious," Sophie told him, and wondered why she suddenly felt so disheartened. She came a little closer, trying to see what it was that held his attention.

He sighed, a sound much like those her father had made when her mother had tried him to the edge of his patience.

"Do you mind?" he asked her, and set the papers down on his desk. In fact, he made a point of turning them over again . . . as though he didn't trust her, and didn't want her nosing over his shoulder.

Why didn't he trust her?

Sophie wasn't about to be dismissed so easily. By Jove, if he didn't trust her, he could just say so! She wanted to hear it from his own two lips! And she wanted to know why!

They stared at each other, at an impasse. Sophie stood her ground.

Chapter 15

S he just didn't know how close she was to finding herself in a very precarious position.

Jack was trying, he really was, but she wasn't making this easy on him.

He'd let her stay mostly because at the first rumble of thunder, his conscience had pricked him, and he hadn't liked the idea of her lying in her bed getting thoroughly drenched.

But he was beginning to regret it now.

His body was tense and he was beginning to feel a bit like a starved, caged lion—except that the object of his hunger had managed to lock herself up with him, and he was almost beyond the point of restraint.

He stared at her, trying to clear the fog from his brain. It was difficult enough to focus on his research with her in the same room, much less with her standing at his back. The scent of her dizzied him. His mouth grew dry with desire and his heart beat like a cannon blasting in his chest.

"I'm working," he told her curtly, and tried not to notice the silhouette of her body beneath her gauzy white gown. His heartbeat quickened. "I see you managed to salvage at least something from your wardrobe?"

She smiled and leaned a hip against his desk. She was too close, way too close.

"A few things actually."

Jack's gaze was drawn down to the V in her gown, and then down again to where the material tucked neatly between her legs, giving him a tantalizing glimpse of the shape of her thighs.

Christ.

His mouth watered.

"I'm . . . uh . . . glad," he said, and closed his eyes, shielding them from the sight of her.

What he wouldn't give just now to sit her on his desk, hike up her gown, and feast on the nectar of her body. His hands shook as he shoved his papers aside.

Hell, he couldn't read anyway, his eyes were clouded with desire. How long had it been since he'd wanted a woman this badly?

He couldn't remember.

Reminding himself that she belonged to someone else—never mind that the man was undeserving—Jack turned to face her, intending to rise from his chair, to walk away from temptation.

Physical evidence kept him firmly planted.

His eyes were drawn to the dark aureoles visible beneath her fine gown, and he swallowed. He tried to ignore the heat filling his loins. He shifted in his seat slightly.

"Jack?" she prompted, his name coming tentatively to her lips.

The sound of it surprised him, pleased him, sent a shock of a different sort leaping through him.

It was the first time she'd used his name . . . but he wanted more. He'd like to hear it whispered in his ear.

He looked up at her to find her hugging herself sweetly, almost like a little girl. "I was wondering . . . did you always know what you wanted to be?"

Her voice was soft and sweet and her mood had shifted one hundred eighty degrees.

No longer was she the vixen ready to do battle. She suddenly was looking at him like an expectant child, ready for her bedtime story.

The image should have cooled his ardor, but only managed to confuse him.

Here she stood before him, alone in his room, prim in her nightgown, her eyes full of curiosity . . . but for something far more innocent than what he wanted to show her.

She was an incredible contradiction—bold enough to share his room without asking permission and pure enough to stand before him in her little girl nightgown, staring up at him with an expression that looked suddenly and very dangerously like . . . admiration.

Was she really interested?

Or was she trying to soften him up?

In any case, he thought about her question

a moment, because it took that long to register. "I think so," he answered, clearing his throat.

Those honey-colored eyes glimmered with intelligence.

He could see so much in them ... passion, excitement, joy. Despite the state of their personal affairs, she seemed intoxicated with life in the way he usually was when he was on the brink of some new discovery.

Was she always so ebullient?

Or was she simply looking forward to seeing her lover as she'd claimed?

That thought soured his mood.

Damned Penn.

Why was it the bastard always ended up with the things Jack most wanted? At the instant, he was feeling bitter in a way he'd never let himself give in to—not even on receiving the news that Penn had been awarded yet another grant. *His grant*. He'd warrant Penn had no idea why he was even out there ... beyond the arguments he had stolen from Jack. He was probably wandering around in a daze, tripping over the very evidence Jack was hungry for.

Which led him to wonder ... what *did* Sophia know about her fiancé's affairs? If she was spying for him, it had to mean she knew something, at least. And if she did ... well, then maybe he could pick her brain ...

"Do you enjoy anthropology, Sophia?"

For an instant, Sophie started at his question.

She didn't ever remember Harlan once asking her, though she'd been greedy for his conversation.

"Actually . . ." She blinked away her surprise and nodded enthusiastically. "Yes."

"I suppose you would have to share a passing interest, at least?" he suggested.

Sophie thought he must be referring to Harlan, and chafed at the reminder of Harlan's letter—his ready dismissal of her curiosity. "I *never* pretend an interest in anything," she told him, and hesitated, unsure why it seemed suddenly inappropriate to address him so formally. ". . . Mr. MacAuley."

Perhaps it was simply because she was standing before him dressed only in her nightgown, a tattered one at that. Honestly, she ought to be more abashed by the fact, but she considered herself a practical woman, and her dress simply couldn't be helped at the moment. She was fortunate, indeed, that she was wearing what she was, and had decided not to dwell on it. What good would it do her now? She couldn't exactly complain when it was her own fault that she was minus a few gowns.

"I wasn't implying you were pretending at all," he countered. "Only that you are no stranger to the field." He sat back in his chair and cocked his head at her. "I imagine your fiancé spoke often of his . . . second love."

Her heart squeezed at his question.

"His second love?" For an instant, the allusion flew past her entirely. Foremost in her mind was Harlan's dalliances. And then she realized what he was implying. "Oh, yes! Well, no, actually," she confessed. "Harlan rarely spoke of his activities to me at all."

She sighed, realizing just how little time they had actually spent together as adults. "In fact," she confessed a little sadly, "I rarely saw him after our engagement."

His brows lifted and he stared at her, scrutinizing her much too closely. "Really?"

Sophie looked away, uncomfortable with his regard. She didn't want him to know anything.

It wasn't any of his affair.

"Really," she replied, and changed the subject at once. "However," she told him with a smile, "When we were children, he often shared his aspirations with me."

"Did he?"

Was he truly interested or was he merely humoring her?

It didn't matter.

Sophie pulled herself up on the desk, hungry for his conversation. "When I was a little girl," she began wistfully, "we went on an expedition into the wilderness. It was the most fun I ever had!"

His brows lifted. "Expedition?"

Sophie giggled, embarrassed though she hadn't a reason to be. It had been a very long time ago, and she'd been merely a child. "At our summer home . . . my mother used to have these picnics where she would invite her closest friends. Because none of them had little girls my age, I usually played alone. But one day the boys asked me to join them on their expedition, and I was absolutely beside myself with joy at my first discovery! A shark's tooth, they'd sworn."

She laughed softly at the memory. "Actually, I'm not sure if, in fact, it was a shark's tooth, but it certainly looked like one. Some part of me couldn't begin to fathom fierce fish had once swam over my yard. But they swore it was a shark's tooth, and somewhere deep down I wanted to believe it."

"Sometimes you have to forget everything you know and see the world with new eyes."

"I think so, too," Sophie agreed. "Sometimes everything you know is just plain wrong." She was talking about Harlan now, her life in general, but he needn't know it. "Sometimes everyone around you is telling you something is right, and you try hard to believe it, and it just doesn't feel it . . ." She chewed her bottom lip, contemplating that truth. "Know what I mean?"

His eyes twinkled a bit. "Sure I do."

"Sometimes," Sophie continued, encouraged by his attention, "nothing feels right until you forget everything you know . . . and follow your heart."

He shook his head. "Your heart will get you in trouble," Jack proposed. "Follow your gut instead. It never lies."

"I suppose that's true." Her gut said she was doing the right thing.

"So what did you do with your shark's

tooth?" he asked her, and smiled. "Did you save it?"

Sophie bit her lip and told him a bit sheepishly, "My mother found it, actually, and was quite horrified by it. She tossed it in the garden, and told me never to get my hands dirty again. But I went back later and found it, took it inside, and hid it in my pillow." She refrained from adding that she would pull it out each night and sleep with it tucked in the palm of her hand, certain he would think that was silly.

"I used to imagine it was my good luck charm, to scare away the ghoulies."

He laughed, the sound of it rich and warm. It made Sophie feel completely at ease.

"I think that's every budding anthropologist's first discovery . . . the infamous shark's tooth."

Sophie grinned at him. "Was it yours?" She lifted her knees up and hugged herself, lying her cheek atop them, feeling perfectly at ease when only minutes before she had felt awkward.

"Actually, no."

"What was yours?"

"A canine tibia."

Sophie scrunched her nose. "A dog's leg?" She laughed. "Yuck!"

He grinned. "Yep. Told my friends it was an ancient breed of horse that belonged to pygmies who migrated from Africa."

Sophie giggled. "You told them that?"

He nodded, looking quite proud of himself,

and Sophie suddenly imagined him as a child, his golden hair white from the sun and his skin deeply bronzed, his teeth flashing in a mischievous grin that was inherently all boy. "Wherever did you come up with a theory like that?"

"Vivid imagination, mostly," he admitted. "But my father was an anthropologist," he told her, "and I picked up bits and pieces from him."

Sophie's brows lifted in surprise. "Was he truly?"

"One of the best," Jack said, and Sophie could see the pride in his face. His eyes filled with admiration and his smile was genuine.

"He must be so proud!" Sophie exclaimed.

He blinked then, and looked away, then back, shuttering emotions from her. "He's dead now, Sophie."

She'd known that.

"Oh." Sophie flinched at her own carelessness. How could she have forgotten? She sat up, her heart twisting a little. "I'm sorry," she offered, and wanted to hug him suddenly.

"Don't be," he told her, and smiled. "He lived a full life."

She wanted to ask more, but didn't dare.

Their gazes held.

Her heart began to beat a little faster, and she swallowed a knot that rose in her throat.

"I guess I should go to bed now," she said after a moment, taking a deep breath and sliding her feet to the floor.

She was feeling strange suddenly, wanting

things she shouldn't dare even think of.

He didn't speak, merely continued to stare, and Sophie's stomach fluttered without cause.

"Well . . . g'night," she whispered and rose, leaving him to his work.

"G'night, Sophia," he whispered back.

Her body shivered at the sound of her name on his lips and she quickly closed the curtain between them. Without another word, she put out the lanterns on her side of the room. She had no idea what had just happened between them, but her head was spinning as she climbed into her hammock.

As she lay there, she tried not to think of him sitting on the other side of the curtain, but was far too aware of every shuffle of his papers . . . every sound that came from his half of the room.

Her heart didn't stop pounding until long after his lantern clicked off and the room lay completely still.

The storm that had been threatening earlier never materialized and the sound of the waves slapping outside the cabin lulled her to sleep.

Chapter 16

It was late afternoon when Sophie finished her self-appointed chores.

She was weary as she made her way back to the cabin for a moment's respite, but filled with satisfaction over the day's accomplishments.

In the last few days, she'd managed somehow to stay out of trouble, and had even made strides toward making amends with Jack. He seemed different toward her today—not that he'd spoken to her much at all, but it seemed to Sophie that every time she'd chanced to look up, he was there, watching her.

She couldn't tell if it was because he didn't trust her, or if he still expected her to find her way into trouble ... or if it was something more ... but something about the way he looked at her sent her pulse skittering.

Maybe he *had* felt what she'd felt that first night in his cabin?

She tried not to think of it, pushed it aside.

Her life was complicated enough, and she

was determined now to uncomplicate it at all cost. Jack MacAuley was a distraction she could do without. She didn't need any man in her life.

At any rate, there were other things to concern herself with this moment. Thanks to Kell, the stove was no longer a complete enigma, and she'd managed to concoct a few edible things. She thought perhaps she was improving, though it wasn't as yet evident in the expressions on the crew's faces. She'd work on her seasoning now, and maybe before long she would see them smile at the prospect of eating the fruit of her labors.

She found the captain's cabin empty and slipped within, closing the door behind her. She had one dress left and contemplated changing into it, soiled as this one was becoming, but she didn't dare. For the first time in her life, she couldn't just *buy* another. Nor was she certain how to wash them without ruining the material. No, she'd have to make do.

Untying her makeshift apron, she tossed it over the rope that separated their rooms, and dared to go and sit at Jack's desk. She really should wash up first, she thought, but she was far too tired to actually do it. She sank back in his chair and set her feet up as she'd seen him do while reading his papers, and smiled to herself at the picture she must present.

She imagined the look he'd wear if he walked in just now, and bit her lip to keep from laughing.

All she needed was a cigar and a brandy

and a pair of pants and she'd be just one of the crew. Which made her wonder. What would it be like to be Jack? To simply be able to go when he pleased? To be in love with his work? To live life by his own rules?

Her gaze was caught by the portrait of Harlan. She removed her feet from the desk and leaned over to snatch it into her hands.

How could she ever have thought herself in love with this man? Somehow, he paled in comparison to Jack. Everything about Jack MacAuley bespoke vitality. He was passion incarnate and Sophie couldn't see him doing anything halfway.

She admired him, she realized.

She set the portrait of Harlan down and scrunched her nose in disgust at it. His looks were deceiving. He seemed far too angelic when he should be wearing devil's horns and an evil goatee.

On a whim, she picked up Jack's quill and dipped it in his inkwell, then drew tiny little horns on Harlan's head. She smiled, satisfied with the impression. Next she drew a small goatee, pointy at the end—almost like another horn—and went on to doodle a mustache as well. Funny, she had never noticed how weak a chin Harlan had before now. The goatee only seemed to accentuate it. She giggled as she drew, imagining the expression on his face were he to see her disfiguring his picture. Next, she drew little money symbols in his pupils . . . so tiny one could almost mistake them for a simple gleam in his eye, and then she smiled at the finished product, her mood improved a hundredfold.

It was strange actually . . . She was no less determined to face Harlan and seize back her honor, but somehow . . . the edge had softened from her anger.

She no longer felt such bitter fury when she thought of Harlan with other women.

It no longer stung so much that he had no wish to see her.

It no longer even seemed to matter that he'd been so willing to leave her on a shelf until he was good and ready to encumbrance himself with the burden of matrimony.

The one thing that did bother her was that he had used her and her father . . . and he continued to use her without compunction.

She set the portrait down again on the desk so that it faced her side of the room, thinking that there was nothing to stop her now from going to Paris to study art.

Or perhaps she would go to Italy . . .

Or maybe she would go dust off some heretofore undiscovered pharaoh's tomb in the great land of Egypt and give Harlan a better example to follow. She leaned forward and flicked her finger at the picture, knocking it on its face, smirking at it. It was really bad of her to feel so vengeful, but she couldn't quite keep herself from it. She hoped it didn't make her a terrible person.

Her thoughts returned to Egypt. Wouldn't it be fun to explore new cultures and to piece together the puzzle of their existence through

their artifacts? She envied Jack fiercely. She
wanted to know the things he knew.

She glanced down at the small silver key
that protruded from the drawer lock. It was
too tempting. Her curiosity beckoned her to
open the desk drawer.

She couldn't resist.

His papers were all neatly stacked within
and she pulled out a handful of them.

The documents were all titled, with myriad
notes scribbled into the margins. Some caught
her attention more than others . . .

"The Phoenician Connection" . . . "Hiero-
glyphics at Closer Inspection" . . . "The Maya
Code." Skimming the material, she noted that
the last appeared to be an in-depth interpretation of the Mayan system of record keeping.
She leafed through a few more, and paused at
one that bore interesting sketches in the margins. It was titled "The Supernatural Associa-
tion."

One sketch appeared to be the body of an
infantile human with the spots of a jaguar and
a rather grotesque face. The figure was lying
on its back and appeared to be having a tan-
trum of sorts. Under that particular drawing
was scribbled "Baby Jaguar, Early Classic Ti-
kal and Caracol." The passage beside it was
about the Bearded Jaguar God of the underworld, and Sophie surmised they were one in
the same—a Mayan version of the devil perhaps?

The next paragraph spoke of a god who sat
on his throne in judgment and destroyed an

early creation by flood . . . How strangely co-incidental.

Or perhaps not strange at all . . .

She flipped a few more pages and found another drawing entitled "The Body and Its Accouterments." It was a gruesome picture of the skeletal remains of a Mayan man, with labeled artifacts outside the boundary of the drawing, and markings showing the position in which they were found.

Fascinating.

There were, after that, pages on pages of crudely drawn maps, depicting what Sophie assumed were tombs. Had he drawn these maps himself? Had he actually, with his own two eyes, beheld the bodies at rest? How must it feel to unearth something that had not been seen by human eyes since the day of its interment?

She read on, devouring information like a hungry beggar, losing track of time. It wasn't until the sun began to set and she was forced to light the lantern on the desk that she realized just how late the hour had grown. Still she couldn't put down the manuscripts. They held her enthralled. Here in these papers were a man's life's work, evidence of the time and heart he had invested in his profession.

Sophie read until her eyes grew weary, until she had to squint to see the letters because the room had grown too dim to make them out. Greedy for knowledge, she turned the lantern light higher, the better to read by, and removed it from its brace, drawing it near. As she huddled over its flickering flame, heat caressed her lips and cheeks, seducing her into a sweet languor . . .

She felt the heat like a whisper touch of his finger, and she closed her eyes . . .

Like a phoenix, his image rose before her, and Sophie dared to imagine what it would feel like if he came to her and took her face in his hands . . . if he kissed her . . .

To her shock, her mouth remembered the taste of him, the feel of him . . . and she touched a finger to her lips . . . caressing them softly . . .

She never failed to surprise him.

Jack had expected Sophie to pout over the loss of her gowns but she hadn't from the first. A simple grimace had been the extent of her lamentation.

She simply made do with what she had.

He'd also expected her to complain about her cabin; she hadn't.

Instead she'd moved in with him.

He had chuckled to himself over that one.

After she'd paid him ten thousand dollars for passage, he'd *never* anticipated she would willingly roll up her sleeves and work, but she had, and without having been asked.

Her meal tonight had even been edible, and it was apparent that she was trying.

She was either a very remarkable woman or a clever little spy who was bound to turn his entire crew against him. He hadn't done a damned thing to her, but a blind man couldn't miss the suspicious looks he was getting from his crewmen. She was winning them over with very little effort, and Jack could damned well see why.

Her smile alone, when she favored them with one, was enough to make a man's gut flop. The thing was, Jack didn't really think she even knew it. She seemed oblivious to the fact.

It had been a long day, and he was tired, but he was actually looking forward to the rest of the evening alone with her.

He whistled a cheerful tune as he approached his cabin, hoping it would be enough of a warning, just in case she was in the middle of her toiletry. There was no telltale scurrying behind the door, and so he knocked lightly and then opened it.

His good mood dissipated at once.

Rage filled him at the sight of her.

Chapter 17

She was a lousy spy!

She'd obviously fallen asleep while snooping through his papers.

"What the hell are you doing?" Jack shouted at the top of his lungs as he came in, slamming the door behind him.

He startled her from her slumber, and she awoke with a gasp, her hands flying out, papers scattering.

Her gaze met his for the briefest instant; confusion in hers, then fear.

It happened too fast to stop it.

She knocked the lantern over. Its flame spilled onto his research, engulfing the papers at once. She shrieked in alarm when she realized and tried to put out the flames, blowing on them.

The fire merely spread faster.

His work was going up, literally, in smoke!

Jack moved quickly; he removed his shirt and began to smack at the flames, yelling for Kell to get water—something—anything!

She was going to kill them all.

She ran out the door suddenly, shrieking, abandoning him to the fire—damned woman!

"Yah, right, save yourself!" he growled after her.

He was thankful the ship was so small.

Someone shouted at him and Jack ordered him to bring water to put out the fire—all the while continuing to slap out the flames, cursing Sophia Vanderwahl under his breath.

Had he begun to soften toward her?

Dangerous prospect.

He was going to have to remember this the next time a good thought about her niggled its way into his brain.

"Kell!" he shouted. "Dammit, someone get in here!"

He heard footsteps and spun to see who was there. Water rushed past him, onto the desk, but not without drenching him first.

Before he could say anything, she ran away again, bucket in hand.

Stunned, he turned again to slap at the flames.

Kell was right behind her with another bucket, and someone else with another. By the time Sophia returned, the flames were extinguished, and she stood in the doorway, looking a little bit dazed and a lot sorry.

Jack wasn't in the mood to be forgiving.

"What were you doing at my desk?" he railed at her. "Looking through my papers?"

She stood there clutching her bucket, and had the nerve to look injured by his anger.

"I should have known you couldn't be trusted!" he told her, slamming his shirt down on the floor at her feet. She winced and took a step backward. Kell came up behind her, but Jack was undeterred.

By God, he had had enough!

"Did Penn put you up to this?"

He wanted to know. To hell with waiting to see. If she was Penn's spy, for whatever reason, he wanted her exposed.

"Jack," Kell objected.

"I . . . I don't know what you are talking about," she answered.

Jack ignored Kell, determined to find out the truth once and for all. "Sure you don't."

"I don't!" she protested, her eyes filling with tears. "I fell asleep and then you scared me and then—"

"I know what happened then," he countered. "What I want to know is *why* you were going through my papers!"

Sophie stood there, trying to make sense of his questions.

She shouldn't have been snooping, that much was true, but she didn't understand why he was so furious with her. She had almost burned down his cabin, that much was also true, but she certainly hadn't intended to do it and it was as much his fault as it was her own for he had scared her to death.

Still . . . it seemed to her that she was missing something . . .

"Did your boyfriend put you up to this?"

he asked her again, and Sophie blinked at the question.

She clutched the bucket in her hand. "Put me up to what? I don't understand."

What did Harlan have to do with this?

"The bloody hell you don't!" he snapped, and his eyes flashed with anger.

She felt Kell's hand on her shoulder and was thankful for it.

"Your boyfriend is a thief, Mizz Vanderwahl—and you're no better if you think you can just come in here and help yourself to my research!"

Sophie's eyes widened in surprise as understanding dawned. "You think I am here to steal your research?"

One brow shot up. "Yes, I do!" His gaze bore into her accusingly.

Sophie couldn't believe what he was thinking. She couldn't even fathom that someone would think her a thief! And Harlan was many things but she hardly thought he would stoop to taking another man's work. And more, that he would employ Sophie to do his dirty work, was simply unthinkable!

However contrite she had felt about starting the fire, she was no longer.

In fact, she was getting quite angry.

The more she thought about it, the more she felt like shouting back. Except that she had not been raised to engage in shouting matches with any man!

Her grip tightened on the bucket in her hands.

"Let me get this straight," she said as calmly as she was able.

His eyes glittered ferociously at her, but he said nothing, merely stared at her.

"You think that Harlan engaged me to spy for him?"

"Damned right, I do," he admitted, and his glare dared her to deny it. The wretch!

"And you think that is why I obtained passage aboard your ship? To spy for Harlan?"

He smiled a merciless smile. "Bright girl we have here!"

Sophie bristled, ready to do battle for her honor, but there was nothing she could say to defend herself if he chose to believe it. There was no proof she could give him to make him see the truth.

She clenched her teeth, fury seeping into her every nerve. She didn't think then, just reacted. She heaved the bucket at him, tossing cold water into his face.

It was the very least he deserved and she didn't bother to feel contrite. It served him right.

He yelped in surprise, and she spun on her heels and left him wiping the salt water from his eyes.

She was gone by the time Jack opened his eyes.

Only Kell remained. The few others who had come to his rescue had slunk away when he'd begun to shout.

"You're not going to like my saying so," Kell told him. "But you deserved that, Jack."

And then he left too, leaving Jack to deal with piecing together the charred remains of his research, and thinking that his entire crew had defected to the enemy's camp.

They'd been blinded by that damnable smile of hers, he decided, and was determined not to succumb to it as well.

The problem was . . . he was afraid he already had.

The night sky was nearly starless—an endless ocean of marbled blue. The moon itself was invisible but for a sliver behind dark ominous clouds. It was almost impossible to distinguish between ocean and sky.

The breeze lifted, cooling her temper as well as her body. Sophie was no expert on the weather but instinctively she sensed the brewing storm. They had been spared the last few days and nights, had merely been teased with a light drizzle late each afternoon.

Tonight would be different, and the electric feel in the air left her agitated.

Jack MacAuley was an impossible man!

She couldn't believe that he thought her a spy and a thief! Nor could she believe he would think it of Harlan and was piqued that she should feel the need to defend the rat even now. And yet she felt terrible for having destroyed his work, unintentional though it had been.

Men were a bane to the human race!

"He's really not so bad a guy," Kell said to her, coming up behind her.

Sophie turned to face him, crossing her arms to keep the chill at bay. It was cool, and getting colder with the increase of wind.

She believed Kell, had seen glimpses of a different man, but wasn't feeling the least bit charitable at the moment. "I don't believe you," she said irascibly.

Kell laughed softly.

Sophie turned again to face the ocean, turning her face up into the breeze. It was peaceful out here, almost as though nothing existed but them.

"You kind of like him anyway, don't you?"

He came to stand beside her, and Sophie peered up at him through her lashes. "He doesn't like me," she countered. "That much is evident."

He stared at her, and she averted her gaze. "You don't believe I've come to spy, do you?"

"No, I don't, but if you'll forgive my frankness, Sophie, I don't think you're telling us the whole truth, either."

Sophie refused to look at him. It wasn't any of their concern why she chose to visit her fiancé. And she hadn't lied about that—she *was* going to see Harlan. Her reason for doing it was her affair alone.

"Jack's not stupid, and he's sensing something," he continued. "He's a good man, a fair man."

"I didn't lie," she assured him. "And I am not a spy!" She turned to meet his gaze. "Why would he think so?"

He hesitated a moment. Sophie could tell he was weighing his words.

"Honestly, I'm not sure it's my place to say so, but he has good reason not to trust your fiancé, I can tell you that."

Sophie tilted her gaze, questioning him, "Why?" she wanted to know. "What has Harlan ever done to him? I thought they were friends!"

He seemed completely surprised by her declaration. "Why would you go and think a thing like that?"

Sophie turned back to stare out over the ocean. "Because ... Harlan mentioned him in his letter to a mutual friend of ours ... I thought perhaps ..."

"You thought wrong," he disclosed without reservation, and his harsh tone caught her attention. She looked up at him then, gauging his expression. "I can safely say there is no friendship at all between Jack and your fiancé."

"Oh," Sophie said, realizing Kell had no reason to lie to her. The look on his face was contemptuous, though it was obvious he tried to shield her from it. Curiosity made her ask, "Tell me, what did Harlan do?" It wasn't as though Sophie thought his integrity impeccable. He had long ago fallen from grace.

"That," Kell replied, "you'll have to ask Jack. It's just not my place to say, Sophie. I'm sorry."

"I see," Sophie answered, but she really didn't at all. Kell's loyalty was unwavering, and commendable, but she wasn't about to ask Jack MacAuley for anything at all.

"You say you found Jack's name in a letter?" Kell asked her, and she could tell by his tone that he was curious.

Sophie decided she had nothing to hide from him. She trusted him. She somehow understood that whatever was said between them would go no further. And she needed someone to confide in. She decided it wouldn't hurt to at least tell Kell the truth.

"I *am* going to see Harlan," she assured him, "but it's not what I've led you to believe. I don't really miss him at all," she confessed.

"That much is obvious, Sophie."

Sophie peered up at him.

Was it?

She wanted to ask why, but wasn't really certain she wished to know the reason he had come to that conclusion. She was heartily afraid the truth was in her eyes.

She told him about the letter then, finishing the story with tears in her eyes.

"You deserve far better," Kell told her, and drew her into his embrace, consoling her in a brotherly fashion.

Sophie was grateful for his support. Her heart squeezed her just a little at the memory of Jack's baleful glare. "Please don't tell Jack?" she begged him. She was angered that he had chosen to believe the worst of her, but she couldn't bear it if he were to pity her.

"It's not my place to," he reassured.

Sophie nodded, grateful for his answer. The

last thing she wanted was Jack's pity.

Anyway, it would be far safer if he continued to loathe her. Judging by the weight she felt in her heart over his obvious disgust of her, she had allowed him to come too close already, and without even knowing it.

Why should she care if he didn't trust her, or didn't like her? After these two weeks he would be of no consequence to her at all. She didn't intend to bother asking about return passage. It would suit her best if she got off this wretched ship and never set eyes on him again.

One heartache a lifetime was more than enough.

Chapter 18

The impact sent her into shock.

Sophie awoke, surrounded by darkness, her body quivering with remembered terror. She'd been dreaming, and the dream had seemed so real that she could still hear the wailing of ghosts in her ears. She whimpered softly.

"It was just a dream," a voice soothed her.

Sophie blinked, trying to orient herself.

"A bad dream," the voice cooed.

"Jack?"

Thunder roared, shaking her to the bone and rattling the ship's shutters. A distant bolt of lightning lit the room for the briefest instant—long enough that she saw Jack's look of concern as he stared down at her.

"I'm here," he replied softly.

"I was locked in a tomb!" she cried out, her body continuing to quiver and her heart pounding until she had trouble catching her breath.

"You fell out of the hammock," he explained, his voice soft and comforting. "Are you all right?"

"I fell?"

"Yes, you did."

She hadn't even realized she was on the floor.

"Are you all right?" he repeated.

"Yes . . . I . . . I think so," she replied a little dazedly, and continued to shiver as the wind howled in her ears.

She sensed, more than saw, that he reached up and pulled the blanket from her hammock. It fluttered down atop her, and he spread it around her, tucking her in like a parent would a cherished child.

Another bolt of lightning lit the room.

He was shirtless. The realization came to her at once.

The ship rolled a bit, sending him sprawling over her. "Sorry," he offered, and retreated from atop her.

Sophie swallowed. "It's all right," she said, stuffing her arms beneath the blankets. "Thank you for the blanket." She didn't know why she suddenly felt so cold. Her teeth chattered, and he slipped an arm around her. Sophie couldn't care less about propriety at the moment; she was grateful for the reassuring embrace.

"It's cold," she complained.

"It's the storm," he told her, and added as the ship listed sharply to the stern, "I'd put you back in the hammock, but I think it'd be a wasted effort."

Sophie was inclined to agree.

"I dreamed that I was locked in a tomb with ghosts and skeletons everywhere!" Her heart was still racing, her body tingly and numb.

He chuckled softly. "No skeletons here," he swore. "But you hit the deck so hard it woke me from a dead sleep. Are you sure you're all right?"

Sophie felt guilty for waking him.

When the ship listed once more, and she slid a bit in the opposite direction, she knew it was not her fault. And, in fact, were it not that Jack caught her, she thought she would have slipped away. "I think I'd prefer the floor just now anyway," she confessed as her stomach rolled in protest to the motion. "I suddenly don't feel so well."

Jack laughed. "Would it make you feel any better if I told you that I didn't, either?"

Sophie didn't think so. She shook her head and tried to steady her stomach, taking deep breaths.

"It feels worse than it is," he disclosed.

How comforting, though at the moment, her stomach wasn't much appeased by his reassurances. She groaned, grateful that the room was dark, because she thought it would be spinning otherwise.

"Kell has everything in hand," he told her. "He says it'll pass before morning."

"That long?"

"Afraid so." He shifted beside her and Sophie thought he meant to get up.

She panicked. "No! Stay with me!" she begged him.

She knew she was being silly, but she couldn't help it. She'd never liked storms anyway, but it was far worse, she realized, to be caught in a squall at sea than to wait out a gale in her cozy little bed.

He squeezed her arm. "I'm not going anywhere," he promised. "Just getting another blanket."

"You can share mine!" she offered at once, and lifted the blanket for him to climb beneath.

He hesitated. "Uhhh . . . maybe that's not such a good idea, Sophia."

"Don't be silly," she scolded him. "It's perfectly all right!" Her chest hurt a bit as though someone were sitting on her, and she couldn't quite catch her breath. The nightmare was with her still, and the ship's rolling was making her anxiety worse. "Please, don't go!"

He didn't sound the least bit assured. "Well . . . all right," he relented, and slipped beneath the covers.

Sophie stiffened at the feel of his bare chest against her arm, and he noted it at once. "I *did* warn you," he told her, his voice low.

Sophie swallowed convulsively.

"It's all right," she assured him, and hoped it didn't seem such a terrible thing that she didn't want him to leave her.

"Should I get my own?" He lifted up the covers to remove himself.

"No . . ." Her objection sounded weak even

to her own ears, and he lifted the covers higher. "No!" she said a bit more resolutely, and he dropped the covers and settled in beside her.

Her anxiety eased the instant he put his arms around her. Outside, the storm raged on, but inside the cabin it suddenly didn't seem so frightening.

For a long time, there was silence between them. Sophie lay still in his arms, listening to the rumble of thunder and the waves slapping at wood. It wasn't long before her stomach felt better. He was a solid barrier and kept her steady.

"When I was a kid," he began, and seemed to understand that his voice would soothe her, "I used to climb out of my window and ride out the storm in the tree outside my bedroom."

Sophie's heartbeat began to slow.

She imagined him straddling a branch, while the tree swayed under the onslaught of wind . . . like a bucking horse . . . and was amused by the image.

"That wasn't the safest place to be!" she scolded him, but there was a smile in her voice. "Though I'm certain your mother told you so."

He held her a little tighter and laid his head down beside her. Sophie could feel the heat of his breath against her cheek. It sent a shiver through her.

"My mother died when I was about four," he disclosed. "It was just me and my dad."

"Oh no!" Sophie exclaimed. "I'm sorry!"

"Don't be," he reassured her, and Sophie heard no self-pity in his tone. "I never really knew her, and my father was the best father a kid could want."

Sophie smiled. "Especially since he let you ride out the storm in a tree?"

He chuckled low at her ear. "No, even better. Because he sometimes rode out the storm in the tree with me."

"Oh my!" she exclaimed, and couldn't imagine her own father or mother sitting out on the limb of a tree in the middle of some raging storm. She laughed.

She tried to imagine Harlan out on a tree limb, even as a lad, and couldn't picture it. He was far too proper.

For that matter, she tried to picture him out in some field, digging up fossils . . . and ruining his nails.

She couldn't and frowned.

Unlike Harlan, she could easily picture Jack there, and she wondered what it was that Harlan did in the Yucatan . . . besides raise women's skirts. She couldn't begin to fathom.

She was still trying to figure that out when Jack whispered against her ear. "I really love the smell of your hair, Sophia."

She thought she misheard him. "Wh-what?" she asked, trying to see him through the darkness.

"I love the smell of your hair," he murmured, and seemed to be nuzzling it softly.

A quiver sped through her at the realization,

and her heart began to beat a little faster. She couldn't speak, and he mistook her silence.

"Forgive me," he begged her, but Sophie wasn't the least offended by his compliment . . . or by his actions.

She tried to speak past the knot that formed in her throat, to reassure him that he hadn't offended her at all, but she couldn't form a coherent sound.

No man had ever titillated her so with mere words.

No man had ever made her yearn for things she shouldn't even think about.

Never with Harlan had her thoughts turned physical in nature . . . never had her body responded so wantonly to his nearness.

Her mouth tingled at the memory of her stolen kiss, and she longed to savor just one more from his mouth.

Only she wasn't about to make the first move this time.

She wanted so much for him to want her.

She wanted him to look at her not with disgust or disappointment, but as he had that first day on the docks, she realized . . . before all the unpleasantness had come between them.

"Sophia," he whispered.

His voice seemed rife with as much confusion as Sophie was feeling . . . confusion about everything . . . save one thing . . .

She closed her eyes, feeling heat flow through her . . . so that she no longer shivered at all.

"Yes?" she replied, breathless now.

Silence met her reply.

The scent of him drew her nearer, and her breath became more labored as she tempted him in the darkness, tilting her head back for his kiss, if only he would take it.

She willed him to . . .

Jack wanted to kiss her.

The scent of her skin intoxicated him.

The air around them grew charged with far more than just the storm, and Jack held her closer against his better judgment. He was wearing only his pants and they were already becoming too snug.

Was she feeling it as well? The electric current in the air? It sent fire racing across his skin.

He was drawn to her in a way he hadn't ever felt toward a woman. His skin burned, craving her touch. The points of his nipples were on fire for the soothing touch of her moist tongue.

What would it feel like to be inside her? To have her legs wrapped around his waist and her tongue dancing on his nipples?

She had no idea how close he was to forgetting she was a lady . . . and remembering he was no gentleman. He was a pretender at best . . . and her kind never let him forget it.

Never in his life had he felt so uncertain around a woman . . . or so attracted . . . or so wary . . . or so confused.

And he'd never considered the word *no* before now . . . not in this way . . . never needed to. He had always been willing to accept the outcome, whatever it might be. For the first time ever, he dreaded hearing it.

Sophie was from a world he could never truly be part of—not that he hadn't tried. *And failed.* He had the money and the brains. He just hadn't the name. And that in a nutshell was why he'd had to purchase this ship himself, and fund his own research.

He drew back, looking down on her, telling himself that he'd be a fool to get mixed up in something that was set against him from the start.

She was off limits, and it didn't take an academic genius to figure that one out.

Except that he had never before let the odds stand in his way.

Sophie waited with bated breath for him to speak again, but he didn't.

She wanted nothing more than to forget all that had passed between them. She wanted to start over. Daring to press herself closer, she closed her eyes, hoping he would respond.

Her body tingled where it met his skin, and she ached to reach out and explore ... to smooth her fingers over the muscles of his bare chest.

"Sophia," he began, his voice hoarse and low. "May I ... kiss you?"

Her heart hammered at the question.

She swallowed and whispered back, sounding more hesitant than she wished to, "I would really like that."

She felt him lean closer, though he didn't

close the space between them. She longed for the feel of his mouth on hers.

"Are you sure?" he asked once more.

Sophie was very certain.

Couldn't he tell how much she wanted to kiss him by the sound of her heartbeat? It was so loud in her ears that her body thrummed to its rhythm. She nodded and, for answer, lifted her hands from under the blankets, finding his face in the darkness. She touched it tentatively and heard his soft gasp.

His hand covered hers just an instant before their lips met.

The shock of it sent Sophie reeling . . . or maybe it was the boat listing once more. She couldn't really tell. He held her close, kissing her passionately, but with restraint . . . and Sophie knew instinctively he was holding back.

She didn't want him to.

He kissed her like a gentleman, not because he was one, she sensed . . . but because he chose to be one, and that knowledge in itself left her breathless and excited in a way she had never experienced before.

His kiss was nothing like the chaste pecks on the lips Harlan had given her.

He cradled her face in his hands, pleading with her. "Open for me, Sophia."

For an instant, Sophie didn't understand what it was he was asking. Her senses were delirious. She closed her eyes and saw tiny points of light bursting before her lids.

Capturing her hands once again, he drew them behind her head and shifted so that he was atop her, pinning her beneath his weight.

There was no escape.

The very thought of it made her body ache in places she had never even known existed.

"Give me your tongue," he whispered against her ear. "Let me taste you, Sophia."

Sophie shuddered in anticipation of his request. She parted her lips as he wished, and the first foray of his tongue sent her heart fluttering out of her breast. Like a wanton, she clung to him. In response, he deepened the kiss. He held her hands behind her head and moved atop her with such delicious slowness that her body instinctively sought him. She arched into him, trying to free her hands, to hold him, but he held them fast, refusing to free her.

"Just as I remembered," he murmured, and Sophie had no notion what he was talking about, only that it gave her a heady rush to hear him say so.

"Kiss me back, Sophia," she heard him beg her, and Sophie tried to obey. She had never kissed a man with openmouthed abandon before. Tentatively, she offered him her tongue, and nearly fainted where she lay when he took it to suckle gently within his mouth.

She whimpered softly beneath him, writhing in pleasure, urging him deeper into her mouth.

She wanted more . . . wanted him to show her more . . .

Jack groaned with satisfaction over the taste of her. Brief as their first kiss had been, he'd remembered exactly. The taste of her had taunted him since, and like a man starved for sustenance, he'd craved her.

His hands needed to roam her body, to touch her, feel her . . . make love to her, but he restrained them, knowing she hadn't given him leave to explore.

But he wanted to—God, he wanted to!

He held her hands behind her head, because if she touched him . . . if she so much as urged him to . . . unwittingly even . . . he would give it to her gladly.

He broke free of the kiss, before he could be tempted further . . . before his hands could slide down over her beautiful body to lift the hem of her flimsy gown. If he did that . . . if he dared to . . . she would need far better armor than what she was wearing.

He stared down at her, very aware of his arousal nestled between them. His body ached. Did she have any idea what he wanted from her?

More than anything, he wanted to be inside her.

She was so beautiful.

Though he couldn't see her, he imagined her lying beneath him, her rich auburn hair spread like molten copper about her perfect face. And those eyes . . . golden like honey, and sprinkled with emerald dust. He cursed the darkness in that instant that he couldn't see them . . . that he couldn't read her expression.

Did she regret it already?

He surely didn't.

Couldn't.

Wouldn't.

She was silent, and Jack told her, "Do you know how long I've wanted to do that, Sophia?"

She sounded breathless, the same as he did. "How long?" she asked him, and he had to smile at her question.

As a matter of fact, he didn't remember a moment when he hadn't wanted to kiss her, and yet he couldn't honestly give her the exact instant he'd first realized.

"Since you first kissed me," he told her, and knew it was a lie.

He'd wanted her even before then.

"Oh!" she replied. He wished he could see the color in her cheeks. And then she added, sounding as though she were holding back an embarrassed giggle, "I don't suppose I should apologize, then?"

Jack grinned down at her. "Not on your life," he assured her, and chuckled.

There was silence between them then, and after a moment she said, "I'm very sorry about your papers, Jack."

Jack didn't want to think about that just now, didn't want to remember who she was. "It's all right. I managed to save most of them anyway."

"Still . . . I'm sorry. I didn't mean to."

He wanted to believe she had nothing to do with Penn, other than the obvious. He wanted to believe her when she'd said she missed her fiancé and wanted only to see him . . . and yet

a part of him recoiled at the very possibility
. . . because he wanted her for himself.

"You don't really believe I would steal from
you, do you?" She sounded hurt by the prospect.

Reality smacked him in the face.

*She was some other man's fiancée . . . engaged to
be married to someone other than him.*

On top of that, he wasn't entirely certain he
could trust her. His answer was honest when
he gave it. "No."

He couldn't believe she would kiss him like
that if she could so easily turn around and stab
him in the back. And still . . . she wasn't being
completely honest with him . . . because no
woman in love with someone else could kiss
another man like that.

At least he hoped like hell it was true.

Chapter 19

"**S**he's not what you think," Kell said, coming up behind him.

Jack glanced up from his work at him, annoyed that the only thing Kell ever seemed to have to talk to him about was Sophie. "No?" he asked, though he was beginning to sense it as much himself.

"No," Kell answered, and came to sit on the desk. The portrait of Harlan Penn caught his attention and he lifted it up, arching a brow as he inspected it.

Jack tried hard not to notice the picture, as much as it irked him. In fact, he'd like to send it flying across the room, and would have happily let his desk burn down just to get rid of it. But it belonged to Sophie and so he just ignored it.

"You know something I don't?" he asked Kell, sensing it was so. Kell never kept anything from him, but somehow Jack felt this time he was.

Kell's reply only provoked him more. "Maybe."

Jack studied his friend. "You like her, don't you?"

Kell flipped the picture down against his thigh and grinned at him. "Everyone likes her, Jack."

Jack knew it was true.

"Except you, ya rotten bastard!"

"I like her just fine," Jack countered, and it was a hell of an understatement. He liked her more than just fine . . . he liked her too damned much.

"Do you?" Kell pried.

Jack sat back in his chair, studying the smug expression on Kell's face.

"What is it you're trying to tell me, Kell?"

Kell stood again, took another look at the picture, and said, "If you're too blind to see the truth then you don't deserve to know." And then he set the picture down facing Jack and walked away.

Jack watched him go with narrowed eyes, thinking they had known each other far too long. He sighed deeply and his gaze returned to the portrait of Penn.

His brows drew together as they focused on the picture, and he reached out to grasp it in his hand.

"I'll be damned," he said, and chuckled.

The artwork wasn't his.

Penn sported two horns on his head and a third on his chin, and his eyes were filled with dollar symbols. The look suited him. Jack shook his head and laughed outright. He glanced at the door and thought about calling Kell back to hound him for whatever information he'd gotten out of her, but he knew Kell well enough to know he wouldn't give it—not if he'd made up his mind not to, and it seemed he had.

"I'll be damned," he said again, and set the picture down facing him, so that he could enjoy it while he worked. His mood, as he sat again, was much lightened.

It was then he heard the shouts, and he nearly knocked the desk over in his haste to discover the cause of the commotion.

"I'm perfectly all right," Sophie assured Randall who was shouting at her to come down, trying to calm him before he managed to rouse Jack. It wasn't as though it were windy and the seas turbulent. The ocean and sky were both at peace after last night's storm, and Sophie didn't see the first reason why she couldn't manage a simple repair. If a man could do it, she could do it. That much was certain.

"Miss Vanderwahl," Randall shouted up at her, "please come down from there!"

Sophie ignored him, climbing higher up the makeshift ladder. Apparently, through the night, the winds had rent the sails enough that it was visible from the deck below and she didn't want the rip to worsen. She would certainly take precautions, but she would not be deterred.

She wanted to do something nice for Jack.

They'd awakened that morn arm in arm on the floor. He'd held her through the night while the storm had raged, and she'd pretended to sleep on while he'd risen with the bright morning sun, taking care to tuck her in before leaving. He'd brushed the hair from her face . . . so tenderly that it had made her heart twist with longing.

"Miss Vanderwahl," Randall protested, and then was joined by Kell, who thankfully remained quiet while staring up at her as though he thought her mad.

And perhaps she was, because all she could think about was Jack. Jack, Jack, Jack. What in damnation was wrong with her?

A crowd began to gather on deck, but Sophie ignored them, determined to be of some use. She had found needle and thread in storage, and by their enormous size she determined they were intended for just such an occasion. She might not know how to repair sailcloth precisely, but she was hardly beyond figuring such things out.

Once she reached her destination, however, the size of the rip dampened her resolve. From below, it had seemed small enough, but up close, she began to wonder if she would do it any good. Even so, it didn't hurt to try. She took the rope she had coiled on her arm and tied it first about the masthead, and then about her waist, securing her position, lest she slip and fall. That done, she braced herself to work and removed the needle from her dress. It was already threaded; she had done that before coming up. And if she should need more thread, she had that at the ready.

All was well until Jack shouted up at her, startling her.

"Goddammit, Sophia! Get down here!"

She dropped the needle.

Sophie peered down at Jack, glaring at him. "Look what you made me do!" she railed at him.

"Get down here, Sophia!"

His tone of voice grated on her nerves. "I will not!" Sophie countered. "How dare you use that tone with me!" If he were concerned about her, there were far better ways to show it! At any rate, she was just fine, except that now she had no needle. Irritation welled up inside her.

"Do you have any idea what the hell you are doing?" he asked her, with the emphasis on *hell*. He set his hands on his hips as he glared up at her. "Or do you make it your duty to run around looking for trouble? In all my blasted days, Sophia Vanderwahl, I have never met a more undisciplined woman!"

If there had been anyone aboard ship who hadn't known she'd climbed the masthead, he certainly knew it now.

Undisciplined, was she?

Anger surged through her. Were she a man up here, Sophie doubted her efforts would have been viewed quite the same way. A man would have been considered conscientious and constructive.

Undisciplined!

"I'm fixing the sails!" she informed him smartly, and tried to look as dignified as she possibly could under his tirade. Everyone was watching. "Not that someone like you would bother to appreciate that," she railed at him. "Ungrateful man," she muttered under her breath.

"I see," he said. "So that's what you are doing up there."

"Yes."

"And you planned to just stitch it up with needle and thread?"

"Of course," Sophie responded. "Isn't that how you fix torn cloth?"

He was silent a moment in the face of her logic, though his fury was evident in his very stance. And then he said, "I don't know how the hell you fix that cloth, but any idiot would know not to try to fix it while the wind is ripping through!"

"It's not windy!" Sophie argued. Merely a gentle breeze. Nothing that should have hampered her repairs. "You are being ridiculous, Jack."

"Sophia," he continued, sounding harassed now. "If you don't come down from there, I'm coming up!"

Sophie bristled at his threat. It made her feel a wayward child, and not even her mother had given her such abuse.

Then again, she'd hardly ever done a single thing for which to be reprimanded, so afraid of her mother she had been.

She refused to be cowed. She was no five-year-old with a muddy dress to be chastened. She was an adult, and a free-thinking one at that!

She smiled down at him, a challenge in her tone. "You just do that, Jack MacAuley—and why don't you bring me the needle you made me drop while you are at it?" All at once, the crew below began to search the deck, as though looking for the needle.

"Sophia!" Jack shouted.

"I think it's there . . . near Randall," she instructed him, ignoring his directive. If he wanted her down, he could very well ask, politely. She had no reason to remain now without her needle, but she wasn't going to bow to his every command.

Randall dropped to his knees, searching. Sophie doubted he would ever find the needle, and in truth, she had no idea where it had fallen. Jack had startled her so.

Rude cantankerous man!

"That's it!" Jack said, throwing up his hands in obvious disgust of her and practically lunging at the masthead before taking hold of the ladder and climbing it much too agilely. Sophie bit her lip, frowning at him. He couldn't very well drag her down against her will. It wouldn't be safe to simply pull her down after him. Instinctively she tightened the knot at her waist, and then just to be certain she tied another and pulled with all her might. She didn't wish to fall victim to his rash anger.

"I was only trying to help!" she assured him

when he was halfway up. She tested the rope once more, growing more anxious the closer he came.

"Don't help!"

"I don't understand why you are so angry!"

Neither did he.

Jack couldn't explain the fear that had knotted in his gut the instant he'd spied her up on the masthead.

The woman was blasted insane!

No more was he merely concerned that she would sink the boat. If she kept this up, she was going to end up six feet under. Jack was going to have to lock her up to keep her from harm!

He climbed swiftly, thinking only of reaching her, not questioning the inexplicable hysteria he felt inside at the thought of her up there.

He almost had her, was within arm's reach, when he placed his foot a bit too heavily on the ladder rung. It gave way beneath him.

"Jack!"

He reached out for the masthead, embracing it as he went sliding downward. In the same instant, he felt a sharp tug on his scalp, only an instant and then it was gone. He landed heavily on the next rung down, and he heard it snap, too. Down he went again, groaning in pain. For an inscrutable moment, all he could think about were his jewels. There had been no way to protect them in his slide down, and he went black now with the pain. The next rung down held fast, and he stood there, hugging the masthead, coming aware next of the burning in his hands.

When reason returned to him, he peered up into Sophie's horrified expression.

She held her hand outstretched and in it she held a lock of his hair. Jack's brows drew together in shock at seeing it. His first instinct was to reach back and find the bald spot, but his arms were wrapped tightly about the masthead, and he'd be damned if he'd let go.

She peered down at it, and then again at him, her brows lifting in supplication. "I'm sorry, Jack. I . . . I tried to stop you."

Words would not form.

In his mind, he imagined tying her to her hammock, wrapping mile after mile of rope around her, cocooning her away from the world. In his fantasy, she shouted pleas to be released, but he steadfastly ignored her, silencing her with a brutal kiss before turning and walking away, then locking the door.

He should have followed his gut instinct, and never let her aboard.

Chapter 20

❦

"**Y**ou're lucky this isn't worse," Sophia scolded him.

Jack merely looked at her.

"I was only trying to help," she defended herself.

"No more helping!"

"But I want to!" she protested.

Stubborn woman.

He admired her fortitude but the pain in his hands made him resolute. It was his turn to sit grimacing while she removed splinters from his hands—big fat ugly splinters. He leveled a stern look at her.

"No more, Sophia, do you understand? No more!"

She sat on his desk before him, digging out splinters, wincing as she worked. "I'm sorry," she said, and sighed. "This is all my fault."

Jack wasn't about to disagree, but neither did he say anything. It was clear by her expression that she was guilt-ridden enough already.

"I suppose my education falls somewhat short of instruction for the world at large."

He smiled at her, softening his insult with a wink. "You do pretty damned well for a spoiled little rich girl."

Sophie laughed softly, but the self-deprecating tone had pricked at his heart.

"You know . . ." He met her gaze and said, somewhat more soberly. "The simple fact that you've rolled up your sleeves to help is a good sight more than I expected from you."

Sophie shrugged. "I wouldn't quite call it *help*."

"Don't be so hard on yourself, Sophia."

Sophie couldn't help it. It seemed everything she attempted, she failed. She'd thought herself so well-schooled because she'd managed her parents' household so smoothly. In truth, she was almost afraid to attempt anything more. Only sheer stubborn will made her keep trying. She refused to be defeated by menial tasks. She was determined to be of some help to Jack, to be an integral member of his crew . . . to make up for the damage she had caused. Much of his research had been ruined. Somehow, she had to atone for it.

Perhaps she could try to redraw the pictures?

She *was* good at that.

She walked over to the washbasin, picked up the soap and a washcloth, tossed them into the basin, and then lifted the basin out of its table and brought it back to his desk, still thinking about his research. Many of the pages had survived, damaged though they were. She could redo them for him.

She soaped up the rag and then lifted it to his hand, cleaning it gently.

"Does it hurt?" she asked him, her tone filled with concern.

"Yes!" he cried out.

"I'm sorry," she offered genuinely, and gentled her touch.

His own drawings had been good enough to give her a vision of the objects he had tried to capture. She would begin as soon as possible.

This was all Jack's fault: Never before had she been embroiled in so many disasters. He was a terrible distraction. She had lived a very reserved life, never indulging in anything that wasn't entirely proper. She didn't know anything about cooking or cleaning, or any of the other domestic chores her parents had hired help for. She'd never even had to lift a finger to turn out her own lights. The servants had always taken care of everything. If she'd fallen asleep with the lights on, reading, they were always there to put them out.

And now that she finally had the opportunity to do things for herself, to prove she didn't need anyone, she was stumbling all over herself and endangering others with her puny efforts.

It made her feel very much a failure.

She couldn't blame Jack for forbidding her to help anymore. She really wouldn't blame him if he locked her up in her cabin and took away everything with which she could possibly cause damage. She couldn't even read without putting everyone at risk. What made her think she could do something so responsible as share in Jack's career?

She only wished she could have proven herself somehow.

She blinked suddenly, looking up at Jack, only just realizing what she had been thinking.

What made her think she could do something so responsible as share in *Jack's* career?

She swallowed uneasily, quite certain she must be mad to even entertain such a notion.

And yet she had thought it.

She brushed the cool, moist cloth over his hands, but his eyes seemed to bore into her own, searching. He looked at her, as though trying to read her thoughts, and Sophie fidgeted under his scrutiny.

Did he know what she was thinking?

Did he think her silly?

The intensity of his gaze set her heart to pounding once again.

"I do know something for sure now," he told her, and Sophie caught her breath, afraid that her secrets had all been revealed in the depth of her eyes.

What did he know?

It was said that the eyes were the mirrors to the soul and if that were indeed true, then Sophie's heart was an open book. Her father had always told her that he could tell what she was thinking simply by the look in her eyes.

Whether that was true or not, her father certainly seemed to read all.

She was almost afraid to ask, and mentally braced herself for whatever revelation Jack had had. "What?"

He smiled at her, and his green eyes glistened like the clearest emeralds, full of good humor. "You don't snore," he said with certainty.

For an instant, the unexpected acknowledgment surprised her.

As far as Sophie was concerned it had never been in question. But she realized he was trying to make her smile and she did manage to appease him.

The cad.

"You are absolutely insufferable!" she told him, trying to keep from laughing.

"You're not the first woman to tell me that," he assured her, quite obviously unrepentant. "And it's not even the first time you've accused me of it."

"I assure you, it is always true!"

"Yah?" His eyes fairly twinkled with mirth, spoiling the effect of his complaint. "Well, you're no great party yourself, Mizz Vanderwahl!"

Sophie tilted him a knowing glance. "If I didn't know better, Mr. MacAuley, I would say you were trying to pick a fight with me."

Like a child who had been caught with his hands in the proverbial cookie jar, he grinned at her, looking in that instant far too boyish and endearing. "Maybe you just don't know better?" he suggested, egging her on. His brow arched.

Sophie had to laugh at his confrontational expression. "I think you must have been a rotten little boy!" she told him, and wished she'd known him then.

"To the core," he allowed.

"I don't doubt it!" Sophie agreed heartily. She wondered at how Jack's provocations made her find strength in herself and bolstered her spirits.

They shared a moment's ease together, and then he glanced down at his hand. "Take it easy on that, will you?"

"Oh!" Sophie started, and let go of his hand.

"I'll make you a deal . . ." he bargained with her.

She dropped the cloth into the basin and waited to hear his suggestion.

"You make sure you keep out of trouble the rest of the trip, and I promise you can make our first breakfast when we get off this boat."

Sophie smiled in answer, delighted that he was willing to give her another chance. And then her breath caught. He was really very handsome . . . especially when he wasn't scowling at her.

She could look into his eyes forever.

"Deal?"

"Deal," she agreed.

"You have only a week left. Think you can manage it?"

He was playing with her, she realized. "Of course!" she exclaimed, pretending offense.

"Starting now," he warned her.

She threw her arms around his neck as much in gratitude as to make him stop. "Hush," she demanded of him, and looked up into his smiling face. She kissed him quickly on the lips when he tried to speak again, and whispered, "Thank you."

He quieted at once, his smile vanishing, and she realized suddenly what she had done.

Her heartbeat quickened.

She tried to disengage herself but his arm went about her waist, preventing it.

"Don't," he whispered, beseeching her, and Sophie could suddenly feel his heart beating against her breast as he pulled her against him . . . or maybe it was only her own.

She couldn't tell.

The breath left her as he tilted his head to kiss her once more.

"Sophia," he whispered hoarsely, as though she should stop him.

She didn't want to.

His eyes closed, and her heart leapt as his lips fitted perfectly over hers.

His mouth was wonderful and Sophie had never wanted anything more . . .

She opened to him, anticipating his tongue with bated breath. At the brush of it against her lips, soft and warm and sweet, she offered her own without protest, without hesitation . . . with total abandon.

Jack had never tasted anything sweeter.

No lips had ever trembled so beautifully.

No tongue had ever felt so much like heaven.

No embrace had ever been so welcome.

He wanted something he knew he could never have, but he was willing to take whatever she would give him. She might not be in love with Penn, but she was still another man's fiancée. Whatever piece of her she gifted to him would be gone soon enough. He didn't feel guilty for taking his share. Jack wasn't so honorable a man that he could walk away clean from the only woman who had ever made his heart beat so hard that it hurt to breathe... who could make him smile, make him feel like he'd never felt before.

He pulled away to look into her face, wanting to see her. Her cheeks were flushed with color, her eyes dark golden, dazed with passion. He could take whatever he wanted of her this moment and she would give it without protest; he knew that instinctively.

And he desperately wanted to taste her.

He could pleasure her, and satisfy himself ... and she would remain virtually untouched ...

Or he could walk away and wonder for the rest of his life.

The choice was his, he knew.

He chose to stay.

"Sophia," he whispered, and bent to kiss her throat. Her head lolled to one side, and her scent tempted him beyond reason, aroused him. His body tightened, hardened. He opened his mouth over her throat and nipped her gently, and she moaned softly in delirious pleasure. He was filled with intense satisfaction at the beautiful sound of her passion. "I want you," he told her, and meant it fiercely.

A slow burn seeped through him at his baser thoughts, and he met her gaze, wanting her to see every move he made . . . while he was making it. If she wanted him to stop, she would just need to say the word, and he would.

He kissed her throat once more, biting it softly, and then kissed her breast over her clothes. When she didn't stop him, he closed a palm over one breast and molded his hand to the tantalizing softness, craving the feel of her bare skin on his lips.

She cried out, soft whimpers.

Sophie closed her eyes and let her head fall back, helpless, to let him do his will.

Her body wasn't her own.

He knew where she ached, and knew how to touch her, and she couldn't have stopped him even if she'd thought to.

But she didn't.

She had wanted this all her life and just hadn't known it . . . or him.

He was kissing her so wantonly . . . biting so softly . . . as though she were his coveted feast . . .

He knelt before her suddenly, clasping her to him, and she gasped in shock as his lips touched her bosom . . . then his hands, and her breath left her in a rush as he dipped a kiss between the valley of her breasts, letting his tongue slide down where no man had ever kissed her before.

Sophie was deliciously scandalized.

Her skin prickled with pleasure and she lifted her hand to his head, urging him to give her more. She knew instinctively that he could . . . that he would, and she wanted it with every fiber of her being.

His lips skimmed her breasts, kissing and gently nipping, and Sophie's heart somersaulted against her ribs. She was vaguely aware that he lifted the hem of her dress, his fingers lightly caressing her calf. He continued to lift it . . . as he kissed her belly . . . moved down to her thigh . . . His tongue caressed her inner thigh, and Sophie swallowed the objection that came to her lips.

Her heart hammered fiercely.

His fingers skimmed the curls at the juncture of her thighs and she gasped in shock that was too laced with bliss to speak out in protest. Instinctively, clinging to a shred of modesty, she pressed her legs together, though not entirely to stop him. It only managed to intensify the feeling . . . and trap his hand between her legs.

He wiggled his finger, brushing her most delicate spot.

"Oh my," she exclaimed, and felt her eyes cross with a pleasure so keen it was almost pain. She leaned back on the desk then, bracing herself with trembling arms, lest she faint. The room went dim, and she was aware only of the man nestled so intimately between her thighs.

He peered up at her, his green eyes burning with something like . . . hunger.

"Spread your legs for me, Sophia."

Sophie's heart jolted at the request. But she was powerless to deny him. His gaze demanded it and she wanted to give him everything he wanted . . . anything he wanted.

Again, she swallowed any protest she might have uttered.

Her legs trembled as she obeyed and he rewarded her with the most wickedly pleased smile Sophie had ever beheld. It made her belly flutter with anticipation.

"That's it, flower," he encouraged her. "Open for me."

He teased her . . . there . . . and Sophie's breath caught at the intensity of sensation that exploded everywhere he touched.

"Jack," she cried out, and sought his gaze.

His eyes glittered like jewels. He didn't stop. He continued without mercy, his fingers dancing magically, eliciting the most delicious sensations she had ever felt in all her life.

"Oh my!" she said again, and thought she would die. "Jack!" she hissed, and it might have been a protest but her body arched toward him, urging him on. Her legs spread of their own accord, opening to him like a blossom to the sun.

Her head fell backward, and her breath faltered as he lifted her skirts higher.

And then she felt something so delightfully

sinful that she wanted to cry out in ecstacy. His mouth replaced his fingers . . . his tongue moving over her with such slow precision that Sophie thought her heart would stop completely. His tongue danced where his fingers had, teasing her. And then he suckled her, and Sophie couldn't bear it any longer. Unable to speak, she cried out for mercy.

She fell backward as a finger slipped within her body, gently, caressing until she was oblivious. And then something suddenly burst within her, and she cried out with a joy so intense that she could scarce contain it.

She heard his answering gasp and felt his ardor as he continued to devour her.

Her own cry of release played like an echo in her ear. As she lay there on his desk, Sophie was aware of only two things . . . three . . .

One, she had never felt so cherished in all her life. Though she knew it was an illusion, an afterglow from the intensity of her pleasure.

Two, she seemed to have given him something he'd desperately wanted, because he was kissing her sweetly still and didn't seem to want to stop.

And three . . . she seemed to have his quill embedded in her spine . . . but damned if she cared if it had skewered her completely through.

At the instant, she was floating on clouds.

Chapter 21

Jack sat at his desk, trying to make sense of the words jumbled before him.

He was reading through reports that had been made by colleagues . . . accounts that had been lambasted and tossed away as inconsequential or erroneous simply because they did not comply with the accepted theory of human evolution.

He was *trying* to read them but he could scarce concentrate over the sounds coming from the other half of the room.

Sophia was preparing for bed.

He didn't feel the least bit tired.

In fact, he could barely sit at his desk; he was too tense. He couldn't stop remembering the taste of her . . . the feel of her sweet shudders as he'd brought her body to climax.

His own body was in dire need of relief . . . relief only she could give him.

His vision blurred and his concentration was reduced to nil.

She was washing.

He could hear her too clearly; buttons being unfastened, the rustle of falling garments, water splashing . . .

She was painfully quiet otherwise.

He tried to concentrate on his work, forcing his attention on the papers before him.

It was his contention that the Mayan civilization, to have evolved to its final state of technological advancement, must have had ample time for said evolution . . .

Water splashed behind the curtain.

Where was she washing?

Images taunted him—soft dark curls—he craved the taste of her all over again. Swallowing, he closed his eyes for a moment, and, when he reopened them he tried harder to focus . . .

It was difficult to believe that, as the present theory would have it, a Mesoamerican civilization could have developed to such a degree as had the Maya if man had migrated to the continent as late as only ten thousand years ago.

Sweet . . . she was sweet.

He blinked away the powerful image of her lying back on his desk . . . and ignored the evidence of his arousal.

Sophie's presence was driving him insane.

What was she doing? Her silence was maddening.

Should he speak to her? Tell her good night? Why the hell was he suddenly behaving as though he were some kid with his first crush? She was a Vanderwahl, sure enough, but those beautiful legs had not too long ago been wrapped around his neck, while her soft passionate cries had filled his ears.

Annoyed with himself, he refocused his thoughts, tapping his fingers impatiently on the desk.

The Mayan accomplishments left Jack incredulous. They had developed knowledge never obtained by comparable civilizations. Their system of mathematics could express sums in the millions, and they'd understood the concept of the quantity of zero a thousand years before anyone else. Among their many other accomplishments, they'd developed a calendar accurate for four hundred million years, and their measure of the year was only a small fraction off target from the actual. An infant society, so to speak, would not have had the necessary time to advance to that point— at least not without outside influence.

Those had been the seeds Penn had run away with . . . literally.

Having worked closely with Jack, Penn had presented to the board Jack's precise body of thought, except that he hadn't truly understood the gist of Jack's theory. It was Penn's contention that because the Mayan civilization never seemed to move beyond the Stone Age— never employing the wheel for any sensible purpose, or developing a phonetic alphabet— the Maya *must* have been *handed* their knowledge by sources outside their own culture.

Having had access to Jack's reports, Penn had shot down his theory point by point before the board, twisting his own arguments against him in the name of religion, to such a degree that Jack found it an insult to his intelligence and a crippling blow to progress. As it was, it wouldn't have been easy to convince them of the validity of his own theories, but after Harlan had finished with them, they hadn't even been inclined to hear him out.

Even though Jack had proof to offer.

The reports he had in front of him by trusted colleagues gave evidence that strongly implied anatomically modern man had inhabited the continent from a far earlier date. That led Jack to believe it more likely that the Maya had indeed developed on their own. But with that theory, he had committed a professional sin: He had dared to question the standard institution.

It seemed incredible to Jack that evidence such as this, given by respected researchers, could be dismissed in favor of that given by someone like Penn. Though Penn's evidence was minimal, relying almost primarily on religious parallelisms, it was he who had received the grants for continued research, and Jack who had been left to flounder.

Jack believed it was because Penn's research not merely supported the accepted theory of evolution, but favored religious doctrine. And it galled him, not that Penn's theories were given credence—all evidence should be considered—but that Penn's theories and those like his were the *only* ones given credit.

Jack sure as hell didn't mind being wrong.

He'd proven himself out of countless theories. But he damned well didn't like being told he was wrong even before he'd set out to do his job—by men who considered themselves the ruling elite.

The curtain opened abruptly.

Sophie stood there, dressed in her tattered nightgown, and somehow still managed to look regal.

Despite his mood, the sight of her brought a smile to his lips.

She smiled back at him.

He was leaning wearily on his desk, chin in hand, staring at his papers with that provoked look he usually reserved for her.

"What is it you're studying?" she asked him, resisting the urge to go and peek over his shoulder. He didn't seem to appreciate her interest in his work, but her curiosity was addling her. She just couldn't help herself.

"Work," he said simply. He continued to smile at her, and Sophie's cheeks heated.

He'd been far more receptive to her since their *encounter* that afternoon—a positive change—but Sophie couldn't quite enjoy it. She didn't like this sudden shyness that had come over her in his presence. She couldn't even seem to glance his way without blushing, and the more care he took to put her at ease, the more embarrassed she became.

Jack MacAuley had seen far more of her than any man had a right to, and her behavior had been abominable. Her thoughts were muddled. Something so beautiful couldn't possibly have been wrong . . . and yet she was technically still engaged to Harlan . . . at least until she faced him. She hadn't any right to indulge in such unseemly behavior with anyone at all.

And yet, though her cheeks burned, she couldn't find true regret for what she'd done.

The very sight of Jack made her heart catch.

He set down his papers, giving her his full attention.

Sophie smiled shyly at him and approached the desk under the pretense of looking at Harlan's picture. Lifting it up, she smiled contentedly at her own handiwork, then set the picture down, tapping it thoughtfully before she glanced back at Jack.

He was watching her intently, secretly amused by something. About what, Sophie had no idea.

His brows lifted. "You can't wait to see him, I take it?"

"No, I really can't," she admitted, and it was the truth. She couldn't wait to read him his own treacherous words and then fling her ring into his face. Let him give it to one of his precious native girls!

"It shows," he said, peering at her. Uncomfortable under his scrutiny, Sophie made an effort to appear serene. She wasn't prepared for explanations just yet.

Somehow, it made her feel a failure.

Her mother had sometimes cautioned her not to show her true nature, because she was certain Sophie would never keep a man. Her temper was too quick, her interests were too masculine, and her hair never remained in place. She reached up and pulled the ribbon from her hair, letting the strands fall free. She'd spent an inordinate amount of time trying to make it presentable, but why even try to restrain it?

It wasn't her fault that Harlan was a philandering fool!

"So . . ." She toyed with the pale ivory ribbon, wrapping it around the thumb of her hand. "What are you working on?" she persisted, hoping her question would turn the attention away from her.

Jack was looking at her far too knowingly and it made her nervous.

"You really want to know?"

"Of course," she told him. "I'd not have asked otherwise."

"I was reading through reports made by colleagues."

"What sort of reports?"

"Evidence discovered along the North American continent which indicates a much older indigenous peoples than is normally accepted."

Sophie unraveled the ribbon from her finger. "In other words . . . the natives have been here much longer than we think?"

"Precisely."

"I see." She was truly interested, but although her fiancé was an expert in the field of anthropology, she hadn't the first inkling how their studies were performed. Harlan never talked to her about anything. "And how would you know such a thing?"

He pushed a paper at her. "Take this article, for example . . ."

Sophie turned the paper around. It was titled "A Relic of a Bygone Age."

"That particular article appeared in *Scientific American*, on June 5, 1852."

Sophie read the scribble at the top of the page, written in what she supposed was Jack's hand, *Metallic vase from Precambrian rock*.

"A bell-shaped vessel was thrown from the rock in the explosion highlighted in this article."

Sophie scanned the letter, and asked, "In Massachusetts?"

Jack nodded portentously. "Yes. The body of the vessel resembled zinc in color and on the side was a design inlaid with pure silver. Around the bottom ran a vine, also inlaid with silver. The chasing, carving, and inlaying were done by a skilled artisan. It was blown out of solid pudding stone, fifteen feet below the earth's surface. That stone dates to the Precambrian Age, which makes it over six hundred million years old."

Sophie's brows drew together. "That's remarkable."

"Yes, it is," Jack agreed. "The standard view is that Asian hunters and gatherers crossed the Bering Strait about twelve thousand years ago."

"That is quite a discrepancy," Sophie remarked.

"An incredible discrepancy. But that report hardly stands alone. There are dozens of the like."

"Amazing," Sophie said with awe.

Hungry for more knowledge, she glanced longingly at the stack of reports Jack had guarded so fiercely.

"Would you like to read them?"

Sophie blinked at his question and tried to gauge his expression. Was he serious? Or merely teasing her? "Really?"

He nodded, and she gasped in surprise.

"You truly don't mind?"

He merely smiled at her question and pushed the stack towards her. "Only if you promise to take them straight to your bed and read them there, and nowhere else."

Sophie broke into a wide smile.

"And no lanterns within five feet," he demanded further.

Sophie laughed, although she wanted to take offense. She couldn't. If she were Jack, she doubted she'd let herself anywhere near them.

"And no water, and no ink anywhere near it! And when you are through you are to place them back in my drawer in a tidy fashion."

"Good lord!" Sophie wanted to laugh out loud. "I am *not* usually so prone to disasters," she assured him.

His brows lifted and his smile widened as well. He sat back in his chair, staring at her, and said very decisively, "I don't believe you."

Sophie took his papers before he could

change his mind, lifting the heavy stack to her breast, hugging them. There was really nothing she could say in her own defense, but she could certainly prove it by putting them neatly back into his desk before morning.

"Thank you, Jack," she offered with an appreciative smile.

He nodded, staring at her still, and his smile seemed suddenly wistful, "Good night, flower," he said.

Sophie's heart leaped at his endearment.

She met his gaze, swallowing. It was the second time he'd said that to her . . . and it made her heart beat just as fiercely the second time around. Although they were standing at least six feet from each other, the mere memory of the first time made her body instantly warm, and the look in his eyes seized her breath.

She felt suddenly dizzy.

"Good night, Jack," she said in a rush, and practically ran to her bed, drawing the curtains shut behind her.

Chapter 22

~~~~~~

Jack sat watching the curtains long after she'd closed them.

Ridiculous as the notion was, he envied that stack of papers she had embraced so protectively.

He could see her silhouette against the makeshift curtains, a gift of the lanterns she had lit on the far side of the room. She was curled up in her hammock with his papers braced on her lap, reading.

He couldn't help but watch her as he put up his own hammock and readied himself for bed ... and wonder. Did Penn know what a gem he had in Sophie?

He was pretty sure she wasn't snooping for Penn, and if she was, he doubted she would find anything in those reports that Penn wouldn't at once scoff at. The man's mind was closed. There was nothing to be lost in letting her read them, and his views weren't any secret, either. But he didn't want to believe any longer that she was in cahoots with Penn.

She was stubborn, definitely, and without doubt the most troublesome woman he had ever laid eyes on. In fact, trouble might be her middle name. Besides that, her temper was a bit Vesuvian in nature. Right or wrong, she took a stand the instant she was threatened, and he wondered if she were always that way, or just with him. In any case, he admired that about her. She wasn't some fainting miss who lost consciousness or pleaded illness the instant a man raised his voice. And she didn't strike him as a liar, or a cheat, either. Her emotions were much too evident in her beautiful face.

Her expression when he'd called her *flower* told him she understood where his thoughts had wandered . . . and more, that her own thoughts hovered near. Her reaction had amused him. Her eyes had flared in comprehension, and she'd stared at him wide-eyed for an instant before she'd scurried away to hide on her side of the curtain.

But she hadn't gone far enough.

He tried his damndest to forget there was only a measly sheet separating them.

He turned out his lights and climbed into his hammock, lamenting the fact that he wasn't gentleman enough to turn the other way so that he couldn't see her. The fact was, he wasn't any sort of gentleman at all, had never claimed to be, and so he lay there watching her without the least trace of guilt . . .

Well, maybe just a little guilt.

He was certain it wasn't the most moral

thing to do ... lying there watching her, but then *she* had asked to share his room, not the other way around. If she didn't like it, she could just leave ...

Though he guessed that before she would consider returning to her damaged room, she would have to be aware of the fact that he could see every deuced thing she was doing, every movement behind the curtain ... every time she brushed her hair from her face ... every time she flipped a page ... every time she took a breath.

Her breast lifted, and he heard her sigh.

Of course ... he couldn't really tell her because he knew it would embarrass her ... so maybe he was being a gentleman after all ...

He decided that what she didn't know couldn't really hurt her in this case.

But it sure as hell left Jack in pain.

His body hardened as he watched her, and his blood began to simmer.

Yep, this was definitely hurting him more than it was hurting her.

And it was without doubt the most dishonorable thing he'd ever done ... maybe ...

There *was* that little Mexican girl who had seduced him on his first trip to the Yucatan ... the one whose father had been his guide. The man had offered him a bed in his home the night before they set out into the jungles. Her father had been asleep in the same room, oblivious to the daughter's endeavors. Maria had been her name. Jack would never forget her.

That was also the first time he'd ever fooled around in a hammock—tricky business but he knew now it could be done, and he'd give anything to be in that other hammock this moment . . . with Sophie.

He blinked, staring as the silhouette curled deeper into the hammock, knees bent to support the papers she was reading. Was she getting sleepy? Just trying to get comfortable? Were her thoughts on the reports she was reading . . . or dared he hope they were on something else?

He couldn't stop thinking of her.

Couldn't stop wanting her.

Couldn't stop remembering the taste of her.

He adjusted himself, couldn't help it. He had to. His body was in too much pain, and his pants were far too snug. For her sake, he slept at least partly dressed and made sure to wake before her and dress before she could happen on him shirtless. But this instant, he needed to be naked . . . needed her to be naked, as well . . . needed to feel her skin against his, soft and warm. He needed to smell the scent of her skin, needed to touch her.

Christ, he was going insane with lust!

He cupped himself, needing to feel the pressure.

It was a poor substitute for what he really wanted.

His skin was burning. Sweat beaded on his brow. His mouth was as dry as desert sand.

The silhouette's head fell backward, hair spilling over the hammock. One hand fell over the side. He heard her sigh again, and desire clawed at his loins, making him burn a little hotter. And then, while he watched, she set the papers aside and lay still in the hammock, staring at the ceiling for the longest time, her breasts rising and falling with every breath she took.

Her movements were exaggerated by the curtain, her breasts full and jutting proudly for his lips to suckle.

God, he wanted his mouth on that tender flesh, wanted to know what it was like to feel her nipples harden against his tongue, wanted to suckle gently and tease them between his teeth.

Never before in his life had he wanted a woman so badly.

Never had he fought so hard to restrain himself.

And then she did something unspeakably erotic, and he nearly fell out of his hammock in shock.

She lifted a hand to her breast . . . at first, a tentative touch . . . and then with an open hand as though she were listening to the beat of her heart through her fingers.

His own heart hammering his ribs without restraint, he lay back in his hammock, his body tense and rigid, watching with delicious anticipation.

It seemed an eternity that her hand lay so still on her breast . . . long enough for Jack to feel a pang of guilt for wanting it to slide down and close over the sweet mound of flesh he craved so desperately to touch for himself.

He willed her hand to move, wanting to experience it vicariously at least.

And then when he thought she was asleep, it did move ... closing softly on her breast. Jack's heart nearly flipped out of his chest. His breath caught, and he realized in that instant that his hand was still wrapped about his shaft. It pulsed between his fingers, and he tightened his grip reflexively, pulling his hips backward slightly, unable to deny himself the instant of pleasure.

As he watched, her hand lifted again, and began to caress the tip of her breast, moving gently back and forth.

He held his breath, watching.

God help him, he was almost beyond the point of reason.

Some part of him urged him to speak out, to tell her that he was awake, that he could see far more than he should, but the words caught in his throat and nothing came out of his suddenly parched lips.

Her head turned to one side then, and her hand moved to her other breast, caressing it, too, and Jack thought he would explode with desire. Sweet mother of Christ, he couldn't have spoken to stop her had he tried.

He would be insane to pleasure himself in her presence, but he was beyond thinking ...

Chapter 23

A gentle ocean rocked her hammock, begging Sophie to sleep. Outside the cabin window, waves sang a sweet lullaby. Otherwise, the night was blissfully silent.

Jack had left the shutters open to the night, and the air was sultry warm, seductively so. A sweet, languorous breeze blew within, kissing her skin and tangling like invisible fingers in her hair.

Good night, flower, she heard him whisper once more, as she lay within her bed.

Sophie closed her eyes and tried to forget, but her body ached with the memory of his touch. Her skin was afire, fevered almost, and she instinctively knew why. That morning Jack had shown her the heights of pleasure of which her body was capable, and no amount of denial could keep the reminders at bay.

His scent permeated the room, speaking to her body like a lover's whisper.

That's it, flower . . . open for me . . .

She shuddered at the sound of his voice in

her ear, imagined though it was. His hands had touched her so knowingly, as though he understood her body, and knew what it cried out for. His words had seduced her so that she'd felt no shame, while his touch had evoked a pleasure so intense she had thought she would die.

She couldn't imagine Harlan ever touching her so . . . didn't even want to think of it. She'd never dreamed any man would do the things to her that she had allowed Jack to do, and never wanted to share the experience with anyone else—not ever. It was Jack she wanted . . . Jack she was falling in love with.

The admission squeezed her heart just a bit.

She *was* falling in love with Jack.

She couldn't seem to help herself, couldn't seem to keep herself from imagining a life at his side.

She hadn't felt this way about Harlan, not even from the first. Harlan had never stolen her breath with only a glance, or made her body quiver at the sound of his voice. He'd never made her heart yearn for his presence.

It was different with Jack.

Everything was different with Jack.

Her body ached to feel him again . . . her mind wandered to unspeakable thoughts . . . thoughts she had never dreamed would creep into her brain.

She closed her eyes, and desire shuddered through her. She wanted to kiss him the way he had kissed her . . . wanted to pleasure him the way he had pleasured her . . .

She wanted to taste him, too.

She wondered what he would do.

Would he be shocked to find her lips there? Alarmed? Would it bring him the same pleasure it had brought her? Would he allow it? For that matter, what did it even look like? Her brows knit at the thought. She had never seen a man unclothed before, or even let her brain wander in that shocking direction.

But he had tasted her . . . and seemed to enjoy it . . . and it left her with a burning curiosity . . .

Her breath quickened at the very thought.

Her heart beat furiously as she dared to lift a hand to her breast, cupping it gently. She needed him to hold her . . . touch her . . . caress her . . .

Dare she?

Could she?

No one would ever know. It was late, and Jack was long abed. She hadn't heard a sound from his side of the room in hours. She tickled her breast with her palm, contemplating her outrageous thoughts. Her body ached for something she knew only Jack could give her, but her curiosity burned as well.

There was nothing to stop her . . . nothing . . . except her conscience.

Reaching down, she seized the hem of her gown, lifting it up to her thighs. She slid her hand between her legs, and froze, unable to touch herself where she needed most to be touched.

Silence screeched at her.

Her heart beat so fast and so hard that it reverberated throughout the room. She knew it would wake him, because it thumped so loud in her ears that she could scarce hear anything else. She held her breath, straining to hear his.

"Jack," she cried softly, and wasn't certain whether it was a plea for help, or whether she wanted only to know if he were somehow still awake . . . watching . . .

It suddenly occurred to her that he might be . . . though the curtain was between them, and she felt nearly certain he was asleep.

Still, her skin tingled and burned at the thought.

For the longest instant, Jack was uncertain how to respond.

His body ached for release, and his breath came labored.

Should he pretend to be asleep?

Should he answer?

He opened his mouth and tried to reply, but nothing came out.

"Jack?" she called out, more urgently this time.

He willed his heartbeat to slow and cleared his throat softly, so that she couldn't hear. But he couldn't speak to save his soul.

"Jack?" she persisted. "Are you asleep?"

He thought about the question an instant, somewhat amused by it, and quashed the urge to answer flippantly. If she thought he'd been awake the entire time, he knew she'd feel ashamed—whether she were aware he could see her or not. And obviously, if he were asleep, he couldn't very well answer.

Apparently she decided he was asleep, and Jack felt a pang of guilt for deceiving her.

Sighing softly, she settled back into the hammock, clasping her hands together as though to force them to behave.

He did the same, mentally checking himself.

Without much success, he tried to shut out the images that had tormented him ... her hand on her breast ... caressing ... and was forced to readjust once more.

He was much too aroused.

Damn.

She was so close, and yet so far. She was right there across the room, but she wasn't his. He had no right to seduce her—or even to try.

But he wanted to.

In fact, he needed to.

His own two hands could bring sweet relief, but not satisfaction, and he rejected the thought where only moments before he had considered it. He wanted Sophie ... not a few mere moments of pleasure.

He wanted to bury himself inside her beautiful body ... wanted to know what it would feel like to be inside her, pulsing ... giving, taking.

A shudder went through him as the silhouette moved once more ...

A sigh escaped her, and her body arched, and Jack's entire body went rigid with anticipation. He recognized that sound, knew what she needed, and knew she would be driven to seek it.

He wanted to give it to her.

He didn't dare move.

Keeping him stilled was the simple fact that she belonged to someone else and he cared enough not to confuse her. But he couldn't stand the thought of Penn touching her—or any man, for that matter.

Her hand lifted once more to her breast, caressing it, but no longer gently. Her fingers embraced it, and she moaned softly. His own body pulsed in response. He watched with bated breath as she lifted up her gown, and her hand slid once more between those beautiful thighs he remembered so well...so soft...

The scent of her was intoxicating...the taste of her like ambrosia...

Again she moaned, and he envied those long, delicate fingers and the dance they now performed.

He sat up in the hammock, drawn despite his resolve to remain quiet. In shadow, her body lifted, her breasts arching higher. The image transfixed him. She began to whimper softly, and it took every ounce of his will to keep from going to her.

He closed his eyes and told himself it was only a dream...a beautiful, heady dream, but when he opened them again, his heart gave a powerful jolt.

Christ almighty, he couldn't take it any longer. He just couldn't take it.

He wanted her.

The curtain was so near . . . the silhouette loomed larger than life . . . her writhing was so sensual . . .

Never in his life had he seen a more beautiful sight.

Never had he experienced something so incredibly erotic.

He reached out to touch nothing but air, his hand seeking the fullness of her breasts. His body thrummed with a desire so intense it was almost painful. She tried to be quiet, but her soft gasps filled his ears and hardened his body to the point he thought it would snap.

She found relief at last, crying out softly, her body shuddering visibly, and Jack could only sit there and watch and listen . . . as she sighed a sated sigh and fell back into the hammock.

Long after her breathing evened out and her body went still, he sat there, unable to move, barely able to breathe.

His body was in pain, but he refused to relieve himself . . . not after seeing the passion of which she was capable.

He wanted her, and nothing else would do.

He'd be damned if he'd settle for less.

But he couldn't have her, and he knew it, and he lay back in his hammock, resentful and bitter, and wanting once again to throttle Penn. He tried to focus on that . . . his hands around Penn's lily throat, hoping to gain some measure of satisfaction in that ignoble thought . . . and instead imagined the soft skin beneath Sophie's gown.

Growling in frustration, he ran his hand through his hair, tugging until it was painful, and prayed for mercy.

"Sweet Jesus," he whispered fervently. "Kill me now; put me out of my misery."

Chapter 24

Sophie spent the entire next day piecing together Jack's research. She worked while he was away, wanting to surprise him. The next day she began meticulously copying his script, everything just as it was, or as she best remembered it. Her eye for detail had often been praised, and she had never been more grateful for the God-given skill as she tried to recreate his work.

Once she was finished, she went back and began to fill in the details of each drawing, using her imagination to render each sketch as vivid an image as possible.

The finished product was not her finest work. It couldn't possibly be in the time she'd had, but she was nevertheless proud of her sketches, and hoped Jack would be pleased with them as well.

She left the completed drawings on his desk and went to the basin to wash her hands, feeling a sense of accomplishment as a reward for her labors.

But after having finished them, she was left with an overwhelming desire to see the original pieces. She would dearly love to draw from real-life images, rather than having to interpret somebody else's renditions.

Perhaps Jack would allow her to stay on to record his findings? He wouldn't have to pay her. She would receive great joy in the task, and would even consider paying him for the privilege.

She would have to speak with him.

But first things first.

After more than a week, Sophie could scarcely stand herself. She didn't even begin to wonder why Jack kept his distance. Given the choice, she would, too.

Sheer desperation drove her into Shorty's cabin.

There had to be *something* among Shorty's deserted belongings that would be of some use to her. The poor man had been left behind, but his belongings all remained aboard, neatly tucked away and awaiting his return. In fact, Sophie dared to hope she would find something of his infamous girlfriend's among them—the one with the *infinite tatas*, as she'd heard Randall put it. She hoped, but in vain. All she found were a few pairs of Shorty's pants and a few of his shirts. Feeling a bit disheartened, she sat on the bed with his pants in hand and pouted.

After more than a week in the same two dresses, she felt terribly . . . foul. There was no other way to put it. She couldn't even stand her own company. She'd washed as best she could, braided her hair out of the way, but her clothes were grimy from her foiled attempts at cooking and she had only the two dresses to choose from, thanks to her own gracelessness.

She inspected Shorty's pants and found them to be clean at least—far cleaner than what she was wearing at the moment. The pungent odor of sour potatoes offended her nostrils, and she made up her mind. Better to look offensive than to smell offensive. There was just no help for it.

As quickly as she was able, she discarded her dirty clothes, keeping an eye on the door. And then she hurriedly wiggled into Shorty's pants, and discovered once they were on how he had earned his name. Sophie wasn't particularly tall, but the man's pants came only to her ankles, at best. What was more, he had obviously been quite thin besides, because she had to put considerable effort into buttoning them, as well. The only place they were the least bit loose was at her waist . . . but that was a good thing, she decided, because then she could tuck in his shirts.

Sophie pulled one of the more colorful plaid shirts out of his trunk and was absolutely certain the same man couldn't possibly have worn the two items. The shoulders were too large and the length of the tails fell easily to her thighs. But she put it on anyway, buttoned it, and began stuffing the tails into the waist of her pants, pushing them down until she was satisfied they were neatly done. Once finished, she was certain of only one thing . . . two . . .

One . . . Shorty was in dire need of a good tailor, and two . . . she was really not as willowy as she liked to think herself.

Her modest curves were more than apparent in a man's clothing—particularly this man's—and the only thing that kept her from undressing again and returning to her own smelly clothing was the simple fact that her bosom was not straining at the buttons of her shirt in the same fashion that her hips were with her pants. She didn't need a mirror to see it. The buttons were clinging precariously to the button holes. If she dared to bend, she thought they might pop.

It couldn't be helped.

She stood there, staring down at herself, grimacing at the sight she must present, and then suddenly decided the shirt would be best left untucked. She pulled it out and let it hang over her pants, assessing it that way. Again she frowned. The look was just about as unflattering as the shapeless smocks she often saw immigrants depicted in. Feeling somewhat hopeless, she glanced at the door.

Vanity wouldn't let her leave the room looking so . . . frumpy.

As it was, Jack was ignoring her . . . though when he did speak to her, he wasn't the least unkind. He simply seemed far too busy of late to have much to do with her. In fact, she felt invisible around him, and almost wished he would go back to sparring with her. She could deal with his sarcasm far better than his silence.

She sighed at the admission.

His lack of attention to her disheartened her, left her feeling oddly empty—empty in a way she had never felt before, not even with Harlan's long absences and neglect. In fact—her brows collided in displeasure at herself—she hadn't even realized she was being neglected by Harlan. She had simply attributed Harlan's continued absence to his undying devotion to his work. And she had simply gone on with her life and spared him little thought, except when she was asked about his welfare.

"Oh, Harlan is very well!" she mimicked herself in the small mirror that hung over the wash table. She couldn't quite achieve a serene expression. "He's working quite hard, indeed!"

Working hard at carving notches in his bedpost!

The wretch.

Sophie now understood the little smirks she had so often received at her dutiful reply to questions about Harlan. She wondered if everyone had known about Harlan but her. How many women had he dallied with since they had become engaged? She remembered one particularly smug expression, and the revelation left a bitter taste in her mouth.

His mother really should have named him Harlot instead of Harlan, she thought indignantly. It suited him perfectly.

But she didn't really care about Harlan any longer.

To her surprise, the only reason she was able to summon any anger at all was for her father's sake, and because Harlan had allowed her to appear a silly little fool. Her pride was a bit wounded and in need of retribution. Otherwise, she felt nothing at all at the thought of him with some other woman. In truth, she couldn't even imagine Harlan doing for anyone what Jack had done for her.

Her heart wrenched a little at the thought of him.

Jack, not Harlan.

It had been only two days that he'd been so involved with his work, but Sophie missed him terribly. It seemed impossible that one could miss someone when one was sleeping in the very same room with him, but she did. Horribly. It didn't make sense to her, but it was true, nevertheless.

It was usually late when Jack came in, and early when he arose, and it seemed to Sophie that despite the size of the ship, she was fortunate if she caught even a glimpse of him now and again.

She needed a belt for this shirt . . . a rope . . . something to cinch the waist a bit. Vain as it was, she needed a waist. She didn't want to look like some dowdy old woman. Sighing, she returned to the trunk and rifled through it. She went through the man's shirts, socks— pulled out a pair of socks to wear when she tried on his shoes, and continued looking through his belongings. She lifted a pair of heavy blue trousers and flung out a shiny silver object. Without meaning to, she tossed it across the room. She caught only a brief glimpse of it as it rolled beneath the wash table, but something about it triggered a sense of familiarity in her, and she dropped the pants back into the trunk and went in search of it.

Lifting the curtain around the small wash table, she spied a flash of silver by the wall, and reached under the table, groping for it. Her fingers found and closed about the cool smooth cylindrical object and she dragged it out.

Shock rippled through her as she stared at the unusual piece of jewelry.

It was quite unlike any other ring she had ever seen—a rare design. A hieroglyphic eye, with a single overlarge multifaceted ruby pupil winking out at her. The sides were etched, but not so finely that it seemed inappropriate for a man to wear. The filigree was reminiscent of ancient scrolls, and the ring, indeed, was old.

Anger crept up her spine.

The thing was, this was not the first time Sophie had seen this particular ring.

Sophie had first noticed it in an old shop. She had been out shopping with her mother when they had stumbled on the novelty. She'd purchased it for Harlan before his first trip to the Yucatan, thinking he would like it to remember her by.

Knowing it was there, she turned the ring to look for an inscription, and found the underbelly had been brushed until it shone a brighter silver than the rest. Gone. Eradicated. Whatever had been written there was lost in the vigorous buffing, but Sophie knew what words had been engraved there: *For Harlan with love.*

She stood up, her face burning with sudden rage, and quickly thrust the hem of her shirt into her pants.

It wasn't as though she were angry on Harlan's behalf because he deserved anything that came to him, but she certainly had no love for thieves!

She didn't much care what she looked like at the instant, and didn't care if he was avoiding her. Someone had to answer for this! She had no idea how Shorty had come by it, but Sophie was certain it wasn't by honorable means. And there was no chance it was merely a good likeness.

Ready to do battle to get answers if she must, she went in search of Jack.

He wasn't in a good mood.

In fact, he was in a downright rotten mood, and it was getting worse by the instant.

His shoulders were stiff and his body tense, and he couldn't stop thinking about Sophie. Every time he closed his eyes, her silhouette materialized before him, beautiful and sensuous, moving like ocean waves under a sultry moon. He tried to block the vision, but her soft cries filled his ears, tormenting him.

The echo plagued him incessantly.

He hadn't been able to face her since that night, because if he did, he was bound to take her into his arms—to hell with Penn—and kiss the fool out of her.

He could no longer deny it; he wanted to make love to her more than he'd ever wanted anything in his life. What wouldn't he give for just a single night in her arms . . . to hear her cry out his name in the throes of her pleasure. She was both curious and passionate—full of life—every man's most fervent dream.

The taste of her lingered on his lips, tempting him . . . driving him to distraction.

If she would allow it, he would show her everything—share all that he had—all that he was.

He wanted Sophie at his side while he muddied his hands in the dirt. He wanted her to be there when he made his greatest discoveries, wanted to jump with joy over them with her in his arms. He wanted to lift her up and carry her to their bed in celebration. He wanted her with him always.

And for the first time in his life, he thought of children. Could he be a good father with the life and career he had chosen?

He wanted to try.

He imagined a little girl . . . like Sophie . . . with wayward curls and a button nose . . . with dirty hands and a pristine white dress . . . pink ribbons falling out of her hair and a joyful smile on her face.

Muttering beneath his breath, he tossed down his clipboard and supply list, his mood spiraling downward. He was never going to get through this inventory with these thoughts bouncing round his head—ricocheting like rubber bullets off his skull.

They were driving him insane. Hunger left him weak. Thoughts of Sophie made him hungrier. And Kell's relentless smirk was beginning to get under his skin.

"You've got it bad," Kell said to him, and chuckled.

Jack shot him a cutting glance, but said nothing.

What was there to say? He *did* have it bad. He wanted something he couldn't have.

"Tell her," Kell suggested.

Jack raked a hand through his hair and shrugged. He gave Kell a harried glance. "Why bother?"

Sophie was engaged to be married to the only man Jack had ever detested. Harlan was more her kind. He came from her world. Jack didn't have the same things to offer: If she wanted high society and prestige, he didn't have a chance of fulfilling those needs. If she needed a conventional home, he wasn't even sure what the hell that was. He and his father had pretty much fended for themselves after his mother's death.

The one thing Jack did have to hold up as an example was that his father had loved him unconditionally, and Jack wasn't the least bit ashamed to say he loved him back just the

same. His father had given him everything—
even the courage to roll up his sleeves and
fight for the things he valued. It had been his
father who had encouraged his education, and
his father who had taken on every opposition
to enroll him in Boston's most prestigious university. He'd taught Jack to fight for the things
he wanted, *and* to stand on his integrity, and
that was the crux of the problem.

Every last bone and fiber in his body
wanted to fight for the woman he loved—
dammit, yes, he was in love with her! But
everything he knew about integrity said he
should walk away before it was too late—before he caused her pain. She wasn't his to love.
She was promised to another man, and it
didn't matter that Jack didn't like the bastard.
It didn't matter that Jack thought he was a
miserable son of a weasel. What mattered was
that Sophie had already made her choice, and
Jack would be the worst kind of rat to en-
courage her to fall in love with him.

And he thought he could: He could see it in
her eyes. He could hear it in her wistful sighs
when she looked at him . . . or maybe the sighs
were his own.

Damn, he couldn't tell.

"You can't avoid her forever," Kell intruded
on his thoughts. At the instant, he didn't much
appreciate Kell's advice.

"The hell I can't."

"Look," Kell argued, "you're stuck with her
from now until the time you deliver her to
Penn."

"Yeah, well . . ." Jack's mood wasn't in the least danger of improving over that remark. "Thanks for pointing that out."

"You made her a deal," Kell continued, ignoring his sarcasm, "and even if you didn't, it's not like you can just take her off the ship in Mexico and point her in the right direction, and say *go*. Anyway, I know you, Jack, and you aren't the kind of man who would let a woman fend for herself. Even if you weren't headed to the same damned place she was, you would have delivered her there anyway—whether you liked her boyfriend or not."

It was true, dammit.

Even if Jack didn't care anything about her—and he did—he wouldn't be able to live with himself if he didn't *know* she'd gotten to her destination safely. He felt responsible for her now. He'd accepted her money, and he'd allowed her to leave the safety of her home and surroundings, and he *was* responsible for her—at least until he handed her over to someone who could look after her just as well.

And that thought left another sour taste in his mouth.

Penn was a lazy, self-aggrandizing mooch. If he cared for Sophie as much he cared for his life's work, she'd be lucky not to suffocate in her tent if it happened to fall down on her, because Penn wouldn't lift a finger to help her. He swore he'd kill the son of a bitch if he let anything happen to Sophie.

"Any way you look at it, Jack, you've got another week or so to spend with her, so you'd better find a way to deal with whatever it is you're dealing with."

A week wasn't nearly enough time.

His gut wrenched at the reminder.

No more than five more days and she'd be gone from his life completely. The most he could hope for would be to catch a glimpse of her with Penn now and again—while she remained on site. After that . . . once she returned to Boston, as she would inevitably . . . what then?

The thought that he might never see her again made him physically ill.

"I still say you tell her the truth."

Leave it to Kell to call the shots as they were.

Jack hadn't told Kell a damned thing about what he was feeling, but he didn't bother to deny it. Much as he hated to admit it, sometimes Kell knew him better than Jack even knew himself. At times it annoyed the devil out of him.

As now.

Kell seemed to be studying him. "You don't still believe she's spying for Penn, do you?"

It would certainly make things easier if she were. He could tell her to take a long walk off a very short pier. He didn't answer, didn't want to.

"We're through here for today," he told Kell, and began to replace the tarp over their supplies. They would need to procure a few more items once they reached port and then hire a guide, but otherwise everything was pretty much in order. "Grab the other end of this and tie it down, will ya."

Kell shook his head. "Stubborn bastard. You're going to lose her."

He'd never had her to begin with.

Jack shot him a glance. "Someone put those telegrams into the stove to be burned," he reminded Kell. "They didn't just magically appear there. If you have a better explanation as to how they got there I'd like to hear it."

Kell shrugged, then shook his head, at an obvious loss for explanations. Without another word, he began to batten down the tarp. Jack secured his end, then lifted up his clipboard from the deck where he'd tossed it, waiting on Kell to finish.

"Think Jose will take us out to the site again?"

Jose Salvatore was Maria's father, their guide on previous trips. Jack sure hoped he'd agree to take them out, but there was no telling what Maria might or might not have told him. For all Jack knew he'd be shot on sight, but the man was a damned good guide, so Jack intended to brace himself for the worst, and ask.

When Kell was done, Jack tossed him the clipboard. "When we get into port, you can go after the items left unchecked, and I'll face Salvatore."

Kell broke into a smile. "Hell's bells!" he exclaimed, "I almost forgot about the fair Maria!" And his grin widened.

Jack threw up a hand. "Don't start, Kell."

"Hell, I'm not starting anything! You go *face* him," he said, and began to laugh, as though Jack's choice of words had struck him as hilarious. "You and your women!"

Sophie wasn't like the others.

Jack rolled his eyes and turned to leave Kell to his merriment.

He wasn't in the mood.

Sophie was different.

He loved her.

He'd been young and stupid once, but it had never really mattered. Now, finally, he'd met the one woman he truly wanted, and she was out of his reach.

"Where is he!" he heard the object of his distraction shout from the opposite end of the ship. "Where is Jack!"

She'd obviously come up from the mess hall and was upset about something. It wasn't difficult to read her mood, particularly when her voice was raised several octaves above usual.

Good, he needed an outlet.

"He's workin' with Kell, Miss Vanderwahl. Over there. But . . . I wouldn't disturb him if I were you."

"You aren't me!" she answered flippantly. Jack couldn't suppress a smile at her saucy response.

"Miss Vanderwahl!" Randall seemed determined to protect her from Jack's present mood. "I wouldn't—"

"Let her go," Jack heard someone say low.

Jack cast a glance over his shoulder at Kell,

warning him without words to keep his mouth shut.

Kell's brows lifted, and he shrugged. "I didn't say a word," he protested, but he didn't have to. His expression said enough. He was divided between his own sordid sense of amusement and a need to protect Sophie.

She brought that out in a man: somehow made him want to take care of her, though she seemed perfectly capable of taking care of herself.

"Stay out of it," Jack warned him.

She was his.

"Jack!" she called out, coming nearer.

She was ready to nail him for something. Jack could hear the attitude in the stomp of her feet as she marched across the deck.

If anyone was going to protect her from his present mood, it was going to be he, but Sophie Vanderwahl didn't need protection. No Vanderwahl he had ever met had backed down before anyone—not even before truth. Sophie was as stubborn as her father was, with a temper besides.

And Jack was ready for her.

Something like birds' wings took off in his belly as he braced himself to see her.

But he wasn't ready: Nothing could have prepared him for the sight of her.

Chapter 25

He stood speechless.

Christ, he didn't know whether to laugh or throw himself overboard to put himself out of his misery.

She came scrambling down the stairs, wearing the tightest pair of trousers he had ever seen in his whole deuced life. That beautiful little bottom wiggled deliciously as she descended, and he swallowed whatever sarcasm he'd had in store for her.

With hands on her hips, she spun to face him, her cheeks blooming with rosy color, her amber eyes flashing with anger. She held out something in the palm of her hand. "I found this in the cook's cabin!"

Jack couldn't take his eyes off her breasts . . . her blouse . . . it wasn't quite buttoned all the way, leaving him a tantalizing view of luscious cleavage . . . and not just for him . . .

He turned and shot Kell another glare.

Kell shook himself out of his stupor and seemed to understand at once. He nodded, sputtering laughter. "I'm going!" And he did so at once, but not without casting Sophie one last glance. He shook his head as he passed.

Reduced to a nearly primitive state, Jack actually growled at Kell, and knew it was true in that instant that man hadn't progressed as far as he liked to believe.

In fact, it was only a thin thread of reason that kept him from tackling Sophie where she stood and devouring her right on deck in front of his crew.

What in God's name had possessed her to dress that way!

He didn't see what she had proffered until she thrust it before his face once more. Something bright red gleamed before his eyes, but his brain couldn't quite wrap around the object . . . not while her breasts were jutting out at him beneath the threadbare shirt. If he looked hard—and he was, he couldn't help it—he could see hardened nipples nudging against the loose fabric.

His brain went dizzy, and his mouth immediately dry.

"I found this in Shorty's cabin!" she said again, her eyes narrowed at him.

Along with the clothes she was wearing, he presumed.

Jack tried to clear the fog of lust from his brain. "What is it?" he asked stupidly.

"It's a ring, of course!"

Of course.

Jack stared at it, blinking.

Sun shone into the monster jewel. It sparkled fiercely before his eyes, nearly blinding him. His gaze returned to her shirt. She waved the ring at him again, recapturing his attention, and he had to pry his eyes free from the object of his desire. He reached out to take it from her, shaking himself out of his stupor. He shook his head and cleared his throat. "What would Shorty be doing with that?"

She jerked it away before he could seize it. "*That's* what *I'd* like to know!" she exploded once more, holding it up as proof of something, though Jack hadn't the slightest notion what.

His brain wasn't working. All the blood had rushed somewhere below.

"No need to shout," he told her. "I'm not deaf." Or blind, either . . . but he was going to be if she didn't stop flashing that damned jewel at him!

"I'm not shouting!" she shouted. "But if I were, I'd have every right to!" she informed him baldly. "This ring belongs to Harlan!"

That definitely caught his attention.

He blinked at her, then at the ring, trying to understand. "Harlan?"

"Yes! Harlan!"

Jack tried to comprehend what it was she was telling him. "Are you sure?" She'd found *Harlan's* ring in *Shorty's* cabin? He reached out, wanting a better look.

She jerked it away. "Of course I'm sure!" she countered, waving the monstrosity at him. "This is Harlan's ring! *I* bought it for him!"

His brows collided as he stared at the enor-

mous ruby eye. He hadn't seen a ruby that big
in his life.

"You bought *that* for Harlan?"

Her eyes sparkled nearly as brightly as the
jewel. "Yes. As a going-away present . . ." Her
face turned brighter pink, but her gaze shifted
away momentarily, and then back—as though
she were embarrassed by the evidence of her
affection for Harlan.

She damned well ought to be. The money
she had spent on that single piece of jewelry
might have fed the entire Yucatan peninsula!

"And you found it in Shorty's cabin?"

"Yes!" she exclaimed, waving it again. "Perhaps you'd like to tell me how it got there!"

How the hell was Jack supposed to know
that?

He shook his head and tried to reach for the
ring once more. This time she let him have it.
Watching her expression, he tested its weight
in his hand. It was solid silver, heavy. He
turned the ring to check for an inscription and
found it had been polished clean.

He eyed her speculatively. "And you're absolutely sure this is Harlan's ring?"

She cocked her head in challenge. "Just how
many rings like that do you think exist?"

She had a point. It was ugly as hell . . . and
assuming the ruby was real, it wasn't very
likely there was another just like it.

She'd found the ring in Shorty's cabin. That fact
reared up at him like a rattler's warning. *The
telegrams had been hidden in the stove.* It didn't
take a genius to deduce the obvious: Shorty

was somehow in cahoots with Penn, and by some stroke of luck, they'd managed to leave the jackass behind. In doing so, they'd been spared whatever Penn had planned.

And Sophie was just plain trouble without the least bit of malice.

He blinked at her.

She was waiting for some sort of explanation from him and Jack suddenly wanted to kiss her. He smiled at her, his mood vastly improved. He handed the ring back to her.

"I don't see what's so blessed funny!" she railed at him, her delicate fingers seizing the ring from his hand.

Jack's grin widened.

He didn't care if he had an audience—didn't give a damn who was watching. He didn't care if they thought him loony . . . or smitten . . . he was.

He reached out, grasping her about the waist, and drew her into his arms. Her hands flew up at once to clutch his shoulders and she gasped in surprise but didn't protest.

She gave him a pouty face. "What do you think you are doing?"

"Kissing you," Jack replied with determination, and didn't give her an instant to protest. He took her mouth in a fierce kiss, thrusting his tongue between her lips to silence her.

All restraint eroded with the first touch of their lips.

Her protest came out sounding garbled.

He gave her waist a little jerk, urging her to

kiss him back, and she suddenly silenced, her hands moving to his neck, clinging for support.

And then ... everything faded from his senses but the woman he held in his arms: the jeers from his men, the sun beating down on his head, the wind in his face.

Sophie's heart surged into her throat as his lips pressed against her own.

His tongue dove inside her mouth without invitation, coaxing ... tasting ... with the same urgency and abandon he had shown her before.

He held her tightly, pressing her greedily against his body, and she was grateful for the support because she suddenly didn't think she could stand on her own. She was acutely aware of her breasts shoved against his chest, and her knees went weak. Her belly fluttered with anticipation.

"What are you doing?" she whispered against his mouth. "Jack ..."

"Shut up and kiss me!" he demanded, never breaking the contact of their lips. He increased his ardor. "Kiss me, Sophia," he pleaded with her.

"But ... the ring," she tried to protest, and was vaguely aware of the shouts and huzzahs that erupted from the crew.

"What ring?" Jack murmured into her mouth.

Sophie suddenly didn't remember what she was even talking about. Her thoughts skittered away.

"It's about damned time!" she heard someone yell at them, and then she was aware only
of Jack.

Everything about them faded but the man
in whose arms she was entrapped.

She gasped for breath, but clung to him
greedily. God help her, she didn't care about
any ring. It slipped from her grasp to the deck,
though she never heard it fall.

Her senses were filled only with Jack . . . his
scent, his warmth, his breath, his taste . . .

She felt his kiss in places that made no
sense: The tips of her breasts burned and her
body ached for something she couldn't quite
comprehend. She clasped him eagerly, kissing
him back without shame.

It seemed she'd wanted this all her life . . .
as though every second she had lived, she had
lived only for this moment.

As he kissed her, clutching her against him,
his knee slid shockingly between her thighs,
unhampered by her dress. His fingers closed
about the waist of her trousers, lifting them up
slightly, and Sophie gasped in delight at the
scandalous sensation that flared between her
thighs. She responded from some sense of instinct that blinded her to propriety, parting her
legs and wrapping them around his hips.

He moaned into her mouth and began to
walk, holding her. Sophie hadn't the slightest
notion where, because he kept right on kissing
her. And as long as he kept kissing her, she
didn't really care where they went.

Chapter 26

Somehow Jack managed to get her down to the lower deck.

They practically stumbled down the stairs into the mess hall. Sophie clung to him all the while, kissing him passionately, heating the blood in his veins beyond self-control. He was grateful his men somehow had vanished.

When he reached his cabin at last, he kicked open the door, kissing her without giving her a chance to breathe—because he was afraid of what she might say if he stopped—because he was terrified she'd regain her senses.

He kissed her as though his life depended on it, because somehow he thought it did. If he didn't make love to her right now—this instant—he was going to explode into a thousand miserable pieces.

He wanted her.

He loved her.

"Sophia!" he gasped.

She answered with a murmur that sent quivers down his spine.

He didn't want to stop kissing her, tasting her, feeling her . . .

His hands cupped her bottom, pressing them fully into his arousal, wanting her to know what it was he craved to give her.

"Jack," she whispered pleadingly against his mouth.

He broke the kiss long enough to kiss her chin, her nose . . . whisper against her cheek, "Yes, flower?"

His hands caressed her bottom . . . firm and round and pert . . . he wanted her naked beneath him. He wanted her legs wrapped around him.

Sophie's heartbeat pounded in her ears.

Her body craved something fiercely.

It remembered far too much, wanted something more . . . something she knew instinctively Jack could give her. "I—"

She didn't know what to ask for, except to plead with him never to stop . . . but she couldn't speak. Her throat constricted with emotion, and her body quivered as he kissed her throat, gently nipped her. The sensation of his teeth pressing softly into her flesh gave her a jolt of pleasure. Her head fell backward in rapture.

"Jack," she whimpered.

"Tell me what you want, flower . . ."

His hand moved between their bodies, caressing her breasts over her shirt, and Sophie moaned in response. "Beautiful," he whispered.

She couldn't protest—didn't want to.

Her legs slid down his, touched the floor, and she stood a bit unsteadily. His hands gripped her shoulders, then moved to the front of her shirt when she could stand freely. His gaze locked with hers as he began to unbutton her shirt, and Sophie's breath quickened. She swallowed convulsively as he freed the first button . . . then moved to the next.

Her heart pounded against her ribs.

His gaze never left her as he moved down her shirt, freeing every last button until the shirt gaped at her breast. His green eyes were intense, filled with hunger, sparkling fiercely.

Sophie's face flushed with heat.

She felt suddenly shy, afraid to show him more. What if he didn't like her? What if he found her lacking? She averted her gaze, but he wouldn't allow it. He reached out, lifting her chin with a finger.

"Do you know what I want?" he asked her, his voice low and seductively soft.

She tried to speak past the knot that formed in her throat. "Yes," she said with a gasp, and her heart thumped in answer.

He cocked his head, smiling slowly, seeming wickedly pleased with her response, and Sophie could do nothing but stand before him as he undressed her.

He stopped short of opening her blouse, and Sophie was afraid . . . afraid he would go on . . . afraid he would stop.

Sucking in a breath, she made up her mind and shrugged out of the blouse, letting it fall down her arms.

"God!" he exclaimed, and closed his eyes for the briefest instant. His nostrils flared slightly, his expression intense. He opened his eyes then, and his gaze fell fully on her breast.

Sophie held her breath as he looked at her.

"You are . . . so beautiful," he told her, and his hands reached out to touch her, tentatively. His palms cupped her, his fingers caressed her . . . his thumb gently flicked across her nipple, and it was Sophie's turn to lose herself in the satisfaction of his touch.

Her eyes closed.

She didn't want him to stop.

Her hands covered his, pressing them gently against her heart. She wanted this desperately. There was no longer anyone to save herself for. Harlan was no longer a part of her life. She would likely never marry now, and she'd be a fool to turn away the one man who had ever made her feel so . . . much.

She never wanted anyone else.

If this moment was all she would ever have with Jack, then it would still be worth it. She would savor the sweet memory in her most private moments.

He wanted only to please her.

With a groan of pleasure, Jack fell to his knees before Sophie, embracing her. His fingers clutched her bottom, pulling her against him.

To hell with the hammock!

They didn't need a bed.

His hands caressed her. With a hungry moan, he pressed his mouth against her, biting through the material of her trousers. His nostrils flared and his tongue stroked the rough material. She gasped softly and stiffened.

He didn't want to stop touching her.

"I want you, Sophia," he said, his voice raw. Silence rang in his ears.

She was afraid, and he didn't want her to be.

"Let me," he begged her. "Let me make love to you, Sophia . . ."

For answer, her fingers tangled in his hair, caressing his scalp, and the feel of them made him dizzy with longing. His heart jolted, and he began at once to unbutton her pants. She whimpered softly, and he cooed to her, soothing her.

"Beautiful," he assured her. "You are so beautiful, Sophia!"

He bared her, tugging her pants down. Her nails pressed gently into his scalp, and his body hardened.

Sophie moaned softly.

She looked down at him, and her heart fluttered within her breast at the sight of him . . . the feel of him . . . his face pressed boldly against her, buried in her dark curls. And then his tongue delved softly within, forcing its velvety way between her legs . . . warm and wet. With the delicious feel of it, Sophie lost any inhibitions she'd clung to.

Gulping in a breath, she parted her legs for him, begging him with her body to take what he wished. She wanted this desperately . . . but wanted to please him as well . . .

He pulled her down to the floor, and Sophie didn't resist. He removed her pants, planting sweet kisses along her thighs ... calves. She swallowed convulsively as he returned to kiss her intimately once more ... and then he lifted himself to her lips.

For the merest instant, he stared into her eyes, his green eyes smoldering, and then he kissed her. Sophie's heart jolted violently. She kissed him back, tasting what he had tasted. Her heartbeat quickened as he deepened the kiss, and her fingers at once sought the buttons of his pants.

She wanted to see him, too.

He moaned, his own fingers moving to assist her.

When his pants were undone, Sophie embraced him, pulling him down atop her. She wanted to feel him, experience him, love him.

Somehow, Jack managed to shrug out of his pants without breaking their kiss. He wanted more than anything to be inside her just now, but he wanted to please her. And he wanted her to want this as much as he did. He wanted no regrets afterward. His hands sought and found her wetness, and the feel of it set his pulse to pounding.

"I love the taste of you," he murmured, and felt her quiver beneath him. He pressed a finger into her body. "This is where I want to be, Sophia."

She gasped softly, her body shuddering as he pushed his finger deeper.

"Can you feel that?" he asked, but knew she

did. Her body arched to accept him. Her eyes closed in pleasure, and she gasped softly.

"Yes," she whimpered, and peered up at him, her eyes fevered with desire. The knowledge pleased him. She was as passionate as she was beautiful.

He pushed higher, more firmly. "I want to be inside you," he told her a bit desperately, leaving no mistake as to his intent. "Here."

She nodded, but seemed unable to speak, and he pushed deeper, stopping at the barrier deep within her body. His heart leaped at the feel of it, and his emotions warred.

She had told him the truth: Penn was not her lover.

His breath quickened painfully and his hunger intensified. His body ached. He wanted to be the first and the last to spill his seed inside her.

He wanted her to carry his babies, wanted her for himself . . . always.

He buried his face against her throat, kissing her as he whispered, "Last chance to run, flower . . . no turning back after this . . . tell me you're sure . . ."

He felt her nod, but it wasn't enough.

His fingers caressed her maidenhead, waiting to breach it. "Tell me yes," he urged her.

She gasped, her hands going about his neck. Her fingers dug into the back of his neck, but he wanted her to speak the words.

"Say it, Sophia," he demanded of her.

Sophie shuddered beneath him. Her body tightened about his finger, hungry for what he would give her. He caressed her body, pleasuring her until she cried out.

"Yes!" she exclaimed, and tilted to urge him deeper.

His fingers pressed harder, deeper, and she whimpered softly.

Wetness, warm and wonderful filled her.

Bliss.

And then suddenly he was atop her, his body pressing into hers.

Sophie opened her eyes and looked into his, her breath coming labored.

"First and last," he whispered enigmatically, and closed his eyes, forcing himself within her.

Sophie arched to receive him fully, crying out in delight at the silky feel of him as he entered her. He filled her deliciously.

She wanted him deeper and clutched his buttocks, pulling him inside her . . . inside her heart.

Forever.

I love you, Jack, she tried to say. But his name was the only word to emerge.

And then she was lost to the sensations his every thrust evoked. She gasped softly with every stroke, and cried out in ecstasy as her body sought that expanding thread of pleasure. It uncoiled within her, teasing her and teasing her until suddenly her body found completion.

The world exploded behind her lids.

Jack felt her release in the intense shuddering of her body. Her tremors and her cry of passion thrust him over the edge. He cried out with his own release and clutched her against him, feeling in that moment an intense satisfaction he had never experienced before now.

If he lived a thousand lifetimes, this instant would be imprinted on his brain . . . if he died tomorrow he would die fulfilled.

This moment was what he had lived for.

This instant he had discovered what he had searched for all his life—he knew that now, because for the first time, joined with the woman in his arms, he felt complete.

He had searched a lifetime, and others as well through his studies of bygone eras and peoples . . . devoting his entire life to discovering the purpose of his existence and that of mankind itself . . . and all the while the answer had lain within Sophie Vanderwahl's arms.

He'd be damned if he'd lose her now.

Chapter 27

The weather was perfect the next morning when they sailed into port: The sky was blue, the water was bluer, and the sun shone crisply.

Sophie's mood was buoyant and filled with anticipation.

She had no regrets over the decisions she had made and even fewer reservations over the task left before her. She had no idea how long it would be before she faced Harlan at last, but she no longer felt the least bit of fear or sorrow over it. Harlan was a burden she was eager to have lifted off her shoulders.

If she was saddened by anything at all, it was the simple fact that her journey was nearly over, and at the journey's end she would be forced to make new decisions . . . decisions that could take her far from Jack.

She didn't want to leave him, and the very thought of it wrenched at her heart.

But maybe she wouldn't have to.

She eyed the papers she had placed on his

desk. He had yet to see them; he'd been so preoccupied.

Sophie wasn't such a fool to believe that simply because of what they had shared she could have a life as his wife, but she did hope that perhaps he would allow her to stay on and assist him in his work. She didn't want to go back to Boston, back to social engagements that bored her out of her wits, back to her mother's home where she was expected to be perfect at all times, back to her restrictive dresses that sucked the breath and life and joy from her.

The thought of having to answer the first question about Harlan made her physically ill. No matter what he had done to her, she would never tell anyone the truth—except, of course, her mother and father, and they would likely try to talk her out of her decision. She could hear her mother now as though she were standing before her this instant, her expression dour.

Sophie, my dear, all men stray at some time or another . . . it bears no reflection on their ability to be a proper husband. Harlan is a favorable match. What will people say if you simply discard him to live your life as a spinster!

Well, Sophie didn't care what people would say!

No one would understand, of course, but she didn't need them to. She was beginning to *like* wearing men's pants and shirts and was looking forward to getting dirt under her nails. The very idea left her as titillated as did

Jack's very presence—Sophie had never felt so breathless. It excited her beyond her wildest dreams. In her entire life she had never felt so alive and vigorous and full of energy and expectation.

She couldn't wait to begin their journey!

Every day would be an adventure!

She couldn't wait to cook Jack and his crew breakfast!

It was silly perhaps, but she wanted to prove she could do it. She refused to give in. Practice made perfect. She knew that much from her drawings.

"Sophia!" she heard Jack call, and hurriedly finished packing the few items she intended to take. She'd discarded her dresses completely— no reason to take them at all. They were dirty and far too unwieldy besides. Instead, she'd borrowed a few more of Shorty's trousers and shirts, stuffing as many as she could into the backpack Jack had let her borrow. She wore a pair of Shorty's boots and socks as well, though the boots were at least three sizes too large for her feet. It couldn't be helped. Jack had advised her they would be far more suitable to the remainder of the journey than were her slippers. So she'd stuffed the toes with socks, and could scarce tell except by looking at them that they were much too big.

"I'm coming, Jack!" she shouted back at him, and shoved a few selected toiletry items into the sack.

He came to the door then, leaning against the frame as he watched her with *that* look in his eyes. He seemed to like to look at her since she'd begun wearing Shorty's pants, and what was more, she *liked* the way that he looked at her.

Her heart leapt a little at the sight of him. "Jack," she said breathlessly.

He always managed to do that . . . steal her breath away. The very sight of him left her dizzy. A single look of his made her heart dance against her ribs.

"Whenever you're ready, princess."

He wasn't upset with her, Sophie knew that by the smile on his face, but she grimaced at his endearment. "Harlan calls me that!" she reminded once more, and hoped he would understand how it grated on her nerves. "Please don't call me that."

He pushed away from the doorframe, straightening.

"Well, I'm ready!" Sophie assured him. "Except . . ." She hesitated, glancing at the papers on his desk, wanting so badly for him to see them.

She went back to the desk, lingering there, plucking Harlan's picture from the desktop. She couldn't very well forget the picture when she'd tucked Harlan's letter into the back of it.

Jack eyed it distastefully as she placed it, too, into her backpack, and gave her a look she couldn't quite decipher. "By all means, you can't forget *that*!" he said caustically, and then pivoted on his heels and left her to follow.

"Jack, wait!"

She wanted desperately for him to see her drawings.

Disappointment surged through her as he disappeared from her sight. It took her an instant longer to realize what it was that had rankled him, but when she did, she smiled a secret smile.

He was jealous, and the fact pleased her.

Quickly she seized the stack of drawings from his desk and placed them into her backpack, then hoisted the backpack over her shoulder.

He would discover her journey's purpose soon enough. In the meantime, it wouldn't hurt him to wonder just a little.

Somehow, telling him about her decision to leave Harlan didn't seem quite as fulfilling as the thought of showing him.

The market square was pungent with the aroma of fish and meats, sweetened only by the more elusive scent of fruits and vegetables.

Jack remembered the way through the tangle of booths, though it had been nearly three years since his last visit. He'd brought Randall and Pete with him, just in case Jose wasn't in a forgiving mood. He would have preferred not to bring Sophie, but she'd been babbling excitedly about the breakfast she intended to make them, and he suspected he'd have had to tie her down to keep her from accompanying him once she'd realized their destination.

Anyway, Kell had gone after supplies, and

the rest of his crew were busy setting up camp. And it wasn't as though he didn't trust them with Sophie, but he really didn't trust Sophie with them.

Besides, he *had* promised her that she could cook for them. She wanted to help and and he couldn't quite bring himself to deny her. Nor could he help but be amused at the look of wonder on her face as she followed him through the market. Instead of overripe fruits and day-old meat that made up the market's wares, one would have thought she were surrounded by nuggets of gold and glinting diamonds.

To her credit, she seemed eager to redeem herself to his men and unwilling to accept defeat. Unfortunately, his men were secretly praying Jack would banish her from more attempts. He'd never met a woman in his life who took such joy in her efforts and failed so miserably every time.

Jack actually found it a charming quality.

It wasn't difficult to find Jose's booth, and he recognized Maria at once. He was grateful Sophie's attention had been momentarily distracted by a batch of particularly colorful peppers two booths away. She lingered to inspect them, lifting several and turning them in her hand as though they were precious gems.

Jack smiled a little at the sight of Sophie, then returned to the unpleasant task at hand, hoping the peppers would keep Sophie's attention.

Maria hadn't changed at all, and her pretty

face brightened as she recognized him. Guilt tugged at him.

"Jack!" she exclaimed, and leaped up from the stool she had been occupying.

"Hello, Maria." He smiled a little uncertainly at her, and cast a hasty glance over his shoulder at Sophie.

Sophie's attention was riveted on the peppers. As he watched, she began to select only the finest peppers for the masterpiece breakfast she intended to prepare.

Jack had a sudden desire to be there at her side . . . to look over them with her . . . smell her hair . . . touch her shoulders.

She was beautiful, and it was killing him that she had to drag that damned picture of Penn around with her.

It turned his stomach to think of the two of them together.

Maria's arms were around his neck the instant he turned around again. She nearly choked the breath from him. "Oh, Jack!" she squealed.

Jack patted her back, grimacing as he cast yet another glance over his shoulder.

Considering the damnable picture she was carrying, he didn't know why it should bother him so much that Sophie might be hurt by Maria's attention. He ought to be more concerned with Maria's feelings . . .

Or his own hide.

Jose came into the booth, his eyes narrowing in displeasure as he spotted Jack with Maria. If he'd had them before, Jack had no doubts any longer that her father knew. His stomach roiled again, and he grimaced at the older man's expression.

"Get away from my daughter!" her father demanded at once, and came to pry Maria's hands from around his neck.

Jack tried to assist him as best he could, hoping his immediate compliance would sweeten Jose's mood, but Maria proved stronger than either of them realized.

She held fast, jumping up and down excitedly, strangling Jack with her enthusiasm. "Oh Jack!" she exclaimed, and hugged him tighter, resisting her father as he railed at her in Spanish to release Jack at once.

Jack had a niggling suspicion suddenly that her enthusiasm had less to do with him and more to do with defying her father, because her grip tightened at his furious demands.

"No!" she refused him outright, her tone petulant. And she hugged Jack even tighter in a show of defiance. He was grateful she was fairly tall, otherwise he'd be a hunchback right now. She continued in Spanish. *"No me puedes ordenar!"*

"Maria!" her father thundered, giving up trying to fight her hold on Jack. There was little affection in the stranglehold.

"Dejar lo, Papa!"

Attempting to follow their conversation, Jack was unclear as to whether she was trying to protect him or merely defy her father. Maybe both. And evidently she was determined to protect him to death.

Jose seemed ready to trounce him—not that Jack was particularly afraid of the man, but it didn't help his own cause that he felt Jose was justified in his anger. Jack wasn't honestly certain he could even hit the man back if Jose decided to hurl a punch.

He concentrated on breathing and gave up the struggle, hoping she'd notice on her own that she was throttling him to death sometime before he passed out at her feet.

His Spanish was good, but not good enough to follow the heated discourse that followed. At last she said something that calmed her father, because he took a step backward, and Maria loosened her grip.

Jack stood there uncomfortably, rubbing the back of his neck while Jose glared at him. His malaise intensified as Sophie came over with her colorful basket of peppers in hand, her attention obviously having been captured by the scene the three of them had made. She cast him a curious glance, and then turned to assess Maria.

Maria stood defiantly beside him, refusing to give up her place at his side, and gave Sophie the very same assessing look in return.

Jack groaned and felt the pit of his stomach tighten. Christ, it was going to be a long day.

As best he could, he explained to Jose what had happened, in Spanish so Sophie wouldn't understand, taking full responsibility for his actions. He didn't want Maria to feel the brunt of her father's wrath so he took all the blame, but Maria apparently wasn't about to allow it.

She interrupted at once, making it clear that she was at an age where she had a right to do what she chose . . . which led to a lengthy argument between father and daughter about a daughter's rights.

"What's happening?" Sophie whispered to him. Her brows were drawn together in confusion. She obviously didn't understand a single word, and for that Jack was grateful.

Jack shrugged. Now wasn't precisely the time for explanations.

Sophie gave him a frown for his effort.

Let her be annoyed with him . . . he wasn't the one carrying around pictures of past lovers.

And it really didn't matter that she hadn't actually been Penn's lover. She apparently still had every intention of becoming just that. He grit his teeth at the thought.

"Jose . . ." He interrupted father and daughter. *"Perdon. La culpa es mío . . . no es Maria's."*

"No!" Jose exploded. *"La culpa es de mi puta hija que no puede cerrar las piernas por nadie!"*

Jack winced: Apparently he hadn't been Maria's only conquest.

Maria turned ten shades of red at her father's degrading remark and averted her gaze. Jack wasn't exactly sure if it was out of anger or embarrassment, but it quieted her at once. He explained his reason for coming—not to cause trouble but to ask for Jose's help.

Jose remained quiet, listening, his thick brows drawn together in a hefty frown. He was much smaller than Jack, but his shoulders must have been twice as broad as Jack's, and they were tense now as he listened, giving Jack a sense of unease.

Jose began to shake his head as Jack went on to explain exactly what he needed from him, refusing him outright. He didn't blame the man, but still he tried. He didn't know who else to ask.

Sophie and Maria went back to inspecting each other.

In the meantime, a man came up to the booth and asked Maria for onions. Maria's cheeks turned pink, and she shook her head briskly to say they had none. She waved him away, eyeing her father warily, and then turned again to the smiling customer. The two shared a brief look, and she tilted him a pleading glance. He nodded and hurriedly left.

Jack lifted his brows, wondering what else the man had wanted besides onions.

"What did that man say?" Sophie asked Jack as Jose launched into a fervent explanation for why he wouldn't guide them. Jack tried to keep up with him and listen to Sophie at the same time.

She tugged at his sleeve. "What did that man say?"

He frowned at her. "What man?" he answered impatiently.

Sophie raised herself on tiptoes to whisper in his ear, while Jose continued explaining that it was not only his anger for his daughter that kept him from agreeing to guide Jack to the jungle ruins, but his sense of responsibility to his family. He could no longer justify traipsing off into the jungles and leaving his family to fend for themselves. It was his fault, he added, that his daughter was so loose with her favors because he hadn't been around to keep her safe. He intended to change all that . . . beginning today.

"The one who was just here," Sophie explained, and pointed out the man in question, who was now lingering at another booth trying to buy his *onions* elsewhere, making flirty eyes at the woman behind the counter. "What did *he* say?"

Jack blinked at her. "He wanted to know if they had onions for sale."

Sophie's brows knit as she considered that, and Jack returned his full attention to Jose.

Sophie tried to remember exactly how he'd worded it: *Tu no tienes sayboyas?* That was it precisely. *Tu no tienes sayboyas? "Tu no tienes sayboyas?"* she repeated to herself, trying to memorize the phrase.

She tapped Jack on the shoulder. He turned to look at her, his expression somewhat harried. She didn't bother to remind him how rude it was to leave her so completely out of his conversation. He hadn't even bothered to introduce her. Was she supposed to twiddle her thumbs until he decided to include her? "I *really* hate to interrupt," she told him, "but how do you say onions in Spanish?"

He blinked at her. "*Cebollas*," he answered.

Sophie nodded.

All right then . . . if *sayboyas* were onions . . .

then *tu no tienes* must mean "do you have." She tried to remember that while she endeavored to ignore the woman who was staring at her so rudely and so suspiciously.

Maria, Jack had called her.

She tried not to acknowledge the attraction Maria obviously had for Jack, and tried not to notice the way her gaze shifted to longing when she managed to pry her eyes away from Sophie to look at him.

But she couldn't help but wonder who the woman was.

And she couldn't help but be just a little jealous . . . even though she told herself she wasn't . . . not at all.

Though whoever she was, she was someone Jack was obviously *very* familiar with . . . judging by the grip she'd had on Jack's throat. Sophie's stomach turned at the thought of Jack and Maria together in any form or fashion.

But then . . . she really didn't want to think of it, so she thought instead of breakfast. She was eager to prove herself, and itching to begin. But first she needed eggs. Should she scramble them or should she make them into perfect little suns, with the yolks bright yellow and the whites perfectly formed?

She patted her basket in approval. She had plenty of the colorful peppers and intended to throw them into the pan along with ham. And she had plenty of smoked ham from the ship's pantry, but she needed bread as well.

Growing impatient to return so that she could begin, she tapped Jack on the shoulder again and whispered, trying not to distract the man he was talking to from his explication, "How do you say eggs?"

He gave her a curious look.

"How do you say eggs in Spanish?" she asked again.

His brows collided, but he answered. "*Huevos.*"

Sophie mentally added that to what she already knew and practiced it to herself a few times, committing it to memory. *Tu no tienes huevos? Tu no tienes huevos? Tu no tienes huevos.*

She kept repeating the phrase to herself, dutifully ignoring the glaring woman. She tried to be patient with the interminable conversation going on between Jack and the man, who, she now assumed through Jack's conversation, was named Jose. He was either the woman's husband or her father . . . and judging by their ages, she assumed father.

Tu no tienes huevos, she repeated mentally while she waited for her chance to speak.

She really ought to ask Jose first, before looking elsewhere. It wouldn't make much sense to run around looking for eggs elsewhere if Jose had them to sell, but their conversation was becoming tedious. She couldn't understand a single word they were saying and she was growing impatient . . . not to mention battling a severe case of jealousy that was growing to monstrous proportions.

Never in her life would she have guessed herself capable of such terrible envy, but she was. She wanted desperately to put her hand possessively on Jack's arm, but couldn't bring herself to do it, so she found herself standing so close to him that she could smell the wonderful scent of his skin.

Her body remembered, and warmed. It drew her nearer, despite her resolve not to appear competitive with *that* woman!

She refused to lower herself to such an unseemly level of behavior. If Jack chose to be with her, then so be it. He wasn't hers to command—and neither was she his!

Still . . . she had every right to stand as close to him as she pleased.

She was the one making breakfast for him after all!

She cast the woman a baleful glare, though she really hadn't meant to, and then became annoyed with herself when the woman gave it back.

What on earth was she doing trading evil glances with a woman over a man who wasn't even her own?

It was ridiculous, and Sophie was ready to go, but Jack seemed to be pleading with Jose for something, determined to win his compliance.

Jose shook his head, stubbornly refusing whatever Jack was requesting of him.

His daughter's hand in marriage?

Sophie's stomach twisted at the ridiculous notion. Her thoughts were running amok. Jack was not the sort of man to make love to her one day and marry another woman the next.

Still, she decided they weren't getting anywhere, and she wasn't going to stand around and watch them butt heads all day long like two stubborn bulls. She decided to go look for her eggs now. At least that would while away some of the time while they argued.

The man continued to shake his head, not speaking, only staring at Jack, and Sophie didn't feel the least bit guilty about interrupting this time. She had shopping to do. It wasn't pleasant for her to stand here and listen to them argue in a language she didn't understand while *that* woman glared at her in a language she couldn't help but comprehend!

Sophie didn't like her, or her father, either, and it must have come across in her tone. *"Tu no tienes huevos?"* she blurted at the man, and was quite pleased with the way it flowed from her tongue.

Jack's head spun about, and the man's did as well.

The woman gasped and put a hand over her mouth.

The man glared at her, and his face began to mottle.

Sophie peered up at Jack. "What's wrong?" she asked, sensing something was terribly wrong.

Jack's expression was full of something like horror.

Something was definitely very wrong.

Sophie's eyes went wide. Her belly fluttered nervously. "What! What did I say?"

Jack had only time to open his mouth, when

the man hurled a fist at Jack's face. It hit Jack's jaw with a sickening thud.

Sophie screamed as Jack went tumbling backward at the unexpected impact. She managed somehow to catch him.

Maria screamed, and then chaos erupted.

Chapter 28

❝I demand to know what I said to cause that much trouble!"

Sophie held a smelly piece of meat to Jack's jaw. His jaw was throbbing and the odor was nauseating him.

Randall and Pete both sported their own bruises, but none as bad as Jack's.

"Let's just drop it, Sophia," Jack persisted. "Jose apologized after I explained what you really meant. Let's just drop it, all right?"

He didn't really want to tell her that she'd accused the man of having no balls.

Her timing couldn't have been worse. Jack had been in the middle of explaining to Jose that most of his other guides had abandoned him long before they'd reached the ruins— that if the snakes hadn't gotten to them, superstition had. Sophie's question had come as an unwelcome punctuation to his own. He'd gotten desperate and had just asked Jose if he'd lost his nerve—and that after Jose had *heard* Jack tell Sophie how to say *huevos . . .* a

307

very strange homonym for both eggs and the male scrotum. Jack could definitely see the connection, but he'd be damned if he would ever understand how the two were used interchangeably. Sophie couldn't have known.

"It was my fault, Jack, and I have every right to know what I said to cause such an uproar! I only asked him if he had eggs! He had no right to hit you like that!"

Jack groaned and pressed the meat more firmly to his aching face. "Sophia," he begged her. "Please . . ."

"Well, if you won't tell me, I'll just have to ask someone else," she said stubbornly, and turned to Kell.

Kell's brows lifted and he looked pleadingly at Jack. Randall and Pete continued to look away. They'd explained everything to Kell well away from Sophie's earshot, and for once Kell was keeping his good humor to himself.

"The odor of this meat is almost as hideous as the bruise swelling on your face!" she declared.

Jack was grateful for the momentary change in topic—even if the diversion was minuscule.

He nodded in agreement. "Can't blame the man for not offering a better piece, considering . . ."

"I paid for it!" Sophie complained. "It wasn't any of his business whether I intended to eat it or bury it!"

She was definitely a spitfire.

A beautiful one at that.

Jack tried to smile up at her, but couldn't quite manage.

"Did Jack ever get you your *huevos*, Sophie?" Kell asked suddenly, trying to sound casual.

Jack glared up at him, curbing his tongue, though not easily.

"Yes," Sophie answered, frowning down at Jack. "I have the eggs." She gave him a beautiful pout.

Jack smiled to himself.

"I suppose I'll go start breakfast!" she said, obviously displeased with him. She spun on her heels and sighed as she left them, and Jack's smile turned crooked as he peered up at Kell.

She had her eggs all right, along with a deuced ton of hot peppers. He hoped Kell would have smoke steaming from his ears when she was through. For himself, he intended to stick to the bread. He tossed the meat away with a grimace.

"Give it to the dog!" he demanded irascibly, and looked up at Randall. The smell was making him sick.

"What dog?" Randall asked.

"Find one," Jack replied curtly.

Randall's eyes widened in understanding, and he bent to pick up the offensive slab of meat at once. He hauled it away, much to Jack's relief.

Kell's grin was annoying. "So you managed to get Jose to guide us, after all?"

"Yeah," Jack said, as he watched Sophie work at a distance.

Pete had followed her and was helping her set up a small camp fire. He was explaining to her how to cook over the open fire with the frying pan she'd insisted on bringing.

She didn't even seem to realize how in tune to her Jack was. He couldn't get enough of her. Couldn't seem to keep his mind even on his work.

"How'd you manage that?"

"Thank Sophie's money. Guess it's true everyone has his price."

"Sure they do," Kell agreed. "Including you," he added with a deliberate nod.

Jack's gaze snapped up to meet Kell's. His brows collided. "What the hell is that supposed to mean?"

Kell shook his head. "You figure it out Jack. She's paying you to deliver her to Penn, isn't she? And you're doing it. Why? Because she paid you?"

"No, I could care less about the money." Jack's shoulders slumped. "I'm doing it because it's what she wants."

"Yeah? And how do you know what she wants, Jack? Have you asked her lately?"

Jack didn't answer.

He didn't have to ask her.

When a woman couldn't leave without dragging a damned picture of her fiancé around with her, it didn't take much to deduce that she had told him the truth to begin with . . . that she did miss the bugger. Her mood, until the egg incident, had vastly improved since getting off the ship. It was obvious to Jack that she couldn't wait to see Harlan.

It needled him.

Who was he kidding?

It hurt.

He was almost grateful for the pain in his face because it reflected the one growing in his chest . . . that aching feeling of loss even before she was gone.

Hadn't what happened between them meant anything at all to her?

How could she sit there humming so cheerily over the damned frying pan?

She *had* paid him—and very well—to do a job, and it was nearly done. Then he could go on with his own work far more comfortably after she was gone.

So why was he feeling as though he'd lost his best friend? Why did he suddenly feel like handing everything over to Penn and just throwing up his hands and going home?

"What's your price, Jack?" Kell asked enigmatically, then walked away.

Jack turned to stare at his back as he went, and questioned how much his life would be worth if he couldn't wake up and face the day . . . if he had to go to sleep at night wondering what might have been . . .

Sophie continued to hum and sing, talking animatedly to several of his crew as they set up camp. Jose was expected shortly and energy was high. The crew seemed to share Sophie's enthusiasm. Every last one of his men had a stake in what they would find. They had applied themselves to learning their chores aboard ship solely for the privilege of muddying their hands in the rich Yucatan soil.

Only Jack's mood was dour.

What price was he willing to pay for his pride?

How much was honor worth?

He thought about it for an instant, and wondered . . . had anyone even bothered to pay for the eggs?

He didn't think so, but hell . . . Sophie's bribe money would more than make up for it.

And *everyone* was bound to pay for it later.

He kept his mouth shut anyway, determined to allow Sophie a chance at her moment of glory. It meant a lot to her, and it meant a lot to him to see her succeed.

But he wasn't about to eat her food.

From this point on, it was every man for himself.

It was no use: She was a disaster as a cook.

Sophie didn't want to pout, but couldn't help it.

It wasn't easy to cook nearly sixty eggs in a single frying pan over an open flame. She took such care with the first few, but it hadn't mattered. In the end they'd all ended up scrambled. And it was just as well.

They were too hot to eat anyway.

She nibbled at her bread as she stared at her plate.

The only thing that kept her from running

away in utter humiliation and pouting in the privacy of the woods was the simple fact that it would be the easy way out. To abandon her food now, and leave everyone else to bravely force his down, was too cruel.

On the other hand . . . if she left, they might pour out their plates on the ground and bury the evidence, rather than sit there with their stoic expressions while they struggled to eat.

Sophie felt sorry for them. They'd been hungry and looking forward to a hearty meal to begin the journey.

"This is . . . very good," Peter offered, as fat tears streamed down his cheeks. His blue eyes glistened with as much sincerity as he could muster considering that his mouth was probably on fire and heat was burning through his nostrils. He struggled to swallow as Sophie watched. She then lifted up her fork and guiltily stabbed at a blackened crumble of egg . . . or maybe it was a pepper . . . or ham.

She couldn't precisely tell.

She swallowed convulsively and lifted the fork to her lips, saying a tiny prayer that she might be spared the pepper. Her water was practically gone . . . and everyone else's as well. Desperation was setting in. She could see them greedily eyeing one another's canteens, their expressions covetous. Sophie would have gladly offered hers . . . except that she was starved as well, and she would literally perish where she sat if she ended up with a mouthful of peppers and no water.

Meanwhile, Jack was feasting on some exotic dish of Maria's.

That woman had arrived with her father and two other men—her brothers perhaps, because the resemblance was strong—and the five of them were seated separately from the rest, discussing something of import.

Jealousy reared again, and Sophie couldn't help but notice how pretty Maria was, with her large, trusting black eyes. She wanted to draw her, capture her spirit, even as Harlan's almost forgotten letter came to mind. His words haunted her:

. . . skin so velvet brown and eyes so deep a black a man may sigh to see his own reflection in her eyes. And hair . . . Christ, I have never had the joy of touching hair so rich it flows through your hands like the mane of a fine riding horse.

Sophie's cheeks heated.

Was Jack enamored of her?

She was certainly lovely enough. Sophie couldn't begin to compete. Her own hair was drab in comparison and her skin too pale, her nose slightly freckled, and her eyes . . . well, her eyes were her best feature, she thought. They were different at least, and Harlan had often commented on their odd golden color.

Maria was the embodiment of everything wildly beautiful.

Sophie sighed wistfully.

It no longer bothered her in the least that Harlan was so smitten with the women here.

But Jack . . .

Her eyes couldn't help but follow him

wherever he went ... whatever he did. She found herself even struggling to hear their conversation and felt guilty for eavesdropping.

Absurd as the notion was, she wanted to go over and sit right in his lap!

She should do it, too, she thought petulantly. And she would ... except ... except that she didn't have any right to. Nor was she quite so bold as to interrupt their conversation and seat herself so rudely in his lap. So she sat there pouting instead, trying to eat her food, endeavoring to be as brave as the rest of the crew, and was near certain that Maria would never, *never* burn her food.

Kell sat down beside her. "Don't mind if I join you, do ya?"

Sophie shook her head, casting Jack a wistful glance.

"Don't sweat it, Sophie," he consoled her. "It wasn't so bad."

Which *it* in particular? Her envy of Maria, or her wretched breakfast? Sophie shrugged.

Kell smiled. "It really wasn't. I swear." She looked at him hopefully. "A little hot maybe," he relented, "but tasty nevertheless."

Sophie tilted him a glance, daring to hope. "Really?"

He nodded without the least hesitation. "Truly."

She eyed her plate a little dubiously. "It *is* hot," she admitted, and glanced up at Randall, who sat across from her at a distance. "Poor

Randall looks as though he could bury his head in a vat of water."

Kell chuckled. "Some like it hotter than others, I suppose." He winked at her. "But Randy is a wimp."

Sophie lifted her brows at him.

"All right, I'm a wimp, too, but I'm telling you . . . there are men who like their food so hot it makes 'em sweat. They aren't happy until they're snorting smoke from their nostrils."

Sophie didn't believe him, but she laughed anyway, and appreciated his efforts.

Her gaze returned to Jack.

He was smiling at Maria, holding his plate before him, lifting it up as though to thank her.

Maria beamed happily in response, her smile radiant only for Jack, and Sophie's heart twisted with envy.

For an instant . . . just a tiny little instant . . . she hoped he would choke on whatever he was eating.

Chapter 29

Maria had brought him chocolate-covered cockroaches.

Jack didn't know whether to be grateful or offended.

Jose had brought his sons along, as well as Maria, and Jack was uncertain whether it was simply because he wanted to do the best job for Sophie's money, or whether it was an added warning for Jack to keep his hands off Jose's daughter. In either case, her father and brothers didn't seem the least displeased with Maria's immediate attention.

He kept studying the four of them, trying to determine whether a bowlful of chocolate-covered insects was a normal thing for them, or whether it was their idea of some sick joke at his expense.

It didn't appear to be the latter.

They didn't give the bowl of *delicacies* a second thought. Only Maria seemed to be eagerly anticipating his verdict.

Damn . . . he cringed at the sight of them. He

knew it would hurt her feelings if he didn't try one . . . but he just couldn't bring himself to put deuced insects into his mouth. He looked about at his men . . . at how they choked and sputtered on Sophie's cooking . . . eyes watering and nostrils flaring . . . and longed to be eating beside them.

Some of his men ran for water, others were determined to sit tough. Jack marveled at how hard they tried for Sophie's sake. She had them all—including him—in her spell.

He glanced down at his bowl of food and spied a bristly leg poking up from the creamy chocolate covering, and nearly spewed his guts out where he sat. First the rotting meat, now this . . . Somehow, he managed to smile up at Maria.

Never again would he dread Sophie's cooking. May God strike him dead the instant he considered it!

He couldn't stand the sight of his dinner. He would have long ago set the bowl down and walked away but Maria continued to stare at him expectantly.

He swallowed convulsively, trying to talk himself into it. It wasn't so bad, he assured himself . . . just one . . . big . . . crunchy bite . . . and it would be all over. Bile rose in his throat.

"You licka dem?" Maria asked him, nodding hopefully.

Licka them? Christ. He didn't even want to *watch* someone *else* lick the disgusting creatures! She meant *like*, he knew. He lifted his brows as he looked at her.

"Yes?" she persisted.

Jack prayed to God ... any God ... that the bowl would suddenly burst into flames. He forced himself to nod and smile appreciatively.

He glanced over at Sophie and saw her with Kell, their heads together in conversation, and wished he were there beside her.

What were they talking about? What was Kell saying?

Did his friend appreciate the scent of her hair the way Jack did? It seemed he did, close as Kell was leaning into her, and Jack's gut churned a bit more violently.

What he wouldn't give to be sitting beside her ... eating her blackened eggs and ham.

He stared wistfully at them. Her laughter made his heart jump, and her smile made his belly flutter. Her scent made him want to kiss her ... and her eyes ... he could look into them a lifetime and never have it be long enough.

She stood suddenly, looking saddened, and Jack's heart twisted for her.

Was she disheartened by her efforts? Had someone said something to her? Jack would skin the bugger, whoever he was!

She slipped into the woods, and he waited a few moments to see if she would return.

She didn't, and he set the bowl down at once, apologizing hastily to Maria, and went after Sophie.

* * *

The woods were lush and cool.

Sophie couldn't bear to sit and watch Jack with Maria any longer. She'd tried to be a big girl about it, but the sight of the two together had been much too painful. No matter that Kell had been kind enough to keep her company, she hadn't been able to stand the sight of them, and she'd retreated like a coward into the sanctuary of the woods.

She hadn't intended to go far, but somehow she lost herself in thought and wandered deep enough to lose her direction.

Everywhere she looked now she found the same thick vines and bush. Still, there was no need to panic. Camp must be somewhere very near. She could still smell the scent of charred food.

Or maybe it was her imagination. Good lord, this was all she needed . . . to lose herself in the woods. Wouldn't that be a perfect addition to her long list of catastrophes?

Barely, she could make out a path in the bracken, and she followed it, hoping it would lead back to camp.

It ended abruptly at the edge of a deep chasm.

Despite the situation, she couldn't find it in herself to be afraid. She gasped in awe at the miracle of nature she had stumbled on.

Mesmerized, she moved carefully to the edge to peer down below and found the chasm filled with crystal-clear water. It was incredible, almost unreal. Magical even. Ten feet below the surface, silvery fish darted in schools among the thick, dark tree roots. Beams of light pierced the green canopy above and stabbed deeply into the pool like airy icicles. They formed a prism of sorts below the water's surface. Color radiated from them, painting fish as they passed through the watery rainbow.

Entranced by the sight, she knelt at the edge of the chasm. Pebbles rolled from beneath her feet to the pool below, startling fish.

Sophie had never seen such a beautiful sight. Her fingers itched to draw it. Sucking in a breath, she knelt there on the brink and stared in fascination, imagining how she would capture it.

"Beautiful, isn't it?"

Starting at the voice, Sophie turned to find Jack watching her. Her heart leaped a little at the sight of him, both in relief and something more. "Yes," she said on an exhale. "I've never seen anything quite like it!"

It left her breathless.

As did he.

She peered down again as Jack came to stand at her side, enthralled by her discovery.

"It's called a *dzonot*," he told her. He placed a hand on her shoulder. Sophie felt it and her breath caught. "They're created when cave ceilings collapse."

Sophie peered up at him. "Cenote?"

He nodded. "The Maya believed these were doors to the watery underworld which were inhabited by rain gods and jaguar spirits. There are many of these pools here. The land is riddled with them, but this one is particularly beautiful."

"It's . . ." She peered down once more into the pool. It was so clear she could see every pebble at its bottom. "There are no words to describe it."

He squeezed her shoulder. "I was going to bring you here later to show you, but you found it on your own."

She turned to smile up at him. "You were going to bring me here?"

The thought that he intended to share something so incredible with her warmed her beyond words. When was the last time anyone had taken the time to bring her into his world? To share with her the things that pleased him? Fascinated him?

She couldn't remember.

He sat beside her. More pebbles scattered into the pool as he boldly hung his legs off the edge.

Sophie smiled and sat as well, sliding one leg over the chasm's edge, and sat on the other.

He looked at her then, giving her a particularly wicked glance. "There is a Mayan legend about an evil princess named Hechicera, who couldn't marry the man she loved. It's said when lovers come too close to the *dzonot*, Hechicera seizes them and drags them into her cave where she turns them into *aluxob*." He arched a brow suggestively, and said, "We're pretty close to the edge."

Sophie blushed at the implication.

They were indeed lovers now. How could she ever forget?

She didn't want to forget a single moment she'd spent in his arms. As scandalous as the thought was, she had not a single regret.

Sophie's breath quickened. She wished he'd kiss her now . . . brush her hair aside as he was inclined to do. "*Aluxob*?"

Jack nodded. "Little people like leprechauns."

Sophie lifted her brows. "And what does she do with these unfortunate lovers?"

His brows knit. "Well, I'm not exactly sure, but small huts are built in cornfields after each harvest. And the first ears of corn are left there to feed the *aluxob*."

He went quiet, staring at her like *that* again . . . like he wanted to kiss her.

Sophie held her breath, willing him to. "Why?" she asked, when he didn't.

His voice was seductively soft as he told her, "For the farmers who honor them, the *aluxob* will push up their corn plants and rock their hammocks at night."

Sophie thought about it a moment, picturing herself in a hammock with Jack, while little leprechauns rocked them beneath the stars. "That's a beautiful legend."

His eyes sparkled as they watched her. "It is," he agreed.

"They must have been a wonderful, benevolent people!"

He shrugged. "I've a suspicion they weren't as benevolent as some wish to believe."

"Why not?" Sophie asked him, truly curious. He was so filled with knowledge. She wanted him to teach her everything he knew.

He looked down into the pool, nodding. "For one . . . there is a place called Chichén Itza."

"Chichén Itza?"

"Yes. The name means 'mouth of the well of the Itzas.' "

"Itzas?"

"Water wizards," he explained. "Anyway, this particular pool measures almost two hundred feet across, and below the surface of green scum are the remains of countless sacrifices and offerings . . . animals and sometimes humans . . . gold and jade jewelry."

Sophie shuddered at the thought. "You mean they just threw people inside . . . and let them . . ."

He nodded.

"How disgusting!"

"That's nothing next to some of their rituals. I'd tell you about them, but you'd blush."

Sophie wished she could stay at his side and discover things along with him. She wished she could spend quiet moments with him just sitting and reading. She wished she knew as much as he did.

She wished more than anything he would shut up and kiss her.

Her face warmed under his scrutiny.

"Then again, you're already blushing," he told her, his expression sobering a bit.

Silence fell between them . . . except for the

trickle of water falling somewhere below. It was a beautiful, musical sound.

"What are you thinking, Sophia?" His voice was as soft as a caress. Her stomach fluttered at the sound of it.

"I was thinking . . ." She blinked as she stared longingly at his mouth. ". . . that I love . . ."

God, she loved him, she truly did.

His hand reached out suddenly, touching her face, startling her, and she swallowed her words.

Jack held his breath, waiting for her to speak.

"Yes," he prompted when she didn't continue.

She blinked, and he could tell she was struggling. "That I love . . . how you know these things."

Disappointment slithered through him.

He caressed her chin with his thumb. "And I love . . . your curiosity, Sophia."

Her eyes seemed to reveal an inner battle. Jack waited . . . silent, hoping she would speak.

"And I really, really love . . ." she began again, her brows twitching a bit with what seemed to be confusion.

"What is it you love?" he asked her, his heart hammering fiercely.

She swallowed visibly. "That you are so willing to share your knowledge with me!"

His thumb touched her lower lip, rested there, and she blinked. "And I really . . . really love your smile, Sophia." Her lip trembled just a bit, and he teased it, willing her with his eyes to speak the words. He encouraged her, telling her also, "And I love the sound of your voice . . . and the way you laugh . . ." He leaned close to her, his nostrils flaring. "And the way you smell." He took a deep breath, craving the taste of her.

She closed her eyes and lifted her face into a ray of sun, and Jack sat there staring at her, mesmerized, his heart swelling with joy at simply being in her presence.

Never in his life had he felt so at peace with someone, so connected . . . so alive.

He bent to kiss her, touching his lips tentatively to hers. His hand moved down to her throat, and he felt her swallow once more. She didn't stop him, and he deepened the kiss, wanting nothing more than to crawl into her body, to be at one with her.

He wanted all of her, body and soul.

He wanted her mind, wanted her heart.

Torn between his desire to show her that her body was not all he wanted of her, that he respected her and loved her spirit and her mind as well, and wanting to make love to her again and again, to take her for his own, he hesitated, drew away.

"Sophie," he began.

There was so much he wanted to say, but he didn't know where to begin. He didn't want her to go back to Harlan, didn't want to lose her, but he wanted her to do whatever made her happy. If Harlan did that for her, then he wanted that for her, too, even if it would kill him to see them together. But he hoped she didn't love the jackass still. He really couldn't bear to see them together . . . to know that he would touch her . . . kiss her . . . make love to her . . .

The thought of it made his gut turn.

The words caught in his throat.

She stared up at him, her golden eyes wide, looking far too vulnerable. "Yes, Jack?"

Jack swallowed his words, unsure how to voice them. He'd never spoken those three words to anyone in his entire life, not a soul. He'd never felt for anyone the way he did for Sophia. He'd never thought to feel this way.

If there was just one thing he'd learned from his studies to be carried into his own life, it was that nothing lasted forever. Nothing. His studies and excavations were proof enough of that fact; societies came and went. He hadn't ever intended to put his heart at risk for something so fleeting. But he didn't care any longer . . .

Sophie was worth it.

He wanted her at his side.

But who was he to ask her to give up her own life on a whim . . . to follow him about? What did he really have to offer her?

His brows knit as he struggled with his thoughts.

What was the right thing to do?

Did she love Penn?

She desired Jack, that was true enough, but desire and love were two different things.

In the end, it came down to just one thing: She had to follow her own heart. He couldn't put words into her mouth, or feelings into her heart.

He sighed heavily and pulled away. Looking down into her beautiful face, he smiled and caressed her cheek.

"You wouldn't happen to have any eggs 'n' peppers left, would you?" he asked her.

"Eggs 'n' peppers?" She blinked up at him. "You're still hungry?"

If she only knew. "Starved," he said.

Her brows knit. "What about the meal Maria brought you ... didn't you eat?" She pulled his hand away from her face, and averted her gaze. "You really don't have to eat my breakfast just to make me feel good, you know! I'm well-aware that it was awful!"

Jack laughed suddenly. "Are you kidding? I'd rather eat pure poison than eat what Maria brought me!"

Sophie gave him an annoyed look. "You're just saying that!" she accused him.

He gave her a sheepish glance. "Uhhh ... no ..."

"Truly?" She tilted him a curious look. "What did she bring you?"

Jack shook his head, disgusted all over again by the mere thought. He grimaced and said, "Chocolate-covered roaches!"

Her eyes went wide. Her hand flew to her mouth.

"Oh, my!"

"Swear to God!" he told her, still grimacing.

In self defense, his hand went to his belly.

She shrieked with laughter.

Deeply offended by her lack of concern for his delicate stomach, Jack was forced to tickle her.

He tickled her until their limbs were tangled and her cheeks were aching with her laughter, until one of her boots flew off and across the pool, and landed in the water with a hearty splash.

"Oops," he said, and stopped suddenly, looking into her eyes. "There went your shoe," he told her.

Sophie grinned up at him. "I guess you'll just have to go down and get it, won't you?"

He grinned back, poking at her chest. "If I go, you go," he assured her.

Sophie held her breath as his finger slid down between her breasts, teasing her.

"Says who?" she asked him a little breathlessly.

His gaze followed his finger. "I'm bigger than you are," he reminded her.

That much was true.

"Yes, but I could scream," she assured him.

His gaze met hers. He arched a brow in challenge. "And who would come? We've wandered too far for anyone to hear us."

Sophie shrugged. "Hechicera."

His smile was wicked. "Let her come," he said, flaunting danger.

He kissed her then, a sweet, gentle kiss that made her heart swell with love.

A knot formed in her throat. She wanted to

make love to him. She wanted to give him her body once more. She wanted him to know how she felt through her touch.

Without a word, Sophie boldly unbuttoned her shirt, reveling in the way he watched her.

"Are you sure?" he whispered against her cheek, kissing her softly.

Sophie lifted her face to him, kissing his lips. "Very sure," she murmured, and he joined her, undressing her eagerly, hunger burning in his eyes.

His hands explored her body with such sweet tenderness that Sophie wanted to weep with joy.

She closed her eyes, torn.

More than anything she wanted to tell him how she felt, but was afraid to open her heart completely ... afraid he wouldn't love her back ... afraid to speak the words aloud ... afraid to be a fool again.

With Harlan she had given everything and had thought she'd received his love in return. She had been wrong, and was afraid to be wrong again. Harlan had never once spoken those words to her.

Three simple words were all she needed to hear ... but she needed Jack to say them first.

They didn't come easily to her lips, though they filled her heart.

But there were no doubts any longer ... she loved Jack with all her soul. Jack was everything she'd ever wanted in a man ... and more ...

And Harlan was simply a bad memory, a

lesson learned . . . growing more distant with every kiss from Jack's tender lips.

She made love to him then, daring Hechicera with every cry from her lips.

Greedy for every precious moment he would give her, she held nothing back . . .

Except three cherished little words.

Chapter 30

S ophie rejoiced in the afterglow of their lovemaking.

She'd never felt closer to anyone in her entire life. More than anything, she wished they could stay in this jungle paradise, just the two of them, forever. The thought of returning to Boston had never been more distasteful.

Jack lay beneath her, sheltering her naked body from the bracken of the forest floor. His eyes were closed, and his arms were around her, his fingers lightly stroking her back.

Her cheeks warmed with the memory of her own boldness, but she had reveled in the moment. She now knew exactly what Harlan had meant when he'd spoken of being ridden. Jack had straddled her over his exquisite naked body, begging her to ride him. And she had, without shame. All the while, he had murmured endearments to her, encouraging her, making her feel like his goddess.

She felt a little like that still, with her Adonis

lying satiated beneath her, his body warm and comforting.

"I suppose we should get dressed," she told him, though reluctantly. "Someone may finally miss us and come searching."

"No one will come," Jack assured her, his eyes closed. Sunlight broke through the canopy above them, warming her back, falling across his face. In his hair, she spied the first signs of silver. It sparkled in the sunlight, and she ran her fingers through his hair, enjoying the feel of it in her hands—thick and soft. And he had a tiny little mole beneath his lower lip. She touched it reverently.

"They might," she argued. "How can you be sure they won't?"

He shook his head and smiled softly and said, "Because you're with me."

Sophie lifted a brow. "Oh my," she said, and knew it was true. She would have preferred not to be so obvious, but they weren't fooling anyone. She doubted anyone but Jack had missed her love-struck glances.

Sighing contentedly, she laid her head down once more, cuddling against Jack's bare chest. It was smooth and soft, the feel of it delicious against her cheek. His hand tangled in her hair, finding something . . . a leaf perhaps . . . and he plucked it out, and began leisurely to search for more. Sophie didn't care if she wore the entire forest floor in her hair. She felt beautiful in Jack's eyes. He had told her so until she dared to believe it.

He lifted his head suddenly, and Sophie did, too.

He was grinning at her. "I think we should both go after your boot," he told her, and shook a brow suggestively.

Sophie laughed. "No doubt we could use a bath," she agreed.

He gently slapped her naked rear, and Sophie yelped in surprise. "Up!" he said, caressing where he'd slapped her. "Before I'm tempted again. If I am, we'll never leave, and then they'll definitely come looking and I'll have to kill any man who sees you like this."

Sophie laughed again, oddly exhilarated by his possessiveness. She rose. So did he, and he grinned at her before jumping into the pool. Sophie moved to the edge, laughing at his boyish antics as he came up shaking his head and sputtering.

He dove under once more and came up with Shorty's boot. "Look what I found!"

Sophie smiled regretfully. "I hope Shorty won't mind terribly."

He tossed the boot up at her. "Shorty's damned lucky not to be in them right now," he told her. "I'd have to kill him." He gave her a look that told her that while his mood was light, his words held a measure of truth. She tried to catch the boot but it landed behind her.

She sat there at the pool's edge. "Because of the ring?" she asked him.

"Because of the ring ..." He gave her a pointed look Sophie didn't entirely understand. They hadn't as yet discussed the ring, or Shorty, or Harlan for that matter, and the realization surprised her. "And because of where he got it," he told her.

Sophie bit her lip as she considered it. She couldn't conceive that Harlan would part with it. And it was far too generous a gift to be used even as payment for services—though whatever services Shorty might have provided for Harlan, Sophie couldn't imagine. "He must have stolen it," she deduced aloud.

"Maybe," Jack said, and nothing more. "Come on down," he commanded her, dismissing the topic. "The water's great." But his mood had sobered, and Sophie wanted to know why.

But then she wanted answers to many questions, and Harlan could certainly provide some. She couldn't wait to move on with her life.

The sooner she confronted him, the better.

"When do you think we'll reach Harlan's camp?" she asked Jack as she climbed down into the pool. "Soon I hope!"

The water was indeed wonderfully warm, and she sighed contentedly.

He stiffened suddenly, his brow furrowing, as though the question had angered him somehow. He didn't answer. He washed his face vigorously, ignoring the question, as though he hadn't heard her, and then he climbed up out of the pool.

"Jack," she called after him, her heart skipping a beat in panic.

He didn't answer.

"Jack, what is it? What's wrong?"

He was angry with her suddenly, and she didn't know why.

"You'd better hurry," he said curtly as he dressed without looking at her. "It's getting late, and we'd best be on our way."

With every step they took toward their destination, Jack's mood grew more sour.

He couldn't believe Sophie could make love to him with so much feeling and then turn around and ask how long before they reached Harlan's camp.

She was somewhere behind him, talking to Kell, but he couldn't bring himself even to look at her. Anger clouded his brain.

Stubborn, beautiful, infuriating woman!

Maria gabbed incessantly at his side, but Jack didn't hear a word she said to him. Her father had brought her along, refusing to leave her alone. Jack, for one, thought it was just too late to worry about her. Her mother had died giving birth to the youngest of her sons when Maria had been just a little girl. As a result, Maria had grown up wild, free to do mischief while her father was away. But her wildness was her greatest appeal. She was full of life and passionate, beautiful even. But now, her voice grated in his ears.

She wasn't Sophie.

Dammit. He couldn't imagine just handing Sophie over to Harlan and then turning around and walking away.

By God, he wasn't going to do it.

He needed her in his life. It lacked any meaning without her—everything did suddenly, including his studies. What would it matter what he discovered, what he learned, if he couldn't see her eyes light up just to hear him tell of it? He felt sick listening to Maria's chatter, imagining a procession of meaningless encounters with women he never cared to see again.

"Sophie!" he heard one of his men call out to her and his heart squeezed hard.

Who dared to taunt him with her name?

He spun to see who had called her, and found Pete waving enthusiastically at her. He barked orders to the boy, commanding Pete to Jose's side. He didn't know what the hell for, so he ordered him to carry Jose's backpack. The youth gave him a confused look, but did as he was told.

Sophie shot him a narrow-eyed glance, and he turned around, ignoring her, angry at her for wanting Penn.

If they kept going at this pace, they'd reach their destination sometime before nightfall.

Dammitall to hell.

Like a spoiled kid, he wanted to plant his feet and toss down his backpack and refuse to take another step toward Penn's camp.

"What is wrong with him!" Sophie asked Kell. She shook her head.

Kell shrugged in answer, though he hid a little smile, and Sophie sensed he knew more than he admitted. "Dunno," he told her.

"He's been cranky like that ever since this morning!" She hiked her backpack a little higher. One boot was still wet and had begun to squeak. Her toes were beginning to feel spongy and raw. She'd attempted to dry the socks she'd had stuffed into the toe of the boot, but they hadn't had much time, and she'd ended up putting them back in still wet. It was either that or fling the boots off at every step as they were far too big.

Jack had rushed them out of camp, and had kept a grueling pace the entire day. They were moving so fast through the forest and she'd been slapped in the face by so many limbs that she began to wonder whether she had leaf prints all over her face.

"What happened this morning?" Kell asked her, obviously curious, but trying to sound casual.

Sophie shrugged. "I don't know." And she really didn't. "Everything was fine..." She blushed, deciding it was best to leave out the finer details, "and then I asked when we'd be arriving at Harlan's camp and he just stopped talking to me."

Kell's brows lifted as he studied her. "Just like that?" he asked her. "He stopped talking to you?"

"Just like that." Sophie nodded. "And he hasn't said a word to me since."

Kell grinned. "Hell, I know exactly what's wrong with him, Sophie, and he'll be fine as soon as we get to Harlan's camp."

Sophie wasn't so certain, but she didn't argue. Kell knew him better than she did.

And neither was she entirely looking forward to Jack's *understanding*. The coming confrontation with Harlan left her feeling mostly renewed ... stronger ... except when she thought of the simple fact that everyone else would know the truth afterward.

That she hadn't been good enough to keep Harlan ... hadn't been pretty enough ... hadn't been smart enough. It made her feel in many ways a failure, though she knew it wasn't entirely so.

But she hadn't betrayed Harlan ... because the instant she had discovered his perfidy, she had turned him away in her heart, only to realize he'd never really been there to begin with.

Jack was.

With every step they took, she grew more anxious to have the ordeal behind her.

"Nervous?" Kell asked her.

Sophie gave him a sheepish look, nodding. "A little, but it's the right thing to do," she assured Kell.

Kell nodded at her and winked. "I'd have to agree. And I'm really proud of you for standing tall and going through with this."

It wasn't easy. And the thought of it left her stomach in knots.

"Harlan doesn't deserve you," Kell reassured her.

Sophie smiled at him. "Thank you," she said softly, and peered up ahead.

Jose was leading them through a narrow

jungle path, and they could barely walk side by side. They kept the pace, never slowing, lest they lose the man directly in front of them. Somewhere ahead, Jack was walking with Maria and her brother, but she couldn't see them, and was glad. She knew in her heart that Jack didn't want Maria, but neither was he at Sophie's side, he was at *hers*.

He was mad at her for something, she knew, but she had no idea what. Well, she didn't intend to concede to him. If he wanted her to know why, then he would tell her. She loved him, but she wasn't his lackey. The one thing she'd learned from her relationship with Harlan was that she was wisest to look after herself. She had given up everything to be what Harlan had wanted in a wife . . . and it had left nothing of what she wanted for herself. In the end, Harlan obviously hadn't respected her for the sacrifice.

No, she would never again be that foolish.

If any man wanted her . . . if Jack wanted her . . . it would have to be Sophie he wanted, Sophie with all her faults, not some token woman whose life's purpose was to bear children and be the model wife only to honor her faithless husband. She wanted a man to want her for herself—not for her name, or her father's money.

She wanted Jack—Jack, who didn't bow to any man—Jack, who went after his dreams by the sweat of his back—Jack, who respected her enough to talk to her about the things he cherished—Jack, who was the first man to actually see *her*, and not her father or her money or her name when he looked at her. And Sophie knew it was so. She saw herself in his eyes. She saw his heart there as well . . . at least she dared to hope.

"How long do you think it will be before we reach Harlan's camp?" she asked Kell, growing restless. Jack hadn't bothered to answer her question. For all she knew they could be days away, or merely hours.

Kell looked about, studying the forest. They'd reached a clearing of sorts, and he scratched his chin and looked at her, smiling, then peered back up again to judge the path ahead. "Actually . . . I think it's just beyond—" He lifted his arm to point, but stopped in mid-sentence.

Sophie looked up to see what had snatched his attention.

It was Jack, coming toward them, his look nearly murderous.

Her heart leaped a little.

His men parted like the Red Sea for him as he made his way to the back of the line where Sophie walked with Kell. They stopped in their tracks as he passed, turning to watch.

"We're stopping here for the night!" he said loudly enough for everyone to hear, and in a tone that brooked no argument.

Sophie winced. He was staring at her so heatedly that she feared to burst into flames.

Kell blinked. "What the hell for?" he asked Jack, his expression clearly dumbfounded. Sophie lingered behind Kell, not that she feared

Jack would ever harm her, but because she just didn't understand his fury. If she didn't even know what he was upset about, how was she supposed to defend herself! "It's just beyond—"

"We're stopping here!" Jack thundered, "because I said we are!"

Kell pointed down the dirt path they had been walking. "But hell, Jack . . . isn't it—"

Jack pointed furiously at his feet. "I said we're making camp here!" he persisted, and his stance was battle-ready.

Sophie winced again, and moved another inch behind Kell.

Kell shook his head, but threw his hands up in defeat. "All right," he agreed, and dared to chuckle. "Whatever you say, Jack."

Sophie looked up at Kell in surprise, wondering if he was insane to laugh. She had never seen Jack look so terrifyingly mad.

The two of them shared a look, and then Jack walked away.

No one else said a word, and they set up camp in the little clearing.

Sophie determined to steer clear of Jack, judging it best to let his mood pass. Whatever it was he was stewing over, she hoped he would work it out before the morning.

She didn't want to fight with him, and she was going to need a shoulder after facing Harlan. Kell was sweet, but it was Jack she needed most right now.

She just didn't know how to tell him the truth.

She didn't want his pity, just his compassion, and she didn't know how to say that her fiancé didn't really want her. She'd rather Jack see for himself that she wasn't Harlan's fool. She was no victim and she wasn't the least bit devastated, and she wanted Jack to see that truth with his own two eyes. Somehow, she didn't think he would believe her if she simply told him so.

In truth, her anger for Harlan had nearly faded now . . . she just didn't like him and was never more determined to set herself free from the *encumbrance* of their engagement.

Harlan Horatio Penn III could do whatever he wished, love whomever he wished. Sophie just didn't care. She really didn't, and the thought left her smiling to herself.

He could stay in the Yucatan for the remainder of his life, even . . . only without her father's money. She intended to do whatever she could to see that her father's honor was redeemed.

As for herself . . . she intended to follow her heart, wherever it should lead . . .

With or without Jack, she intended to follow her dreams. She was wiser, stronger, and ready to face whatever tomorrow would bring.

Chapter 31

J ack remained long enough to be certain his orders would be followed, and then set off again down the jungle path, confident that he wouldn't be missed while they were busy setting up camp.

Not that he was overeager to protect Harlan's reputation from Sophie, but he damned well didn't want Sophie to be hurt if they showed up to find Harlan *otherwise occupied*.

Jack had worked with the man for nearly a year and his labors had been spent almost entirely in his tent, fondling women's bare breasts. Before having met Sophie, Jack's greatest disgust with Harlan's behavior was in the simple fact that he seemed to have so little respect for his vocation. If he took advantage of the women who came to him, it was nearly as much the women's fault as it was his own. They flocked to the campsites, hoping to win themselves a husband who would take them away from the poverty of their villages, but their affections were calculated, at best. Jack had long ago resolved to mind his own business.

Except that now everything was different.

But the irony of his situation did not escape him. He was on his way to warn the fiancé of the woman he loved that she was on her way so that the cheating bastard could clear his tent of incriminating evidence.

How insane was that?

Still, he didn't want Sophie to find out this way. It wasn't Jack's place to tell her of her fiancé's dalliances—particularly not after he'd seduced her himself.

He hadn't gone far down the path before he reached his destination. Jose had guided them well, and they'd made good time. He broke from the forest into the clearing in which Harlan had set up camp.

Jack didn't bother asking where Harlan was, or which tent was his. It was the biggest, of course. And he was always within it—the sun bruised his skin, the night dampness gave him vapors, just about any excuse not to work. Jack headed straight toward it, resentment in his every stride. He loved Sophie. He wanted Sophie. And Harlan was a dirty, stinking bastard who didn't deserve her.

He found Harlan sitting at a small makeshift table, hunched over his reading material, his brows knit deep in thought, and a dark-skinned woman at his back, massaging his shoulders.

Cold fury seized hold of him.

Jack didn't say a word. He went straight to

the desk, slammed down the telegrams that
had been in the stove, and before Harlan could
say a word, Jack seized him by the collar and
dragged him outside.

Harlan scarcely struggled, so addled was he.
"MacAuley!" he said in surprise.

Jack tightened his hold on Penn's collar.
"Yep, it's me, Harlan! Surprised to see me?"
he asked, squeezing a little harder. Of course
he was surprised, he'd hired a saboteur to
make sure Jack's presence in the Yucatan
didn't become a ball and chain around his lily
neck.

"No, no!" Harlan objected. "I don't know
what you're talking about!"

Jack lifted Harlan up by the collar and dug
into his pockets for more evidence. He drew
out the ring he'd borrowed from Sophie, and
showed it to Harlan. "No?"

Harlan's face visibly paled, though Jack continued to throttle him.

Jack smiled ruthlessly. "I see you recognize
it," he told Harlan, and closed his fist around
it.

"I didn't do it!" Harlan said, and began to
scream. "I didn't send those telegrams to
Shorty!" His crew came running, hearing his
screams. Jack reared back and hurled a punch
at Harlan's jaw, releasing his collar as he did
so. Harlan flew back onto his rear, and his
crew stopped and stared.

"You didn't send the telegrams to Shorty,
did you?" Jack said, flexing his empty hand.

"No!" Harlan declared, scrambling backward.

Jack opened his fist. "And you didn't give him this ring, either, did you, Harlan?"

"He must have stolen it!" Harlan swore, his eyes narrowing furiously. "I didn't give that to him!" Jack read the truth in his eyes. He probably hadn't given up the ring to Shorty. Shorty might very well have stolen it, but it didn't matter. The evidence still pointed in the same direction. Harlan was a cheater and a thief!

He advanced on Harlan once more, lifting him up and hurling another punch. "That's for Shorty!" he said with cold deliberation as Harlan fell back on his rear.

None of his crew moved a finger to help him, Jack noticed—not that it would have stopped him.

He seized Harlan up once more, dusted him off while Harlan babbled to him, and then hurled another punch. "And that one's for Sophia!" he informed him. One last time Harlan went tumbling backward, and Jack told him, "I hope you're enjoying yourself, Harlan! Hope the wench was worth it!"

He left him on the ground that time, blood seeping from the corner of Harlan's mouth. Harlan narrowed his eyes, and he was suddenly provoked. "What do you mean that one was for Sophia?"

Jack was encouraged by the look in his eyes. "Fight with me, Harlan!" he demanded. "It's no damned challenge to scrap with a man who's too much of a coward to defend himself!"

"I'm a gentleman!" Harlan fervently protested and swiped at his mouth. "I'm not going to fight with you!" he assured Jack, his tone as haughty as a man could manage while still sprawled on his ass and spitting blood through his teeth.

"Of course not," Jack replied. "You'd much rather pay a man to sabotage anyone who's the least bit of a threat to you!"

"I didn't pay Shorty to sabotage you!" Harlan denied hotly.

"Yeah, well, how did you know it was Shorty?" Jack countered, his eyes narrowed. "I didn't tell you it was Shorty, now did I?"

Harlan opened his mouth to speak and then closed it again. Jack took a step toward him, and he scurried backward to evade him.

"You're a sorry excuse for a man, Penn!" Jack told him. "I'm not going to hit you again, but I am going to give you one solid piece of advice!"

Relief lit within Harlan's muddled blue eyes. "Wh-what is that?"

Jack looked at him, willing the words to come out right. He wanted to say nothing that would reflect poorly on Sophie.

"Sophia is here," he said at last, his words carefully measured. His hands trembled at his sides, and he gulped hard, swallowing the emotions that barreled up within him.

Harlan started visibly, looking about for her. "Sophia's here! Where is she?"

"Don't piss your pants, Harlan! She's not *here*. I'm not stupid enough to bring her waltzing into your orgyfest, but she damned well will be here bright and early tomorrow morning!" He gave Harlan a pointed glance. "You don't deserve the advance warning, but I'm here to tell you that if I catch your mitts on even one set of breasts before she gets here, or if you hurt her, I swear to God I will kill you with my bare hands!"

Harlan stood at once. "You wouldn't dare!"

"Make her cry, Harlan, and see what I dare!"

"I don't understand!" Harlan exclaimed suddenly, squaring his shoulders. "What is she doing with *you*, MacAuley?" He brushed himself off, giving Jack an accusing glare.

Jack held his tongue.

"And why should you concern yourself over my relationship with Sophia!"

Jack stood there, wanting to say so much more, but determined to protect Sophie at all costs. Whatever she wanted, he wanted for her.

"Because I love her, that's why!" he blurted, and blinked in surprise at his own words.

Harlan blinked as well, but stared speechless otherwise.

Jack nodded. It was the truth, dammit. He did love her. And that was all he'd come to say.

He spun on his heels, leaving Penn staring openmouthed after him.

The rest was up to Sophie.

Chapter 32

Needing time to think, Jack didn't return right away. When he did, it was to find the camp mostly slumbering.

Only a few tents were left illuminated, Sophie's included, and considering her past experience with lanterns, the light drew him to her. There wasn't much danger in her starting a fire as long as the lanterns were left in their braces, but just to be certain, he felt compelled to poke his head inside.

His heart leaped at the sight of her.

She was so beautiful lying there, with her hair spread about her face like gleaming copper. She had fallen asleep with her pad at her side and her pencil still in hand. The sketchpad was still open to the page where she had been drawing. Curious, Jack lifted it up, marveling at the details she had captured so accurately on paper.

It was the *dzonot* where they had spent the previous afternoon. Never in his life had he seen a more . . . spiritual drawing. There was no other way to describe it. In the rays of sunlight it was almost possible to see the sanctity of the place, and in the lush greenery, it was almost possible to spy Hechicera's face. She wasn't there, but somehow she was ... an almost indistinguishable face among the great canopy of leaves.

It was incredible.

Curiosity made him turn the page, and his heart jolted at the face that stared back at him. It was his own, captured with a sense of perfection that he knew he did not possess. The face was almost godly, the eyes piercing and intelligent, the lips full with sensual knowledge ...

It was him, and yet it was not him.

It was his face as Sophie saw him, and the realization made his heart swell with emotion. He was still reeling from it as he turned the page to find another. He cocked his head at the image. It was ... horrific ... the eyes bulging in anger and the mouth wide open as though shouting. Christ, if he had been the least flattered by the previous portrait, this one left him wincing in pain.

He turned more pages ... more images of him, growing progressively more hideous and repulsive. Good God! he'd come a deuced long way in her eyes. The very sight of them left him both amused and offended at once ... and amazed.

Her work was extraordinary.

Sophie stirred at his feet and he closed the pad, setting it down next to her backpack, along with the rest of her drawings. He glanced at them, and then back again, caught by the familiarity of them.

He began to leaf through them, and was stunned by his discovery. His own research. She had recreated the drawings with incredible accuracy . . . the jaguar god . . . even the mapped tombs. Her attention to detail was astounding. Her drawings were not only accurate, they were damned good, capturing more of the spirit of his subjects than he ever could have hoped for.

He could use her talents . . .

With an overwhelming sense of gratitude, he set the drawings down and went to her, hovering over her as she slept, watching her. The shadow of her lashes fell long over her cheeks, brushing them softly.

He was overcome with the desire to kiss her.

"Jack?" she whispered sleepily, and he swallowed, pushing aside the thought that tomorrow she would no longer be with him.

He didn't want to think of that now.

Didn't want to feel angry.

Didn't want to feel lonely.

He wanted to make love to her.

He kissed her lips softly, his heart beating harder at the feel of them so soft against his mouth.

"Sophia," he murmured desperately, and deepened the kiss.

"Jack," she said, waking. She smiled sweetly at him and stretched lazily, then lifted her arms around his neck. She opened her mouth to speak.

"Shhh," Jack demanded, afraid she would refuse him. He silenced her with a brutal kiss of his mouth, willing her to feel what was in his heart.

Like a flower, she opened to him, and he made love to her as he'd never made love to anyone in his entire life.

Before Sophie, he hadn't known the real thing.

Before her . . . everything he ever did was simply in preparation for this . . .

Chapter 33

⌒◡◠⌒

Jack had assured her they would reach Harlan's camp bright and early the next morning, but Sophie had had no idea how near to it they'd encamped.

They'd walked, at most, a mile, and then had burst forth from the forest into a lush, beautiful clearing that was littered with the nearly vanquished remains of a bygone age. The buildings stood a silent testament to the people who had erected them, but the forest had long ago begun to choke the ruins into silence and submission. Flora and fauna alike conspired to conceal the very buildings themselves from human eyes. So deep in the jungle they lay, they were not ruins any man would easily stumble over.

Except that someone *had* found it, and Sophie could see evidence of the jungle stripped away in places, reluctantly unveiling the masterpiece of some forgotten culture.

The sight of it all momentarily took her breath away.

She stood staring at the clearing in surprise, at the multitude of tents her father's money had purchased, and wondered which was Harlan's.

Her gaze sought Jack's.

He was watching her at a distance, his feet planted stubbornly, though she willed him to her side.

Had he realized how near they were?

Why hadn't he told her so?

Despite the intensity of their lovemaking, for whatever reason he was still angry with her. Suddenly, as she stood in the shadow of these august ruins, beyond the bounds of Harlan's sleeping camp, she felt more alone than she'd ever felt in all her life. Never had she felt so minuscule and unimportant, her purpose so insignificant in the greater scheme of life.

Some part of her wanted to kneel in homage. Some part of her wanted to forget all she had come for and simply sit and capture the heart of this place. The greatest part of her wanted to turn and run, but she'd come so far to face Harlan, she intended to see it through till the end.

Sucking in a breath for fortitude, she heaved the backpack off her shoulders and laid it on the ground. Her heart began to hammer as she knelt to retrieve her picture of Harlan.

Their arrival had been noted.

As the sun rose, bursting through the tree-tops, Harlan's camp began to stir. One by one, they crawled out from their tents to watch the interlopers.

Somehow, it seemed everyone watched her ... Jack's crew and Harlan's, as well. They stared at her, waiting to see what she would do.

Her fingers shook as she withdrew the picture, and she refused to look up into anyone's eyes, especially not Jack's.

Kell came and patted her on the back ... at least she thought it was Kell by the friendly way he patted her.

She looked up to find Jack, and her heart did a quick little somersault against her ribs. "Jack," she exclaimed, and wanted to throw herself into his arms.

Panic began to take hold of her. Her meticulously memorized speech flew out of her head completely.

He dragged her up, seizing her by the arms, his fingers digging gently into her flesh.

"Sophia," he said, and the look in his green eyes was fervent. Sophie wanted to weep at the intensity visible there. "I'll back you ... however you choose to handle this. I'll make it right ..."

She knew he would. That wasn't her concern. She wanted to tell him everything, but it wouldn't be long before he knew. "Oh, Jack!" she cried, and tried to embrace him, but he held her at bay.

"I'll tell him it was all my fault," he assured her. "But you don't have to confess anything at all."

"Jack," she protested. "I have to—"

He shook her gently, but urgently. "No, listen to me!" he begged her.

Sophie suddenly wanted to sob, and she didn't even know why. Tears pricked at her eyes, and she admonished herself for being so silly.

It wasn't as though this were goodbye.

Why was she crying?

"Sophia . . ." He swallowed visibly. "I just want you to know . . ."

Her heart squeezed her painfully. She stared into his eyes, willing him to speak. "Yes, Jack?"

"Before you go . . ."

His fingers clutched her harder, almost desperately, but Sophie didn't care. The look in his sparkling eyes gave her hope.

She waited with bated breath to hear his next words.

"Jack," she prompted when he stopped and merely stared, the look in his eyes something like fear, as though he were afraid to speak the words. But that was impossible, because Jack MacAuley wasn't afraid of anything at all.

She swallowed convulsively.

He was her hero, her lover, her friend, and lately her mentor. She loved him fiercely, and respected him even more. She wanted to please him always.

Harlan's camp had come completely alive in the few moments while they stared at each other, while Sophie willed Jack to speak the words.

I love you, her heart cried out.

Say it, Jack.

"Sophia!" someone shouted. It was Harlan.

Sophie peered over her shoulder to see him coming toward them, and panic beset her all over again. She clutched Jack's arm, looking frantically at him. She didn't want him to let go of her because if he did, she would fall flat on her face and humiliate herself before one and all.

"Jack!" she cried softly, terror-stricken, but not for the reasons he might have thought. The picture of Harlan slipped from her fingers and fell to her feet.

She was afraid he would never say it, afraid the real world would somehow take him away, afraid he wouldn't wait for her . . . that he would walk away without knowing the truth—and still afraid of being a fool for any man.

His eyes seemed to be pleading with her.

She tilted him a beseeching glance.

His hand suddenly lifted from her arm, and gently reached out to caress her face. "I love you, Sophia," he said, speaking the words she most needed to hear.

Her heart lifted into her throat, and tears sprang to her eyes. Her throat constricted, and she couldn't speak for an instant.

"Sophia!" Harlan shouted once more, his tone sounding overly pleased. "Here I am . . . over here!" he hailed her.

With a strength of determination, she hadn't known she possessed, she pulled away from

Jack, but he held her fast. "You don't have to go," he urged her.

Sophie pushed him firmly away, wanting so much to explain, but Harlan was nearly on them. "Yes, I do!" she assured him, and sucked in a breath. "I have to do this, Jack!" And she extricated herself from his iron grip, suddenly dizzy with joy.

He loved her!

Dear God, he loved her!

Never in her life had anyone spoken those words to her.

Never in her life had she wanted someone to say them more.

Her heart felt near to bursting.

She didn't care about Harlan at all.

This wasn't the least painful, only necessary, and she was suddenly eager to do it! She straightened her shoulders, picked up the picture of Harlan from where she'd dropped it at her feet, gave Jack one last heartfelt glance, and said again, "I really have to do this."

And she grinned at him.

She actually grinned at him.

As she tore away from him, Jack swallowed so hard that it hurt his heart. She began walking toward Harlan, never looking back, and he stood there, feeling as though she'd ripped out his insides and then smiled as she'd done so.

He let her go.

He had no choice but to do so.

He'd laid out his heart for the taking, and she'd refused it and left him anyway.

He couldn't bear to watch.

His gaze sought Kell's and he found his friend grinning as well. The realization gave him pause.

What the hell was wrong with everyone?

He turned once more to Sophie, watching her stride . . . full of confidence and purpose. She was a woman with a mission. In her hand she clutched Harlan's vandalized picture as though it were a weapon. As he watched, she lifted it up suddenly when she was almost near Harlan and quickly removed the back, tossing it over her shoulder. She removed something and then tossed the picture as well. And just when Harlan would embrace her to welcome her, she unfolded something and thrust it into his face.

He'd be damned if Kell wasn't laughing to himself. You couldn't hear him, but his shoulders shook with mirth.

What the hell was going on?

And how did Kell seem to know so much?

Jack moved closer to eavesdrop, thinking maybe he could bear to hear this after all.

"Harlan, guess what Jon has shared with me!" she declared as she waved a paper in his face.

"What?" her fiancé asked her, trying to examine the paper she held.

And then, evidently, he recognized it, because he paled visibly at the sight of it, and Sophie said to him, "I see you recognize it, Harlan dearest!"

Curiosity needled Jack and he moved closer to Kell. "What the hell is that in her hand?"

"A letter," was all Kell felt inclined to reveal, and he grinned at Jack.

Jack shot him a glare, and turned to watch Sophie again, his attention riveted to her now as she began to recite something aloud to everyone who cared to listen.

" . . . *and the women here are the most lovely any man has ever beheld*," she read, her tone melodramatically poetic, "*skin so velvet brown and eyes so deep a black a man may sigh to see his own reflection in her eyes!*"

"How did you get that?" Harlan suddenly exploded, his face turning deep red.

"*And hair*," Sophie continued, unfazed by the hysteria in his voice, "*Christ, I have never had the joy of touching hair so rich it flows through your hands like the mane of a fine riding horse!*"

"Sophia!" Harlan protested with a gasp and tried to take the letter from her.

"And in parenthesis . . ." she added as an aside, turning to Jack. She actually winked at him then, and laughter burst on his lips, despite his utter confusion.

She wasn't even angry. He'd be damned. Had she planned this all along? Why didn't she tell him? He would have reveled in her purpose, egged her on, even. Hell, he'd have given her free passage.

She went back to the letter, waxing poetic once more. "*And they love to be ridden, Jon . . . I know this firsthand!*"

"Sophia!" Harlan objected, his tone growing angry now. His face turned a mottled shade of red.

Everyone had gathered around them now, and every eye remained on Sophie.

"*. . . never have I known women so earthy in nature,*" she continued, louder than before, with an artistic flair of her hand. "*If you experience the carnal joy of one woman's bosom, you must not think her the exception because the next will make you yearn to feel forever her native soil between your toes and run like a savage through the jungles of her birth. You will nearly forget you are a civilized man and never again wish to languish in the misery that is Boston!*"

Harlan had written that? If so, he was more an idiot than Jack had ever supposed.

Laughter erupted from the crowd.

"Sophia, I can explain!" Harlan pleaded with her. "Give me the letter, please!"

She jerked it out of his reach. "*Not for all the Vanderwahl money would I be dragged so soon from this paradise!*" she finished passionately.

"I can explain," he said again, but his plea fell on deaf ears.

"Don't bother!" Sophie said, turning away, returning to Jack.

Harlan started after her. "Sophia, my darling princess, I can explain everything!"

She whirled to face him, rounding on him once more. "Don't ever again call me that again! I have good news for you, Harlan! You don't have to worry about the encumbrances of matrimony! Not with me! Not ever!"

Jack shook his head, realizing in that instant that this had, indeed, been her intent the entire time. This moment was what she had come for.

And he was damned proud of her for standing up for herself.

"And furthermore, you don't *ever* have to leave this place if you don't wish to!" she told him, and folded the letter in her hand, keeping the evidence. "And better yet you never again have to worry an inkling about Vanderwahl money!" she assured him.

She turned once more, leaving Harlan looking as though he'd been slapped in the face by his mother. She walked proudly toward Jack, looking every bit the woman she was, and handed the letter to him.

"It was never your money I cared for!" Harlan lied without hesitation.

"I love you, too," she told Jack, ignoring Harlan, smiling, and then she spun on her heels once more, going back to Harlan, her demeanor suddenly fierce again.

Jack found himself grinning.

She loved him.

Damn, she'd actually said so.

"Oh no?" She poked a stunned Harlan in the ribs, and said, "Every man should have such an understanding fiancée, eh? And a father-in-law willing to plunk down good money in support of his cause?"

Harlan remained speechless.

"Well, you were right about one thing Harlan Horatio Penn III! I am *not* wasting away! But I won't be bearing *your* children—not in this lifetime!" She poked his chest once more.

"How dare you think to make me wait for you five, six more years for you to deign to return to me! And how dare you belittle my interest in your studies! And how dare you suggest that women have no patience or capacity for learning! And perhaps you couldn't have chosen better," she said in finale, "but I certainly can! And have!" she added with a nod.

And then she turned and left him one last time, coming toward Jack, her smile radiant.

Jack's heart swelled with love for her.

And pride.

And joy.

She returned to him with shoulders squared, and a determined stride, confident.

"You can't do this to me!" Harlan railed at her back. "You can't choose *him* over *me*, Sophia! It's utterly disgraceful!"

Sophie ignored him.

"What will your father say?"

"I don't care!" she replied, without turning.

Harlan advanced on them suddenly, his hand raised and pointing indignantly at the skies, "And don't think I won't tell him you've been carrying on with that . . . that . . ."

Jack set Sophie aside when she reached him, entrusting her into Kell's arms.

Harlan was close at her heels.

"Excuse me an instant," he told her calmly, and then hurled a punch at Harlan, catching him completely unawares with his false sense of security and interminable arrogance. It sent him flying backward once more onto his rear, adding another bruise to the collection on his face.

Some men never learned.

"What the hell was that for?" Harlan asked him, outraged, glaring at him.

Jack shrugged and brushed himself off. "For the hell of it," he answered glibly, and then turned and took Sophie into his arms.

He kissed her thoroughly, thrusting his hand into her beautiful hair, reveling in the feel of it between his fingers, soft and fine. He looked at her with pride in his heart. "Ready to go, flower?"

Sophia nodded, feeling joy as never before.

He shook his head, chiding her. "Why the hell didn't you tell me this was what you came for?"

She wrapped her arms around his neck and said, laughing, "Because it wasn't any of your business, Mr. MacAuley."

"Saucy wench!" Jack said, and grinned at her. "Is that any way to speak to your fiancé?" He pecked her lips softly, caressing her back. "Call me Jack," he demanded of her.

Sophie kissed him back, ignoring Harlan's lunatic raving. She laughed softly. "Was that your arrogant way of asking me to marry you, Jack MacAuley?" She tilted him a coy look, and he teased her lips with his tongue, biting them softly.

He whispered into her mouth, "It just might be at that."

"And I might just say yes ... only under one condition ..."

"And what might that be?"

"That you let me stay with you . . . no matter where you are."

"It's a deal," he agreed, sealing the bargain with another kiss. "Guess I'll just have to make you my new partner."

"Hey!" Kell protested, though his tone was tinged with laughter.

"We'll have to discuss the terms in depth," Sophie assured him, smiling as she caressed the hair at his nape.

"That's easy enough," Jack disclosed. "You can have anything you want . . ."

"I already do," Sophie said. "I have you."

"I'm going to write your father at once, Sophia!" Harlan threatened as Jack lifted her up and carried her away.

"So am I, Harlan," Sophie assured him, and she sighed as Jack kissed her once more. "I think this is where we're supposed to sail away into the sunset and live happily ever after," she proposed.

"How 'bout we walk into the sunrise instead?"

Sophie laughed and clung to him tighter. "And live in a little white house by the lake?" he asked her playfully.

She nuzzled against him. "A tent will do just fine, thank you very much."

"A woman after my own heart," Jack declared.

Penn could have every grant he pleased. He

could have the money and the prestige. He could have anything and everything. Jack no longer cared.

All he wanted was the woman in his arms.

Epilogue

Sophie worked by the light of a single lamp. She had crawled out of bed once Jack had fallen asleep, even though he had forbidden her to work any longer tonight.

"You're tired, Sophia," he'd said. "You can always finish the drawings tomorrow."

He didn't understand, she knew. She had to finish them tonight, before the image blurred in her mind's eye. It wasn't work that compelled her, however. Years ago, she had painted a wedding scene, a perfect replica of the one her mother had dreamed of . . . except that the bride and groom had had no faces. Somehow, it had never dawned on her why she could not depict them, but now . . . now she understood.

She peered back at the bed . . . they had bought a bed for the ship and nailed it in place. The hammocks just didn't have enough room for the two of them, and she couldn't imagine sleeping without his arms curled protectively about her. He was so beautiful lying in the moonlight, and she hoped she depicted every perfect feature in her drawing. He was beautiful, and she loved him fiercely. And she understood now that she had never loved Harlan . . . that Harlan had never loved her. She understood because never in her life had she felt such a glowing warmth for any human being. It was a joy that touched every aspect of her life, like a brilliant ray of sunshine that penetrated even through the darkest clouds, banishing every shadow.

It was late but she wanted to complete the drawing before the morning when they would reach port in Belize . . . to send along with her letter home. She hoped her mother would see it and understand. And her father . . . she knew he would. As she'd lain there in bed with Jack her father's words of wisdom had come back to her like a light flipped on in the darkness. While she'd worried and fretted how he would view her decision to wed Jack she'd remembered something he'd said to her a night so long ago . . . a night not so unlike tonight, when she had labored over one of her pieces. She had been only eight years old, but the memory of it was as clear now as though it were yesterday that he had knelt at her bedside.

"Sometimes it takes a lot more courage," he'd told her, *"to follow your own dreams instead of those of the ones you love."*

Well, she was following her own dreams, and she was happier than she'd ever been in her life. And she had so much joy in her heart that wanted everyone to be as happy as she was!

She finished the painting at last, and stared at it.

A pristine white gazebo, decorated with pure snow-white ribbons, sat in stark contrast to the opulent green lawns of her sprawling family home. Golden rays of sunshine penetrated a vibrant, rich green canopy of trees, and shone down like the touch of God himself on the couple in the gazebo. On the horizon, shiny black horses galloped in a distant meadow. She wondered if her father would understand its significance. She wondered if he would remember the tale he'd told her. She couldn't live their lives for them, or even counsel them in matters she had no right to. But it wasn't too late for them.

Satisfied with the results, she set the painting aside, lifted the pen, and withdrew a clean sheet of paper from Jack's desk.

She began to write.

September 12, 1899

Dearest Mother and Father,

Please forgive me for having taken so long to write. I do hope your visit abroad was as lovely as ever.

You will be quite relieved to know I did not murder Harlan, after all. In fact, I have much to thank him for. And oh, I got married, though not to Harlan, I'm pleased to say. I will explain

*everything in detail when I return to Boston—
as soon as Jack and I complete the current expedition.*

*It was a lovely ceremony held in a quaint
chapel in Mexico and presided over in Spanish
by a native priest. Now Mother, don't fret because despite that I didn't understand a word he
said, Jack speaks the language quite eloquently,
and he was sweet enough to translate everything. You will adore him, I assure you, as I do,
and we promise to get married all over again
when we return. You may, in fact, begin decorating the lawn, just as you so often described
to me.*

*In the meantime, I know you are happy for me
because I am deliriously so!*

*In case you are not . . . Mother, a very wise
man once told me that happily ever after isn't
something someone can give, not even a mother
who loves a daughter very much. It's a place
inside your heart. I've found that place, Mother.*

*I truly hope you'll understand, and if not, at
least forgive me for following my heart. I love
him, Mother, and I am happier than I have ever
been. And for the first time I have found a sense
of purpose in my drawings. I am cataloguing
Jack's artifacts and discoveries, and doing quite
well, Jack says. Enclosed you will find a few of
my finest examples, along with a new picture I
have just completed. Enclosed also is a letter
written by Harlan as delivered to me by Jonathon Preston. It will explain much, I believe, and
Father will find it of particular interest.*

Daddy, I wonder if you have considered pur-

chasing that horse farm you spoke of so long ago? It's never too late. And I do agree, Mother truly has the most lovely smile.

Sophie lifted her brows after writing that particular remark. Her mother did, of course, have a lovely smile . . . when she happened to smile, that was . . . which wasn't particularly often.

A slightly crooked smile came to her lips as she wondered at her own matchmaking. Was it painfully obvious? To her it was, though her remarks were subtle enough that only her father should take them for what they were.

"Until we meet again," she signed the letter. *"I remain your loving daughter, Sophia Vanderwahl MacAuley."*

She signed the last of it with as much precision as she was able, every precious letter fashioned with painstaking love.

Sophia Vanderwahl MacAuley.

Jack stirred at her back, his timing impeccable.

"Come to bed, flower," he told her.

She turned to see that he had lifted his head from the pillow where they had both lain their heads, peering at her sleepily.

"I can't sleep without you."

Sophie laughed softly. "You can too, you rotten cad! I heard you snoring!"

He managed a throaty chuckle. "Impertinent brat. Come back to bed. The drawings can wait until tomorrow."

Sophie smiled at him. "I'm coming, my darling," she said, and stood, abandoning her letter on the desk until morning. He was right, it could wait.

Feeling invincible, empowered, she went to the bedside. Staring down at him, she undressed so that he could see her by the moonlight, and knew by the expression on his face that he wanted her . . . cherished her. And somehow she knew that he would look at her that way even when she was old and her hair was gray.

No words were necessary between them.

With that knowledge and wearing only her most wicked smile, she climbed into bed beside her husband.

And they did, indeed, live happily ever after.

Avon Romantic Treasures

*Unforgettable, enthralling love stories,
sparkling with passion and adventure
from Romance's bestselling authors*

✻✻✻✻✻✻✻✻✻✻✻✻✻✻✻✻✻✻✻✻✻✻✻✻✻✻✻✻✻✻✻✻✻

BECAUSE OF YOU   *by Cathy Maxwell*
                             79710-0/$5.99 US/$7.99 Can

SCANDAL'S BRIDE   *by Stephanie Laurens*
                             80568-5/$5.99 US/$7.99 Can

HOW TO MARRY   *by Julia Quinn*
A MARQUIS   80081-0/$5.99 US/$7.99 Can

THE WEDDING NIGHT   *by Linda Needham*
                             79635-X/$5.99 US/$7.99 Can

THE LAST MAN   *by Susan Kay Law*
IN TOWN   80496-4/$5.99 US/$7.99 Can

TO TEMPT A ROGUE   *by Connie Mason*
                             79342-3/$5.99 US/$7.99 Can

MY BELOVED   *by Karen Ranney*
                             80590-1/$5.99 US/$7.99 Can

THE BRIDE OF   *by Lori Copeland*
JOHNNY MCALLISTER   80248-1/$5.99 US/$7.99 Can

Dear Reader,

Next month, we have some wonderful romantic treats in store for you, beginning with a fantastic Avon Treasure by a writer destined for stardom—Victoria Alexander. Her unforgettable Regency-set romance, *The Wedding Bargain*, is witty, sensuous, and completely tantalizing. A society scoundrel strikes a wager with one of the most eligible ladies of the *ton*. If he wins, he gets her hand in marriage. If he loses...you'll have to read to find out!

Lovers of contemporary romance won't want to miss *A Kiss to Dream On*, the latest from Neesa Hart. Neesa's trademark blend of heartfelt emotion and memorable sensuality are in full force here, as a toughened journalist falls under the spell of an idealistic teacher. Remember to keep your tissues handy, because I guarantee that *A Kiss to Dream On* is a laugh-and-cry romance.

Adrienne deWolfe makes her Avon debut with a smart, sassy western, *Scoundrel for Hire*. A sexy scoundrel is hired to break up the marriage of a wealthy young woman's father and his gold-digging bride-to-be, never dreaming that he'd begin to have designs of his own in this saucy heiress. Filled with delicious twists and turns, you won't want it to end!

If you love headstrong heroines and maverick men, you won't want to miss Rebecca Wade's *Unlikely Outlaw*. A young western miss is ordered to get married, or else, by her father. So she picks the worst possible prospect for a husband...only to discover that opposites are sometimes the best match.

Until next month, happy reading!

Lucia Macro
Lucia Macro
Senior Editor

ael 1199